Big Jack

Titles by J. D. Robb

NAKED IN DEATH
GLORY IN DEATH
IMMORTAL IN DEATH
RAPTURE IN DEATH
CEREMONY IN DEATH
VENGEANCE IN DEATH
HOLIDAY IN DEATH
CONSPIRACY IN DEATH
LOYALTY IN DEATH
WITNESS IN DEATH
JUDGMENT IN DEATH
BETRAYAL IN DEATH
SEDUCTION IN DEATH
REUNION IN DEATH
PURITY IN DEATH
PORTRAIT IN DEATH
IMITATION IN DEATH
DIVIDED IN DEATH
VISIONS IN DEATH
SURVIVOR IN DEATH
ORIGIN IN DEATH
MEMORY IN DEATH
BORN IN DEATH
INNOCENT IN DEATH
CREATION IN DEATH
STRANGERS IN DEATH
SALVATION IN DEATH
PROMISES IN DEATH
KINDRED IN DEATH

Anthologies

SILENT NIGHT
(with Susan Plunkett, Dee Holmes, and Claire Cross)

OUT OF THIS WORLD
(with Laurell K. Hamilton, Susan Krinard, and Maggie Shayne)

REMEMBER WHEN
(with Nora Roberts)

BUMP IN THE NIGHT
(with Mary Blayney, Ruth Ryan Langan, and Mary Kay McComas)

DEAD OF NIGHT
(with Mary Blayney, Ruth Ryan Langan, and Mary Kay McComas)

THREE IN DEATH

SUITE 606
(with Mary Blayney, Ruth Ryan Langan, and Mary Kay McComas)

IN DEATH

THE LOST
(with Patricia Gaffney, Mary Blayney, and Ruth Ryan Langan)

Turn to the back of this book for an excerpt from

HOT ROCKS

by #1 *New York Times* bestselling author Nora Roberts

Big Jack

Previously published in *Remember When*

J. D. Robb

BERKLEY BOOKS, NEW YORK

THE BERKLEY PUBLISHING GROUP
Published by the Penguin Group
Penguin Group (USA) Inc.
375 Hudson Street, New York, New York 10014, USA
Penguin Group (Canada), 90 Eglinton Avenue East, Suite 700, Toronto, Ontario M4P 2Y3, Canada
(a division of Pearson Penguin Canada Inc.)
Penguin Books Ltd., 80 Strand, London WC2R 0RL, England
Penguin Group Ireland, 25 St. Stephen's Green, Dublin 2, Ireland (a division of Penguin Books Ltd.)
Penguin Group (Australia), 250 Camberwell Road, Camberwell, Victoria 3124, Australia
(a division of Pearson Australia Group Pty. Ltd.)
Penguin Books India Pvt. Ltd., 11 Community Centre, Panchsheel Park, New Delhi—110 017, India
Penguin Group (NZ), 67 Apollo Drive, Rosedale, North Shore 0632, New Zealand
(a division of Pearson New Zealand Ltd.)
Penguin Books (South Africa) (Pty.) Ltd., 24 Sturdee Avenue, Rosebank, Johannesburg 2196, South Africa

Penguin Books Ltd., Registered Offices: 80 Strand, London WC2R 0RL, England

Previously published in *Remember When* by Nora Roberts and J. D. Robb.

BIG JACK

A Berkley Book / published by arrangement with the author

PRINTING HISTORY
Berkley mass-market edition / March 2010

For information, address: The Berkley Publishing Group,
a division of Penguin Group (USA) Inc.,
375 Hudson Street, New York, New York 10014.

ISBN: 978-0-425-23490-7

BERKLEY®
Berkley Books are published by The Berkley Publishing Group,
a division of Penguin Group (USA) Inc.,
375 Hudson Street, New York, New York 10014.
BERKLEY® is a registered trademark of Penguin Group (USA) Inc.
The "B" design is a trademark of Penguin Group (USA) Inc.

PRINTED IN THE UNITED STATES OF AMERICA

10 9 8 7 6 5 4 3 2

All things change; nothing perishes.

—OVID

Commit the oldest sins the newest kind of ways.

—WILLIAM SHAKESPEARE

Chapter 1

NEW YORK, 2059

She was dying to get home. Knowing her own house, her own bed, her own *things* were waiting for her made even the filthy afternoon traffic from the airport a pleasure.

There were small skirmishes, petty betrayals, outright treachery and bitter combat among the cabs, commuters and tanklike maxibuses. Overhead, the airtrams, blimps and minishuttles strafed the sky. But watching the traffic wars wage made her antsy enough to imagine herself leaping into the front seat to grab the wheel and plunge into the fray, with a great deal more viciousness and enthusiasm than her driver.

God, she *loved* New York.

While her driver crept along the FDR as one of the army of vehicles battling their way into the city, she entertained herself by watching the animated billboards. Some were little stories, and as a writer herself, and the lover of a good tale, Samantha Gannon appreciated that.

Observe, she thought, the pretty woman lounging poolside at a resort, obviously alone and lonely while couples splash or stroll. She orders a drink, and with the first sip her eyes meet those of a gorgeous man just emerging from the water. Wet muscles, killer grin. An electric moment that dissolves into a moonlight scene where the now happy couple walk hand in hand along the beach.

Moral? Drink Silby's Rum and open your world to adventure, romance and really good sex.

It should be so easy.

But then, for some, it was. For her grandparents there'd been an electric moment. Rum hadn't played a part, at least not in any of the versions she'd heard. But their eyes had met, and something had snapped and sizzled through the bloodstream of fate.

Since they'd be married for fifty-six years this coming fall, whatever that something had been had done a solid job.

And because of it, because fate had brought them together, she was sitting in the back of a big, black sedan, heading uptown, heading toward home, home, home, after two weeks traveling on the bumpy, endless roads of a national book tour.

Without her grandparents, what they'd done, what they'd chosen, there would have been no book. No tour. No homecoming. She owed them all of it—well, not the tour, she amended. She could hardly blame them for that.

She only hoped they were half as proud of her as she was of them.

Samantha E. Gannon, national bestselling author of *Hot Rocks.*

Was that iced or what?

Hyping the book in fourteen cities—coast to coast—over fifteen days, the interviews, the appearances, the hotels and transport stations had been exhausting.

And, let's be honest, she told herself, *fabulous in its insane way.*

Every morning she'd dragged herself from a strange bed, propped open her bleary eyes and stared at the mirror just to be sure she'd see herself staring back. It was really happening, to her, Sam Gannon.

She'd been writing it all of her life, she thought, every time she'd heard the family story, every time she'd begged her grandparents to tell it, wheedled for more details. She'd been honing her craft in every hour she'd spent lying in bed as a child, imagining the adventure.

It had seemed so romantic to her, so exciting. And the best part was that it was her family, her blood.

Her current project was coming along well. She was calling it just *Big Jack,* and she thought her great-grandfather would have gotten a very large charge out of it.

She wanted to get back to it, to dive headlong into Jack O'Hara's world of cons and scams and life on the lam. Between the tour and the pretour rounds, she hadn't had a full hour to write. And she was due.

But she wasn't going straight to work. She wasn't going to think about work for at least forty-eight blissful hours. She was going to dump her bags, and she might just burn everything in them. She was going to lock herself in her own wonderful, quiet house. She was going to run a bubble bath, open a bottle of champagne.

She'd soak and she'd drink, then she'd soak and drink some more. If she was hungry, she'd buzz something up in the AutoChef. She didn't care what it was because it would be her food, in her kitchen.

Then she was going to sleep for ten hours.

She wasn't going to answer the telelink. She'd contacted her parents, her brother, her sister, her grandparents from the air, and told them all she was going under for a couple of days. Her friends and business associates could wait a day or two. Since she'd ended what had passed for a relationship over a month before, there wasn't any man waiting for her.

That was probably just as well.

She sat up when the car veered toward the curb. Home! She'd been drifting, she realized, lost in her own thoughts, as usual, and hadn't realized she was home.

She gathered her notebook, her travel bag. Riding on delight, she overtipped the driver when he hauled her suitcase and carry-on to the door for her. She was so happy to see him go, so thrilled that he'd be the last person she'd have to speak to until she decided to surface again, she nearly kissed him on the mouth.

Instead, she resisted, waved him off, then dragged her things into the tiny foyer of what her grandmother liked to call Sam's Urban Doll House.

"I'm back!" She leaned against the door, breathed deep, then did a hip-shaking, shoulder-rolling dance across the floor. "Mine, mine, mine. It's all mine. Baby, I'm back!"

She stopped short, arms still flung out in her dance of delight, and gaped at her living area. Tables and chairs were overturned, and her lovely little settee was lying on its back like a turtle on its shell. Her screen was off the wall and lay smashed in the middle of the floor, along with her collection of framed family photos and holograms. The walls had been stripped of paintings and prints.

Sam slapped both hands to her head, fisted her fingers in her short red hair and let out a bellow. "For God's *sake,* Andrea! House-sitting doesn't mean you actually sit on the goddamn house."

Having a party was one thing, but this was . . . just beyond. She was going to kick some serious ass.

She yanked her pocket 'link out of her jacket and snapped out the name. "Andrea Jacobs. Former friend," she added on a mutter as the transmission went through. Gritting her teeth, she spun on her heel and headed out of the room, started up the stairs as she listened to Andrea's recorded message.

"What the hell did you do?" she barked into the 'link, "set off a bomb? How could you do this, Andrea? How could you destroy my things and leave this mess for me to come home to? Where the hell are you? You'd better be running for your life, because when I get my hands . . . Jesus Christ, what is that smell! I'm going to kill you for this, Andrea."

The stench was so strong, she was forced to cover her mouth with her hand as she booted open the bedroom door. "It *reeks* in here, and, oh God, oh God, my bedroom. I'm never going to forgive you. I swear to God, Andrea, you're dead. Lights!" she snapped out.

And when they flashed on, when she blinked her eyes clear, she saw Andrea sprawled on the floor on a heap of stained bedclothes.

She saw she was right. Andrea was dead.

She'd nearly been out the door. Five more minutes and she'd have been off shift and heading home. Odds were someone else would have caught the case. Someone else would be spending a steaming summer night dealing with a bloater.

She'd barely closed the last case and that had been a horror.

But Andrea Jacobs was hers now. For better, for worse.

Lieutenant Eve Dallas breathed through a filtered mask. They didn't really work and looked, in her opinion, ridiculous, but it helped cut down on the worst of the smell when you were dealing with the very ripe dead.

Though the temperature controls of the room were set at a pleasant seventy-three degrees, the body had, essentially, cooked for five days. It was bloated with gases, had voided its wastes. Whoever had slit Andrea Jacobs's throat hadn't just killed her. He'd left her to rot.

"Victim's identification verified. Jacobs, Andrea. Twenty-nine-year-old mixed-race female. The throat's been slashed in what appears to be a left-to-right downward motion. Indications are the killer attacked from behind. The deterioration of the body makes it difficult to ascertain if there are other injuries, defensive wounds, through visual exam on scene. Victim is dressed in street clothes."

Party clothes, Eve thought, noting the soiled sparkle on the hem of the dress, the ice-pick heels kicked across the room.

"She came in, after a date, maybe trolling the clubs. Could've brought somebody back with her, but it doesn't look like that."

She gazed around the room while she put the pictures in her head. She wished, briefly, for Peabody. But she'd sent her former aide and very new partner home early.

There wasn't any point in dragging her back and spoiling what Eve knew was a celebration dinner with Peabody's main squeeze.

"She came back alone. If she'd come back with someone, even if he was going to kill her, he'd have gone for the sex first. Why waste it? And this isn't a struggle. This isn't a fight. One clean swipe. No other stab wounds."

She looked back at the body and brought Andrea Jacobs to life in her mind. "She comes back from her date, her night out. Had a few drinks. Starts upstairs. Does she hear something? Probably not. Maybe she's stupid and she comes upstairs after she hears somebody up here. We'll find out if she was stupid, but I bet he hears her. Hears her come in."

Eve walked out into the hall, stood there a moment, picturing it, and ignoring the movements of the crime-scene team working in the house.

She walked back, imagined kicking off those sky-high heels. Your arches would just weep with relief. Maybe she lifted one foot, bent over a little, rubbed it.

And when she straightened, he was on her.

Came from behind the door, Eve thought, or out of the closet on the wall beside the door. Stepped right up behind her, yanked her head back by the hair, then sliced.

Lips pursed, she studied the pattern of blood spatter.

Spurted out of the jugular, she thought, onto the bed. She's facing the bed, he's behind. He doesn't get messy. Just slices down quick, gives her a little shove forward. She's still spurting as she falls.

She glanced toward the windows. Drapes were drawn. Moving over, she eased them back, noted the privacy screen was engaged as well. He'd have done that. Wouldn't want anyone to notice the light, or movement.

She stepped out again, tossed the mask into her field kit.

Crime scene and the sweepers were already crawling around the place in their safe suits. She nodded toward a uniform. "Tell the ME's team she's cleared to be bagged, tagged and transported. Where's the witness?"

"Got her down in the kitchen, Lieutenant."

She checked her wrist unit. "Take your partner, start a neighborhood canvass. You're first on scene, right?"

He straightened a little. "Yes, sir."

She waited a beat. "And?"

She had a rep. You didn't want to screw up with Dallas. She was tall, lean and dressed now in summer-weight pants, T-shirt and jacket. He'd seen her seal up before she went into the bedroom, and her right hand had a smear of blood on the thumb.

He wasn't sure if he should mention it.

Her hair was brown and chopped short. Her eyes were the same color and all cop.

He'd heard it said she chewed up lazy cops for breakfast and spit them out at lunch.

He wanted to make it through the day.

"Dispatch came through at sixteen-forty, report of a break-in and possible death at this address."

Eve looked back toward the bedroom. "Yeah, extremely possible."

"My partner and I responded, arrived on scene at sixteen-fifty-two. The witness, identified as Samantha Gannon, resident, met us at the door. She was in extreme distress."

"Cut through it. Lopkre," she added, reading his name tag.

"She was hysterical, Lieutenant. She'd already vomited, just outside the front door."

"Yeah, I noticed that."

He relaxed a little, since she didn't seem inclined to take a bite out of him. "Tossed it again, same spot, right after she opened the door for us. Sort of folded in on herself there in the foyer, crying. She kept saying, 'Andrea's dead, upstairs.' My partner stayed with her while I went up to check it out. Didn't have to get far."

He grimaced, nodded toward the bedroom. "The smell. Looked into the bedroom, saw the body. Ah, as I could verify death from the visual from the doorway, I did not enter the scene and risk contaminating same. I conducted a brief search of the second floor to confirm no one else, alive or dead, was on the premises, then called it in."

"And your partner?"

"My partner's stayed with the witness throughout. She—Officer Ricky—she's got a soothing way with victims and witnesses. She's calmed her down considerably."

"All right. I'll send Ricky out. Start the canvass."

She started downstairs. She noted the suitcase just inside the door, the notebook case, the big-ass purse some women couldn't seem to make a move without.

The living area looked as if it had been hit by a high wind, as did the small media room off the central hallway. In the kitchen, it looked more like a crew of mad cooks—a redundancy in Eve's mind—had been hard at work.

The uniform sat at a small eating nook in the corner, across a dark blue table from a redhead Eve pegged as middle twenties. She was so pale the freckles that sprinkled over her nose and cheekbones stood out like cinnamon dashed over milk. Her eyes were a strong and bright blue, glassy from shock and tears and rimmed in red.

Her hair was clipped short, even shorter than Eve wore

her own, and followed the shape of her head with a little fringe over the brow. She wore enormous silver hoops in her ears, and New York black in pants, shirt, jacket.

Traveling clothes, Eve assumed, thinking of the cases in the foyer.

The uniform—Ricky, Eve remembered—had been speaking in a low, soothing voice. She broke off now, looked toward Eve. The look they exchanged was brief: cop to cop. "You call that number I gave you, Samantha."

"I will. Thank you. Thanks for staying with me."

"It's okay." Ricky slid out from the table, walked to where Eve waited just inside the doorway. "Sir. She's pretty shaky, but she'll hold a bit longer. She's going to break again, though, 'cause she's holding by her fingernails."

"What number did you give her?"

"Victim's Aid."

"Good. You record your conversation with her?"

"With her permission, yes, sir."

"See it lands on my desk." Eve hesitated a moment. Peabody also had a soothing way, and Peabody wasn't here. "I told your partner to take you and do the knock-on-doors. Find him, tell him I've requested you remain on scene for now, and to take another uniform for the canvass. If she breaks, it might be better if we have somebody she relates to nearby."

"Yes, sir."

"Give me some space with her now." Eve moved into the kitchen, stopped by the table. "Ms. Gannon? I'm Lieutenant Dallas. I need to ask you some questions."

"Yes, Beth, Officer Ricky, explained that someone would . . . I'm sorry, what was your name?"

"Dallas. Lieutenant Dallas." Eve sat. "I understand

this is difficult for you. I'd like to record this, if that's all right? Why don't you just tell me what happened."

"I don't know what happened." Her eyes glimmered, her voice thickened dangerously. But she stared down at her hands, breathed in and out several times. It was a struggle for control Eve appreciated. "I came home. I came home from the airport. I've been out of town. I've been away for two weeks."

"Where were you?"

"Um. Boston, Cleveland, East Washington, Lexington, Dallas, Denver, New L.A., Portland, Seattle. I think I forgot one. Or two." She smiled weakly. "I was on a book tour. I wrote a book. They published it—e, audio and paper forms. I'm really lucky."

Her lips trembled, and she sucked in a sob. "It's doing very well, and they sent—the publisher—they sent me on a tour to promote it. I've been bouncing around for a couple weeks. I just got home. I just got here."

Eve could see by the way Samantha's gaze flickered around the room that she was moving toward another breakdown. "Do you live here alone? Ms. Gannon?"

"What? Alone? Yes, I live by myself. Andrea doesn't—didn't—Oh God . . . "

Her breath began to hitch, and from the way her knuckles whitened as she gripped her hands together, Eve knew this time the struggle was a full-out war. "I want to help Andrea. I need you to help me understand so I can start helping her. So I need you to try to hold on until I do."

"I'm not a weak woman." She rubbed the heels of her hands over her face, violently. "I'm not. I'm good in a crisis. I don't fall apart like this. I just don't."

Bet you don't, Eve thought. "Everybody has a threshold. You came home. Tell me what happened. Was the door locked?"

"Yes. I uncoded the locks, the alarm. I stepped in, dumped my stuff. I was so happy to be in my own space again. I was tired, so happy. I wanted a glass of wine and a bubble bath. Then I saw the living room. I couldn't believe it. I was so angry. Just furious and outraged. I grabbed my 'link from my pocket and called Andrea."

"Because?"

"Oh. Oh. Andrea, she was house-sitting. I didn't want to leave the house empty for two weeks, and she wanted to have her apartment painted, so it worked out. She could stay here, water my plants, feed the fish . . . Oh Jesus, my fish!" She started to slide out, but Eve grabbed her arm.

"Hold on."

"My fish. I have two goldfish. Live fish, in my office. I didn't even look in there."

"Sit." Eve held up a finger to hold Samantha in place, then got up, stepped to the door and signaled to one of the sweepers. "Check out the home office, get me the status on a couple of goldfish."

"Huh?"

"Just do it." She went back to the table. A tear was tracking down Samantha's cheek, and the delicate redhead's skin was blotchy. But she hadn't broken yet. "Andrea was staying here while you were gone. Just Andrea?"

"Yes. She probably had someone over now and again. She's sociable. She likes to party. That's what I thought when I saw the living area. That she'd had some insane party and trashed my place. I was yelling at her machine through the 'link when I started upstairs. I said terrible things." She dropped her head into her hands.

"Terrible things," she murmured. "Then there was that

horrible smell. I was even more furious. I slammed into the bedroom, and . . . she was there. She was there, lying on the floor by the bed. All the blood, that didn't even look like blood anymore, but, you know, somehow, you know. I think I screamed. Maybe I blacked out. I don't know."

She looked up again, and her eyes were shattered. "I don't remember. I just remember seeing her, then running down the stairs again. I called nine-one-one. And I was sick. I ran outside and got sick. And then I was stupid."

"How were you stupid?"

"I went back in the house. I know better. I should've stayed outside, waited for the police outside or gone to a neighbor's. But I wasn't thinking straight, and I came back in and just stood in the foyer, shaking."

"You weren't stupid, you were in shock. There's a difference. When's the last time you talked to Andrea?"

"I'm not sure. Early in the tour. From East Washington, I think. Just a quick check." She dashed a second tear away as if irritated to find it there. "I was awfully busy, and I didn't have a lot of free time. I called once or twice, left messages. Just to remind her when I was heading home."

"Did she ever say anything to you about being concerned? About anyone giving her trouble, making threats?"

"No. Nothing like that."

"What about you? Anyone making threats?"

"Me? No. No." She shook her head.

"Who knew you were out of town?"

"Ah . . . well, everyone. My family, my friends, my agent, publisher, publicist, editor, neighbors. It wasn't a secret, that's for sure. I was so juiced about the book, about the opportunity, I pretty much told anyone who'd listen. So . . . It was a burglary, don't you think? God, I'm sorry, I can't keep your name in my head."

"Dallas."

"Don't you think it was some sort of burglary, Lieutenant Dallas? Somebody who heard I was gone and figured the house was empty, and . . . "

"Possibly. We'll need you to check your belongings, see if anything's missing." But she'd noted the electronics, the artwork any self-respecting burglar would have taken. And Andrea Jacobs had been wearing a very nice wrist unit, and considerable jewelry. Real or knockoff, it hardly mattered. A B-and-E man wouldn't have left them behind.

"Have you had any calls, mail, any contact of an unusual nature recently?"

"Well, since the book was published, I've gotten some communications. Mostly through my publisher. People who want to meet me, or who want me to help them get their book published, or want me to write their story. Some of them are pretty strange, I guess. Not threatening, though. And there's some who want to tell me their theory about the diamonds."

"What diamonds?"

"From the book. My book's about a major diamond heist in the early part of the century. Here in New York. My grandparents were involved. They didn't steal anything," she said quickly. "My grandfather was the insurance investigator who took the case, and my grandmother—it's complicated. But a quarter of the diamonds were never recovered."

"Is that so."

"Pretty frosty, really. Some of the people who've

contacted me are just playing detective. It's one of the reasons for the book's success. Millions of dollars in diamonds—where are they? It's been more than half a century, and as far as anyone knows, they've never surfaced."

"You publish under your own name?"

"Yes. See, the diamonds are how my grandparents met. It's part of Gannon family history. That's the heart of the book, really. The diamonds are the punch, but the love story is the heart."

Heart or no heart, Eve thought cynically, a few million in diamonds was a hell of a punch. And a hell of a motive.

"Okay. Have you or Andrea broken off any relationships recently?"

"Andrea didn't have relationships—per se. She just liked men." Her white skin turned flaming red. "That didn't sound right. I mean she dated a lot. She liked to go out, she enjoyed going out with men. She didn't have a serious monogamous relationship."

"Any of the men she liked to go out with want something more serious?"

"She never mentioned it. And she would have. She'd have told me if some guy got pushy. She generally went out with men who wanted what she wanted. A good time, no strings."

"How about you?"

"I'm not seeing anyone right now. Between the writing and the tour, juggling in the day-to-day, I haven't had the time or inclination. I broke a relationship off about a month ago, but there weren't any hard feelings."

"His name?"

"But he'd never—Chad would *never* hurt anyone. He's a

little bit of an asshole—well, potentially a major asshole—but he's not . . ."

"It's just routine. It helps to eliminate. Chad?"

"Oh Jesus. Chad Dix. He lives on East Seventy-first."

"Does he have your codes and access to the house?"

"No. I mean, he did but I changed them after we broke up. I'm not stupid—and my grandfather was a cop before he went private. He'd have skinned me if I hadn't taken basic security precautions."

"He'd have been right to. Who else had the new codes?"

Samantha scrubbed her hands over her hair until it stood up in short, flaming spikes. "The only one who had them besides me is Andrea, and my cleaning service. They're bonded. That's Maid In New York. Oh, and my parents. They live in Maryland. I give them all my codes. Just in case."

Her eyes widened. "The security cam. I have a security cam on the front door."

"Yes. It's been shut down, and your disks are missing."

"Oh." Her color was coming back, a kind of healthy-girl roses and cream. "That sounds very professional. Why would they be so professional, then trash the house?"

"That's a good question. I'm going to need to talk to you again at some point, but for now, is there someone you'd like to call?"

"I just don't think I could talk to anyone. I'm talked out. My parents are on vacation. They're sailing the Med." She bit her lip as if chewing on a thought. "I don't want them to know about this. They've been planning this trip for nearly a year and only left a week ago. They'd head straight back."

"Up to you."

"My brother's off-planet on business." She tapped her fingers against her teeth as she thought it through. "He'll be gone a few more days at least, and my sister's in Europe. She'll be hooking up with my parents in about ten days, so I can just keep them all out of this for now. Yeah, I can keep them out of it. I'll have to contact my grandparents, but that can wait until tomorrow."

Eve had been thinking more of Samantha contacting someone to stay with her, someone to lean on. But it seemed the woman's initial self-estimate was on the mark. She wasn't a weak woman.

"Do I have to stay here?" Samantha asked her. "As much as I hate the idea, I think I want to go to a hotel for the night—for a while, actually. I don't want to stay here alone. I don't want to be here tonight."

"I'll arrange for you to be taken anywhere you want to go. I'll need to know how to reach you."

"Okay." She closed her eyes a moment, drew in a breath as Eve got to her feet. "Lieutenant, she's dead, Andrea's dead because she was here. She's dead, isn't she, because she was here while I was away."

"She's dead because someone killed her. Whoever did is the only one responsible for what happened. You're not. She's not. It's my job to find whoever's responsible."

"You're good at your job, aren't you?"

"Yeah. I am. I'm going to have Officer Ricky take you to a hotel. If you think of anything else, you can contact me through Cop Central. Oh, these diamonds you wrote about. When were they stolen?"

"Two thousand and three. March 2003. Appraised at over twenty-eight million at that time. About three-quarters of them were recovered and returned."

"That leaves a lot of loose rocks. Thanks for your cooperation, Ms. Gannon. I'm sorry about your friend."

She stepped out, working various theories in her mind. One of the sweepers tapped her shoulder as she passed.

"Hey, Lieutenant? The fish? They didn't make it."

"Shit." Eve jammed her hands in her pockets and headed out.

Chapter 2

She was closer to home than to Central, and it was late enough to justify avoiding the trip downtown. Her equipment at home was superior to anything the cops could offer—outside of the lauded Electronic Detective Division.

The fact was, she had access to equipment superior than the Pentagon's, in all likelihood. One of her marital side bennies, she thought. Marry one of the world's wealthiest and most powerful men—one who loved his e-toys—and you got to play with them whenever you liked.

More to the point, Roarke would talk her into letting him help her use that equipment. Since Peabody wasn't around to do any drone work, Eve was planning to let him, without too much of an argument.

She liked the diamond angle, and wanted to dig up some data on that. Who better to assist in gathering data regarding a heist than a former thief? Roarke's murky past could be a definite plus on that end.

Marriage, for all its scary pockets and weird corners, was turning out to be a pretty good deal on the whole.

It would do him good to play research assistant. Take his mind off the revelations that had reared up out of that murky past and sucker punched him. When a grown man discovered his mother wasn't the stone bitch who'd slapped him around through childhood then deserted him, but a young woman who'd loved him, who'd been murdered while he was still a baby—and by his own father—it sent him reeling. Even a man as firmly balanced as Roarke.

So having him help her would help him.

It would make up, a little, for having her plans for the evening ditched. She'd had something a little more personal, and a lot more energetic, in mind. Summerset, her personal bane and Roarke's majordomo, was spending ten days at a recuperation spa off-planet—at Roarke's insistence. His holiday after breaking his leg hadn't put all the roses back in his cheeks. Like those sunken, pasty cheeks even *had* roses. But he was gone, that was the bottom line. Every minute counted. She and Roarke would be alone in the house, and there'd been no mention, that she remembered, of social or business engagements.

She'd hoped to spend the evening screwing her husband's brains out, then letting him return the favor.

Still, working together had its points.

She drove through the big iron gates that guarded the world that Roarke built.

It was spectacular, with a roll of lawn as green as the grass she'd seen in Ireland, with huge leafy trees and lovely flowering shrubs. A sanctuary of elegance and peace in the heart of the city they'd both adopted as their own. The house itself was part fortress, part castle, and somehow had come to epitomize home to her. It rose and spread, jutted and spiked with its stones dignified against the deepening sky, and its countless windows flaming from the setting sun.

As she'd come to understand him, the desperation of his childhood and his single-minded determination never to go back, she'd come to understand, even appreciate, Roarke's need to create a home base so sumptuous—so uniquely his own.

She'd needed her badge, and the home base of the law for exactly the same reasons.

She left her ugly police-issue vehicle in front of the dignified entrance, jogged up the stairs through the filthy summer heat and into the glorious cool of the foyer.

She was already itching to get to work, to put her field notes into some sort of order, to do her first runs, but she turned to the house scanner.

"Where is Roarke?"

Welcome home, darling Eve.

As usual the recorded voice using that particular endearment had slivers of embarrassment pricking at her spine.

"Yeah, yeah. Answer the question."

"He's right behind you."

"Jesus!" She whirled, biting back another curse as she saw Roarke leaning casually in the archway to the parlor. "Why don't you just pull a blaster and fire away?"

"That wasn't the welcome home I'd planned. You've blood on your pants."

She glanced down. "It's not mine." Rubbing at it absently, she studied him.

It wasn't just his greeting that spiked her heart rate. That could happen, did happen, just by looking at him. It wasn't the face. Or not just the face, with its blinding blue eyes, with that incredible mouth curved now in an easy smile, or the miracle of planes and angles that combined into a stunning specimen of male beauty framed by a mane of silky black hair. It wasn't just that long, rangy build, one she knew was hard with muscle under the business elegance of the dark suit he wore.

It was all she knew of him, all she had yet to discover, that combined and blew love through her like a storm.

It was senseless and impossible. And the most true and genuine thing she knew.

"How did you plan to welcome me home?"

He held out a hand, linking his fingers with hers when she crossed the marble floor to take it. Then he leaned in, leaned down, watching her as he brushed his lips over hers, watching her still as he deepened the kiss.

"Something like that," he murmured, with Ireland drifting through his voice. "To start."

"Good start. What's next?"

He laughed. "I thought a glass of wine in the parlor."

"All by ourselves, you and me, drinking wine in the parlor."

The glee in her voice had him lifting a brow. "Yes, I'm sure Summerset's enjoying his holiday. How sweet of you to ask."

"Blah blah." She strolled into the parlor, dropped down on one of the antique sofas and deliberately planted her boots on a priceless coffee table. "See what I'm doing? Think he just felt a sharp pain in his ass?"

"That's very childish, Lieutenant."

"What's your point?"

He had to laugh, and poured wine from a bottle he'd already opened. "Well then." He gave her a glass, sat and propped his feet on the table as well. "How was your day?"

"Uh-uh, you first."

"You want to hear about my various meetings, and the progress of plans for the acquisition of the Eton Group, the rehab of the residential complex in Frankfurt and the restructuring of the nanotech division in Chicago?"

"Okay, enough about you." She lifted her arm to make room when Galahad, their enormous cat, landed on the cushion beside her with a thump.

"I thought so." Roarke toyed with Eve's hair as she stroked the cat. "How is our new detective?"

"She's fine. She's loaded down with paperwork yet. Clearing up old business so she can start on the new. I wanted to give her a few days as a desk jockey before she takes her shiny new detective's badge out on the street."

He glanced down at the bloodstain on Eve's pants. "But you've caught a case."

"Mmm." She sipped the wine, let it smooth out the edges of the day. "I handled the on-scene solo."

"Having a little trouble adjusting to having a partner rather than an aide, Lieutenant?"

"No. Maybe. I don't know." She gave an irritable shrug. "I couldn't just cut her loose, could I?"

He flicked a finger down the shallow dent in her chin. "You didn't want to cut her loose."

"Why should I? We work well together. We've got a rhythm. I might as well keep her around. She's a good cop. Anyway, I didn't tag her for this because she had this whole big night planned, and she was already gone. You get enough plans fucked in this job without me pulling her in and botching her big celebration."

He gave her a kiss on the cheek. "Very sweet of you."

"It was not." Her shoulders wanted to hunch. "It was easier than hearing her bitch and moan about losing reservations and wasting some fancy dress or something. I'll fill her in tomorrow anyway."

"Why don't you fill me in tonight?"

"Planned on it." She slid her gaze in his direction, smirked. "I think you could be useful."

"And we know I love being useful." His fingers skimmed up her thigh.

She set down her glass, then lifted the tonnage of Galahad, who'd sprawled his girth over her lap. "Come along with me then, pal. I got a use for you."

"That sounds . . . interesting."

He started out with her, then cocked his head when she stopped halfway up the stairs. "Problem?"

"I had this thought. You know how Summerset took that header down the steps?"

"I could hardly forget."

"Yeah, well, I'm sorry he busted his pin and so on, even over and above the fact that it delayed his getting the hell out of the house for several days."

"You're entirely too sensitive, darling Eve. It can't be good for you to take on the weight of the world this way."

"Ha-ha. So it's like bad luck. The stairs, I mean. We need to fix that or one of us could be next."

"How do you propose to—"

It was impossible to finish the question, and difficult

to remember what that question was when her mouth was hot on his, and her hands already busy tugging at his belt.

He all but felt his eyes roll up in his skull and out the back of his head.

"Can't have enough good luck, to my mind," he managed, and spun her around so her back hit the wall and he could yank off her jacket.

"If we don't fall and kill ourselves, then we've broken the curse. This is a really good suit, right?"

"I have others."

She laughed, pulled at his jacket, bit his throat. He hit the release on the weapon harness, shoved at the straps so it and the weapon thudded down the steps.

Restraints followed, and pocket 'links, a raw-silk tie, a single boot. He had her pinned to the wall, not quite naked, when she came. Her nails bit into his back, then slid down so she could squeeze his butt. "I think it's working."

With a breathless laugh, he pulled her down to the steps. They bumped and rolled. Thumped down, climbed up. In self-defense, she flung out a hand and gripped one of the spindles of the banister, hooked her legs around him like a vise to keep them both from tumbling down in a heap to the bottom.

He ravaged her breasts while her arching hips drove him toward delirium. When she shuddered, when she choked out his name, he pressed his hand between them and watched her crest again.

For all that he'd wanted the whole of his life, he'd never wanted anything as he did her. The more he had of her, the more he craved in an endless cycle of love and lust and longing. He could live with whatever had come before, whatever would come after, as long as there was Eve.

"Don't let go." He cupped her hips, lifted them. "Don't let go." And drove himself into her.

There was a moment of blind, blasting pleasure, and her fingers trembled on the wood. The force of his need for her, and hers for him, rammed together, all but stopped her heart. Dazed, she opened her eyes, looked into his. She could see him lose himself, as linked with her now as if there'd been steel forging them.

So she wrapped herself around him and didn't let go.

They sprawled together on the stairs like two survivors of an earthquake. She wasn't entirely sure the ground didn't tremble still.

She had on one boot, and her pants were inside out and stuck on one leg at the ankle. She had no doubt it looked ridiculous, but couldn't drum up the energy to care.

"I'm pretty sure it's safe now," she commented.

"I hope to Christ, as I don't fancy having a go at it on these stairs a second time right at the moment."

"I'm the one with a tread in my back."

"So you are. Sorry." He rolled off her, sat up, skimmed back his hair. "That was . . . I'm not entirely sure. Memorable. I'd say memorable."

She wouldn't forget it anytime soon. "Most of our stuff's at the bottom, or nearly."

He looked down, as she did. For a moment, while they pondered, there was no sound except their ragged breathing. "There, you see, this is where having someone come along picking up after you comes in handy."

"If a certain someone—who shall remain nameless

for the next wonderful three weeks—was here to pick up after us, you wouldn't have gotten your rocks off on the steps."

"Point taken. I suppose I'll go gather things up then. You're still wearing a boot," he pointed out.

She debated for a moment, then decided working the boot off would be simpler than untangling the trousers. Once she had, she picked up whatever was reasonably in reach.

Then she sat where she was, chin on fist, and watched him tidy up the mess they'd made. It was never a hardship to look at him naked. "I've got to dump this stuff, throw something on."

"Why don't we eat while you tell me how else I might be useful?"

"Deal."

Since they'd eat in her home office for her convenience, she let him pick the menu. She even manned the AutoChef herself for the lobster salad he had a yen for. She decided the sex had burned the alcohol out of her system and allowed herself a second glass of wine as they ate.

"Okay, woman who owns the residence—private town house, Upper East—was out of town for two weeks. A female friend was house-sitting. Owner comes home this afternoon, late this afternoon, sees her living area trashed. Her statement is that the doors were locked, the security alarm set. She goes upstairs. There's a strong odor, which pisses her off as much as the mess downstairs. She walks into her bedroom, finds her house sitter dead. Dead for five days, according to my on-site. Throat slit. No other visible injuries. Indications are the attack came from behind. The security camera at the entrance was deactivated, disks removed. There's no sign of forced entry. The victim was wearing a lot of baubles. Possible—even probable—they're fake, but her wrist unit was a good brand."

"Sexual assault?"

"My prelim on-scene indicates no. I'll wait and see what the ME says on that one. She was still dressed in club clothes. When the owner settles down some, we'll have her check to see if anything was taken. I saw what appeared to be antiques, original artworks, upscale electronics. My initial search of the crime scene turned up some jewelry in a drawer. It looked like good stuff, but I'm no judge. Possibly, it was a standard B and E that went wrong, but—"

"And here you are a judge."

"It didn't look like it. It doesn't feel like it. It looks like, and feels like, somebody breaking in looking for something, or someone, specific. It looked like this woman came home before he was finished."

"Bad timing, all around."

"Absolutely. It was known that the owner was out of town. Could be he wasn't expecting anyone to be there. She walked into the bedroom, he stepped in behind her, slit her throat from ear to ear, and either continued his search or left."

"No, not your average B-and-E man. They want in and out quickly, no mess, no fuss. No weapons. You get an extra boot on your time if you get tagged carrying."

"You'd know."

He merely smiled. "As I was never tagged, or booted, I find that dry sarcasm inappropriate. He didn't burgle in the traditional sense," Roarke continued, "so traditional burglary wasn't the purpose."

"My thought. So we run Gannon and Jacobs—owner, victim—and see if anything pops that would make someone want them dead."

"Ex-spouses, lovers?"

"According to the witness, Jacobs liked to play. No specific playmate. Gannon has a recent ex. Claims they parted ways amicably, and no hard feelings, about a month back. But people can be really stupid about that sort of thing, hold grudges, or torches."

"You'd know."

She went blank for a moment, then had an image of Roarke pounding the crap out of one of her colleagues and a former one-nighter. "Webster wasn't an ex. You have to be naked with somebody for more than two hours for them to qualify as an ex. It's a law."

"I stand corrected."

"You can stop looking smug anytime. I'll run the ex. Chad Dix. Upper East addy." It wasn't pizza, she mused, but the lobster salad wasn't bad. She scooped up more as she flipped through her mental files. "The victim was a travel agent, worked for Work or Play Travel, midtown. Know them?"

"No. Don't use them."

"Some people travel for reasons other than work or play. Smuggling, for instance."

He lifted his glass, contemplated his wine. "To some points of view, smuggling might fall into the categories of either work or play."

"It'll get boring to keep saying 'you should know.' We'll look into the travel agency, but I don't think Jacobs was a target. It was Gannon's house, Gannon's things. She was out of town, known to be out of town."

"Work or play?"

"Work. She was on some sort of a tour deal for a book. It's the book that interests me."

"Really? Now you have my attention."

"Look, I read." She scooped up more lobster. "Stuff."

"Case files don't count." He gestured with his fork. "But go on. What interests you about this book?"

"Do too count," she retorted. "It's some sort of family story, but the big hook is a diamond heist, early twenty-first, here in New York. It—"

"The Forty-seventh Street job. *Hot Rocks.* I know this book."

"You read it?"

"As a matter of fact. The property was auctioned last year. Starline acquired."

"Starline? Publishing? That's yours."

"It is. I caught the pitch from the acquiring editor in one of the monthly reports. It interested me. Everyone—well, everyone with certain interests—knows about the Forty-seventh Street job."

"You'd have those certain interests."

"I would, yes. Close to thirty million in diamonds walks out of the Exchange. About three-quarters of them are scooped back up. But that leaves a lot of sparkling stones out there. Gannon. Sylvia . . . Susan . . . no, Samantha Gannon. Of course."

Yeah, Roarke was a guy who came in handy. "Okay, so you know what you know. Her grandfather recovered or helped recover the stones they got back."

"Yes. And her great-grandfather—mother's side—was one of the team who stole them."

"Is that so?" She leaned back, considered. "We didn't get into that end."

"It's in the book. She doesn't hide the connection. In fact, the connections, the ins and outs, are strong selling points."

"Give me the highlights."

"There were four known members of the heist team. One was an inside man, who handled the switch. The others posed as clients or part of the investigative team after the diamonds were discovered missing. Each scheduled a meeting with one of the designers or wholesalers upstairs. Each picked up a novelty item planted by the inside man. A ceramic dog, a rag doll, and so on."

"Back up. A doll?"

"Hide in plain sight," he explained. "Innocuously. In each blind was a quarter share of the take. They walked in, walked out in broad daylight. Legend has it—and Samantha Gannon perpetuates this in her book—that two of them had lunch a block or so away with their share on their person."

"They just walked out."

"Brilliant in its simplicity, really. There's a retail section, street level. Almost a bazaar. And in those days—still in these from time to time—some of the jewelers walk from store to store, from shop to shop, carrying a fortune in gems tucked into paper cups they call *briefkes*. With enough balls, data and some inside assistance, it's easier than you might think to walk off with sparkles in the daylight. Easier by far than an after-hours job. Do you want coffee?"

"Are you getting it?"

"I will." He rose to go into the kitchen. "They'd never have gotten away with it," he called out. "There are careful records kept for stones of that sort. It would take a great deal of patience and willpower to wait until enough time had passed to turn them, and careful research and a strong sense of character to select the right source for that liquidation. Human nature being human nature, they were bound to get nipped."

"They got away with a chunk."

"Not exactly." He came back in with a pot and two cups. "Things went wrong almost immediately, starting with dishonor among thieves—as there invariably is. One of the lot, who went by the name of Crew, decided why take a quarter when you can take all. He was a different sort than O'Hara—that's the great-grandfather—and the others, and they should've known better than to throw in with him. He lured the inside man—probably promising a sweeter deal. He gave him two bullets in the brain. They used bullets with alarming regularity back then. He took his dead partner's share, and so had half."

"And went after the others."

"He did. News traveled, and they rabbited before he got to them. And that's how they ended up bringing O'Hara's daughter into it. It got messy, as you'll see when you read the book yourself. Another of them was killed. Both Crew and the insurance cop sniffed out the trail. The cop and the thief's daughter fell in love, happily enough, and she helped him with the recovery of the half O'Hara had access to. Though they rounded up Crew as well, with some drama and heroics, he was killed in prison less than three years after his term began. They found his original share tucked away in a safe-deposit box here in the city, tracked from a key he had on his person at the time of arrest. But he never revealed where the other portion of the diamonds was."

"More than fifty years ago. They could be long gone

by now. Right back in some jewelry case in the form of rings, bracelets, whatever."

"Certainly. But it's more fun to imagine them hidden inside some ceramic cat getting dusty on a shelf in a thrift store, isn't it?"

The fun didn't register with her, but the motive did. "She talks about the family connection in her book, missing diamonds. Sexy stuff. Somebody's going to decide she must have them, or know where they are."

"There's a disclaimer in the book, of course. But yes, some are bound to wonder if she or someone in her family has them. If they're still out there, and unset, they'd be worth a great deal more today than they were at the beginning of the century. The legend alone bumps the value."

"How much?"

"Conservatively, fifteen million."

"There's nothing conservative about fifteen million. That kind of number could push a lot of people to go on a treasure hunt. Which, if pursuing that angle, narrows the field to, what, a couple million people?"

"More, I'd think, as she's been on a media tour. Even those who haven't bought or read the book could have heard the basic story in one of her interviews."

"Well, what's life without a challenge? Did you ever look for them? The Forty-seventh Street diamonds?"

"No. But it was always entertaining to speculate about them with friends over a pint in the pub. I recall, in my youth, there was some pride that Jack O'Hara, the one who got away, was an Irishman. Some liked to imagine he'd nicked the rest of them after all and lived out his days hog high on the proceeds."

"You don't think so."

"I don't know. Had he managed it, Crew would have rolled on him quick as a dog rolls on a flea that bites his back. It's Crew who had that ice, and took the location to hell with him. Out of spite, perhaps, but more—I think, more because it made them his. Kept them his."

"Obsessed, was he?"

"He's painted that way in the book, and from what I've gleaned, Samantha Gannon made it a mission to be as truthful and accurate as possible in the telling."

"All right, let's take a look at our cast of characters." She moved over to the computer on her desk. "I won't have the ME's or forensic reports until tomorrow earliest. But Gannon stated the place was locked and security was on when she returned. I took a good look, and entry wasn't forced. He either came in with Jacobs or got in himself. I'm leaning toward the latter, which would require some security experience, or knowledge of the codes."

"The ex?"

"Gannon states she changed the codes after the breakup. Doesn't mean he didn't cop to the changes. While I'm looking at him, you could get me whatever you can on the diamonds, and the people involved."

"Much more entertaining." He topped off his coffee, took it with him to his adjoining office.

She set up a standard run on Chad Dix, and brooded into her coffee while her computer pooled the data. Cold, wasteful, pointless. That was how Andrea Jacobs's murder struck her. It wasn't a panic kill. The wound was too clean, the method itself too deliberate for panic. Coming up from behind, it would've been just as easy, just as effective, to knock her unconscious. Her death had added nothing.

She discounted any real possibility of a professional hit. The state of the house put that in the low percentile. A botched burglary was a decent enough cover for a target murder, but no pro would so completely botch the botch by leaving so many portable valuables behind.

> Dix, Chad, her computer began. Resides number five, 41 East Seventy-first Street, New York, New York. DOB, March 28, 2027. Parents Mitchell Dix, Gracia Long Dix Unger. Divorced. One sibling, brother Wheaton. One half-sibling, sister Maylee Unger Brooks.

She skimmed over his education, highlighted his employment record. Financial planner for Tarbo, Chassie and Dix. A money guy, then. It seemed to her that guys who fiddled with other people's money really enjoyed having bunches of their own.

She studied his ID photo. Square-jawed, high-browed, clean-shaven. Studiously handsome, she supposed, with well-trimmed brown hair and heavy brown eyes.

"Computer, does subject have any criminal record? Include any arrest with charges dropped or suspended."

> Working . . . Drunk and disorderly, fine paid, November 12, 2049. Possession of illegals, fine paid, April 3, 2050. Destruction of public property, public drunkenness, restitution made, fine paid, July 4, 2050. Drunk and disorderly, fine paid, June 15, 2053.

"Got a little pattern working here, don't we, Chad? Computer, records of alcohol and/or chemical rehabilitation?"

Working . . . Voluntary rehabilitation program, Stokley Clinic, Chicago, Illinois. Four-week program July 13–August 10, 2050, completed. Voluntary rehabilitation program, Stokley Clinic, Chicago, Illinois. Two-week program June 16–30, 2053, completed.

"Still clean and sober, Chad?" she wondered. Regardless, his record showed no predilection for violence.

She'd interview him the next day, dig deeper if it was warranted. For now, she brought up the data on the victim.

Andrea Jacobs had been twenty-nine. Born in Brooklyn, only child, parents still living, still married to each other. They resided in Florida now, and she'd shattered their lives a few hours before when she'd notified them that their only child was dead.

Andrea's ID picture showed an attractive blonde with a wide, brilliant smile. There was no criminal record. She'd worked for the same employer for eight years, lived in the same apartment for the same amount of time.

Moved over from Brooklyn, Eve thought. Got yourself a job and a place of your own. New York girl, beginning to end. Since she had next of kin's permission to go into the victim's financials, she coded in, brought up the data.

She'd lived close, Eve noted, but no closer than any young, single woman who liked fancy shoes and nights at the club might live. Rent was paid. Saks bill was overdue, as was someplace called Clones. A quick check informed her Clones was a designer knockoff shop downtown.

With the data still up, she switched to her notes and began to order them into a report. It helped her think to take the facts, observations and statements and link them together into a whole.

She glanced over as Roarke came to the doorway.

"There's quite a bit of information about the diamonds, including detailed descriptions, photographs. A great deal more on each of the men allegedly responsible for the theft. It's still compiling. I'm having it sent to your unit simultaneously."

"Thanks. You need to oversee the run?"

"Not really, no."

"Want to go for a ride?"

"With you, Lieutenant? Always."

Chapter 3

She went back to the scene. It was dark, she thought. Not as late as it had been on the night of the murder, but near enough. She uncoded the police seal.

"How long would it take to deactivate the alarm, uncode the locks? Average?"

"But, darling, I'm not average in such matters."

She rolled her eyes. "Is it a good system? Would you need experience to get through, or just the right tools?"

"First, it's a good neighborhood. Safe and upscale. There's considerable foot and street traffic. You wouldn't want to bungle about, have anyone wondering, Now what's that guy doing over there? Even in the middle of the night. What time was the murder, by the way?"

"Time of death's estimated due to the condition of the body. But between twelve and one A.M."

"Not so very late then, particularly if we believe he

was inside already. Shank of the evening, really. So you'd want to get in without too much time. If it were me—and it hasn't been for many the year—I'd have studied the system before the event. Either gotten a good firsthand look at it or done my research and found what sort was installed and studied it at the supplier's, or online. I'd've known what I had to do before I got here."

Sensible, she thought, in a larcenous way. "And if you'd done all that?"

He made a low, considering sound and studied the locks. "With any sort of skill, you'd have the locks lifted inside four minutes. Three if you had good hands."

"Three to four minutes," she repeated.

"A longer space of time than you'd think when you're standing somewhere you shouldn't be, doing something you've got no business doing."

"Yeah, I get that."

"If you're an amateur, it would take considerably longer. The alarm, well, you see our resident has graciously put this little warning plaque here, telling those with an interest that she's protected by First Alarm Group."

Eve hissed out a breath in disgust. "Hey, Mr. Burglar Man, let me give you a hand with this break-in. Her grandfather was a cop, then went private," Eve added. "Wouldn't he have told her how stupid it is to advertise your security system?"

"Likely. So it could be a blind. For argument's sake, we'll assume, or assume our killer assumed, she's giving the honest data. Their bestselling residential package is wired into the lock itself. You'd need to take it out while you were at the lock, and that takes steady fingers. Then you'd need to reset it on the panel she's likely to have just inside the door. So that might take your man another minute, even two, providing he knew what he was about. He'd have done better if he'd purchased the system himself, then practiced on it. Did you bring me here so I could have a go at it?"

"I wanted to see—" She broke off as a man hailed them from the sidewalk.

"What're you doing there?"

He was mid-thirties, with the look of a regular health-club goer. Solid muscle over a lean frame. Behind him, across the street, a woman stood in the light spilling from an open front door. She had a pocket 'link in her hand.

"Problem?" Eve asked.

"That's what I'm asking you." The man rolled his shoulders, rocked up on the balls of his feet. Combative stance. "Nobody's home there. If you're a friend of the person who lives there, you should know that."

"You a friend of hers?"

"I live across the street." He gestured with his thumb. "We look out for each other around here."

"Glad to hear it." Eve pulled out her badge. "You know what happened here?"

"Yeah. Wait a sec." He held up a hand, turned and called out to the woman in the doorway, "It's okay, honey. They're cops. Sort of figured you were," he said when he turned back to them. "But I wanted to make sure. Couple of cops came by and talked to us already. Sorry about jumping on you. We're all a little edgy right now."

"No problem. Were you around last Thursday night?"

"We were home. We were right there across the street while . . . " He stared hard at the Gannon house. "Jesus, it's tough to think about. We knew Andrea, too. We've been to parties at Sam's, and she and my wife did the girls'-night-out thing a couple times with friends. We were right across the street when this happened."

"You knew Andrea Jacobs was staying here while Ms. Gannon was out of town?"

"My wife came over here the night before Sam left for her book tour deal—just to say goodbye, wish her luck, ask if she wanted us to feed the fish or anything. Sam told her Andrea would be around to take care of stuff."

"Did you see or speak to her, to Andrea Jacobs, during the time Samantha Gannon was out of town?"

"Don't think I saw her more than once. A quick wave across the street kind of thing. I leave the house about six-thirty most mornings. Hit the gym before the office. Wife's out by eight. Andrea kept different hours, so I didn't expect to see much of her. Never thought anything when I didn't."

"But you noticed us at the door tonight. Is that because of what happened, or do you usually keep an eye out?"

"I keep an eye. Not like an eagle," he said with a half smile. "Just try to stay aware, you know. And you guys were sort of loitering there, you know?"

"Yeah." Like someone might who was trying to lift the locks and bypass the alarm. "Have you noticed anyone who doesn't belong? Did you see anyone at the door, or just hanging around the area in the last couple weeks?"

"Cops asked me the same thing before. I've thought and thought about it. I just didn't. My wife either, because we've talked about it since we found out what happened. Haven't talked about much else."

He let out a long breath. "And last Thursday, my wife and I went to bed about ten. Watched some screen in the sack. I locked up right before we headed up. I'd've looked out. I always look out, just habit. But I didn't see anything. Anyone. It's terrible what happened. You're not supposed to know people this happens to," he said as he looked at the house. "Somebody else is supposed to know them."

She knew them, Eve thought as she walked back to Roarke. She knew countless dead.

"See how long it takes," she said to Roarke, and gestured toward the door.

"All right then." He drew a small leather case out of his pocket, selected a tool. "You'll take into consideration that I've not researched nor practiced on this particular system." He crouched.

"Yeah, yeah. You get a handicap. I just want to reconstruct a possible scenario. I don't think anybody casing this house would've gotten past Joe Gym across the street. Not if they spent any time in the neighborhood."

"While you were talking to him, a half dozen people came to doors or windows and watched."

"Yeah, I made that."

"Still, if you were casing, you might walk by, take photos." He straightened, opened the door. "And you might invest in a remote clone, if you could afford one." While he spoke, he opened the security panel inside the door, interfaced a mini pocket unit to it and manually keyed in a command. "Dress differently, take another walk. You'd just need some patience. There, that's done."

"You said three or four minutes. That was under two."

"I said someone with some skill. I didn't say me. It's a decent system, but Roarke Industries makes better."

"I'll give you a plug next time I talk to her. He went upstairs first."

"Did he?"

"He went up first because if he wasn't expecting anyone to come in, he'd have left the lights on after he hit the privacy screens. She'd have noticed that when she came in. She'd have noticed the lights, and the mess in the living area. But she didn't. Assuming she had a working brain, if she'd walked in on that, she'd have run right out again, called the cops. But she went upstairs."

She opened the front door again, let it slam shut. "He heard her. She checks the locks, the alarms. Maybe she checks the 'link down here for messages." Eve walked through the living area, skirting around the mess, ignoring the chemical smell left behind by the sweepers. "She's been clubbing, probably had a few drinks. She doesn't spend much time down here. She's wearing arch-killing shoes, but she doesn't take them off until she's in the bedroom. Can't see why she'd walk around down here in them for long with nobody around to admire her legs. She starts upstairs."

She moved up the steps. "I bet she likes the house. She's lived in an apartment for nearly a decade. I bet she likes having all this room. She turns into the bedroom, kicks off the fuck-me shoes."

"Minor point, but how do you know she didn't take off the shoes downstairs, walk up barefoot, carrying them?"

"Hmm? Oh, their position—and hers. If they'd been in her hand when she got sliced, they'd have dropped closer to her body. If she'd carried them up, she'd have turned toward, or at least have tossed them closer to, the closet. Seems to me. See where I'm standing?"

He saw where she was standing, just as he saw the splotches and splatters of blood on the bed, the floor, the lamp, the wall. The stench of it all was barely hidden under the chemicals. And he wondered how, how in

God's name, anyone could come back and sleep in this room again. Live with the nightmare of this room.

Then he looked at his wife, saw she was waiting. Saw her cop's eyes were cool and flat. She lived with nightmares, waking and sleeping.

"Yes, I see."

"Closet doors were open. I'm betting the closet. He didn't start in here. I think he started in the office down the hall. I think that was his first stop, and he didn't get very far."

"Why?"

"If he'd tossed this room, she'd have seen the mess as soon as she opened the door. No defensive wounds, no sign she tried to run or fight. Second, there's a workstation in the office, and it's still neat as a pin. I figure that was his starting point, and he'd planned to be careful, to be tidy. Jacobs comes in, screws that plan for him."

"And Plan B is murder."

"Yeah. No way he missed her workstation, but he didn't mess it up. He went through everything else, and wasn't worried about being neat, but he'd already searched the workstation. Why mess with it again?"

Roarke looked at the horror of blood and fluids staining the floor and walls. "And slicing a woman's throat is more time efficient."

"That could factor. I think he heard her come in, and instead of waiting until she went to sleep and getting the hell out, instead of knocking her senseless, he slipped right in here, slid back into the closet and watched her come in and kick off her fancy shoes. Push that stuff out of the way, will you? We've already been through here, scene's on record. Stand in the closet."

"Christ." He pushed the heaps of clothes and pillows aside, stepped back inside the open closet.

"See the angle? This had to be the angle from the way she landed. She's standing like this, facing away. He came up behind, yanked her head back by the hair—she had long hair, and the angle of the wound—had to be. Slice down, left to right. Do that. Just fake the hair."

He reached her in two strides, gave her short hair a tug, feigned the swipe with a knife.

She imagined herself jerking once. The shock the system experienced, the alarm screaming in the brain even as the body died. And looked down at the floor, brought the position of the body back into her mind.

"Had to be. Had to be just like that. He couldn't have hesitated, not for a second. Even a second warning, she'd have turned, changed the angle some. Had to be fast and smooth. See, she hit the side of the bed when she fell. Spatter indicates. Hit the side of the bed, bounced, rolled, landed. Then he went back to work. He had to do most of this after he'd killed her. He must've spent another hour, maybe two, in the house with her, some of that right in this room with her while she was bleeding out. He's got steady hands. And he's got cold blood."

"Have you got a watch on Samantha Gannon?"

"Yeah. And it's going to stay on her until I take him down. Let's get out of here."

He waited until they were outside again, in the hot summer air. Until she'd resealed the door. Then he ran his hands down her arms, drew her against him and kissed her lightly.

"What was that for?" she asked.

"We needed it."

"Guess you're right." She took his hand, walked down the steps. "We did."

• • •

The media had already caught the scent. Eve's office 'link at Cop Central was clogged with requests, pleas, demands for information. She dumped them all, with some pleasure, shooting them to the media liaison. They could sniff for blood all they wanted, but they weren't getting any from her until she was ready.

She expected to get a personal visit from Nadine Furst before much longer. She'd deal with that when the time came. The fact was there was probably a way for her to use Channel 75's hotshot on-air reporter.

She programmed coffee and decided it was never too early to nag the ME or the lab.

She was arguing with the ME assigned to her case, disgusted to be informed Chief Medical Examiner Morris was on leave, when she heard hoots and whistles erupt from the bull pen outside her office.

"I don't care if it is the summer crunch in your line of work," Eve snapped. "Sending in bodies doesn't happen to be my little hobby. I need results, not excuses."

She broke transmission, decided her first ass-kicking of the day put her in the perfect mood to bitch at the lab. Then scowled at the clicking sound approaching her office.

"Morning, Dallas."

The stalwart Peabody, newly promoted to detective, no longer wore her spit-and-polish uniform. And Eve was discovering that was a damn pity. Her sturdy body, which showed a lot more curves out of her blues, was decked out in a pair of pegged lavender pants, a snug purple top and a floaty sort of jacket that picked up both colors in thin stripes. Instead of her clunky and perfectly respectable cop shoes she had on pointy-toed purple shoes with short skinny heels.

Which explained the clicking.

"What the hell have you got on?"

"Clothes. They're my clothes. I'm trying out different looks so I can settle on my particular work style. I'm thinking about new hair, too."

"Why do you have to have new hair?" She was *used* to Peabody's dark bowl of hair, damn it. "Why do people always have to have new hair? If you didn't like the old hair, why did you have the old hair? Then you won't like the new hair, and you'll have to have new new hair. It makes me crazy."

"So much does."

"And what the hell are those?" She jabbed a finger at the shoes.

"Aren't they great?" She turned her ankle to show them off. "Surprisingly comfortable, too."

"Those are girl shoes."

"Dallas, I don't know how to tell you this, but I am a girl."

"My partner's not a girl. I don't have girl partners. I have cops. My partner is a cop, and those are not the shoes of a cop. You click."

"Thanks, Lieutenant." Peabody smiled down at herself. "I do think it all works well together."

"No, Jesus Christ in spandex. You click when you walk."

"They just need to be broken in." She started to sulk, then saw the case file, the crime-scene stills, on Eve's desk. "What're you doing? Are you working on a cold case?"

"It's hot. I caught it yesterday, right before end of shift."

"You caught a case and you didn't tag me?"

"Don't whine. I didn't call you in because you had The Big Night. Remember how you kept saying it, like it was a vid title? I know how to work a scene, Peabody. There was no reason to screw up your plans."

"Despite your opinion of my shoes, I'm a cop. I expect to have my plans screwed."

"This time they weren't. Shit, I wanted you to have it. If you're going to make a big deal here, you're just going to piss me off."

Peabody folded in her lips. Shifted her stance as the shoes weren't quite as comfortable as she'd claimed. Then she smiled. "I'm not. I appreciate it. It was important to me, and McNab went to a lot of trouble. So thanks. We had a great time. I drank a little more than I should, so I'm a little fuzzy this morning. But a hit of real coffee should help that."

She looked hopefully toward Eve's AutoChef, where there was real as opposed to the sludge disguised as coffee in the bull pen.

"Go ahead. Then sit down. I'll bring you up to speed."

"Missing diamonds. It's like a treasure hunt," Peabody decided. "Like booty. It could be fun."

Saying nothing, Eve passed her one of the on-scene stills of Andrea Jacobs's body. Peabody let out a hiss between her teeth. "Okay, not so much. No sign of forced entry? Sexual assault?"

"None apparent from the on-scene."

"She could've brought someone home with her. Bad choice. People make them."

"We'll check that out. I ran her debit card. Her last transaction, which looks like clearing the evening's tab, was at Club Six-Oh. Sixtieth and Second, at eleven forty-five on Thursday night. Estimated time of death was between midnight and one."

"So she'd have gone straight to the Gannon residence from the club. If she had company, she found it there."

"We're in the field," Eve said, gathering the file. "We talk to Gannon's ex, Jacobs's employer and coworkers, hit the club and swing by the morgue to harass people."

"I always like that part. I get to flash my new badge," she added as they walked out. She flipped her jacket open to reveal the detective's badge hooked to her waistband.

"Very nice."

"My new favorite accessory."

The powers-that-be at Tarbo, Chassie and Dix obviously subscribed to the theory that a display of excess drew in clients whose finances needed planning. The midtown offices were spread over four floors with a main information center the size of the Yankees' outfield. Eight young men and women, certainly hired as much for their perky good looks as their communication skills, manned an alarm-red island counter that could have housed a small suburb. Each wore a personal communicator and manned slick minidata and communication centers.

Each obviously practiced superior dental hygiene if their dazzling, identical smiles were any gauge.

Around them were smaller counters with more perky, toothy men and women in snappy suits, three waiting areas with cushy-looking chairs, equipped with screens for passing the time with magazines or short vids, and a little, tastefully planted garden with its own tiny blue pool.

Bouncy, repetitive music danced through the air at a discreet volume.

Eve decided she'd be in a padded room for mental

defectives in under a week if she worked under similar conditions.

She walked to the main counter over a springy silver carpet. "Chad Dix."

"Mr. Dix is on forty-two." The beaming brunette tapped her screen. "I'll be happy to have one of his assistants escort you. If I might have your name, and the time of your appointment?"

Eve laid her badge on the glossy red counter. "Lieutenant Dallas, NYPSD. And I'd say my appointment is now. We can get up to forty-two ourselves, thanks, but you might want to tell Mr. Dix we're on our way."

"But you have to be cleared for the elevator."

Eve picked up her badge, wiggled it back and forth. "Then you'd better take care of that." She pocketed the badge and strode to the bank of elevators with Peabody.

"Can I be bitch cop next time?" Peabody whispered as they waited for the doors to open. "I really need to practice."

"Seems to me if you need to practice, it's not a true calling, but you can take a shot." She stepped onto the elevator. "Forty-two," she demanded. And leaned back on the side wall as the car whisked them up. "Take the assistant they're going to toss in our way."

"Hot dog." Peabody rubbed her hands together. Then rolled her shoulders, circled her neck.

"Definitely not a true calling," Eve muttered, but let Peabody lead when the doors opened on forty-two.

This floor was no less opulent than the other, though the color scheme was electric blue and silver rather than red. The waiting areas were bigger, with the addition of wall screens tuned to various financial programs. This information station was the size and shape of a small wading pool, but there was no need to bother with it as the assistant clipped hurriedly through the double glass doors that slid soundlessly open at her approach.

This one was blonde with the sunshine hair done in a mass of corkscrew curls that spilled and spun around her head like a halo. She had pink lips and cheeks and a body of impressive curves tucked snugly into a narrow skirt and jacket the color of cotton candy.

Not wanting to miss her chance, Peabody stepped forward, flipped her jacket open. "Detective Peabody, NYPSD. My partner, Lieutenant Dallas. We need to speak to Chad Dix regarding an investigation."

"Mr. Dix is meeting with a client, but I'd be happy to review his schedule and clear some time for you later today. If you could give me some idea of the nature of your business, and how much time you'll require."

"The nature of our business is murder, and the time we require will depend entirely on Mr. Dix." Peabody dipped her head, lowered her eyebrows in a stern look she enjoyed practicing in the bathroom mirror. "If he feels unable to meet with us here and now, we'll be happy to take him downtown and hold our meeting there. You can come with him," Peabody added.

"I . . . If you'll give me just a moment."

When she scurried off, Peabody elbowed Eve. " 'Our business is murder.' I thought that was good."

"It didn't suck." She nodded as the blonde came bustling back. "Let's check the scores."

"If you'll come with me, Mr. Dix will see you now."

"I thought he would." Peabody started to saunter after her.

"Don't rub their noses in it," Eve muttered. "It's tacky."

"Check."

They moved through a fan-shaped hallway to the wide end and another set of double doors. These were opaque and opened when the assistant tapped.

"Detective Peabody and Lieutenant Dallas, Mr. Dix."

"Thank you, Juna."

He was behind a U-shaped workstation with the requisite window-wall at his back. His office suite had a luxurious sitting area with several wide chairs and a display shelf holding a number of antique games and toys.

He wore a stone-gray suit with muted chalk stripes, and a braided silver chain under the collar of his snowy white shirt.

"Officers." His expression sober, he gestured toward chairs. "I assume this has something to do with the tragedy at Samantha Gannon's. I heard about it last night on a media report. I haven't been able to reach Samantha. Are you able to tell me if she's all right?"

"As much as can be expected," Eve answered. "You also knew Andrea Jacobs?"

"Yes." He shook his head and sat behind his desk. "I can't believe this happened. I met her through Samantha. We socialized quite a bit while Samantha and I were seeing each other. She was . . . It probably sounds clichéd, but she was one of those people who are just full of life. The reports are vague, even this morning. There was a burglary?"

"We're in the process of verifying that. You and Ms. Gannon are no longer seeing each other?"

"No, not romantically."

"Why is that?"

"It wasn't working out."

"For whom?"

"Either of us. Sam's a beautiful, interesting woman, but we weren't enjoying ourselves together any longer. We decided to break it off."

"You had the codes to her residence."

"I . . ." He missed a beat, quietly cleared his throat. "Yes. I did. As she had mine. I assume she changed them after we broke up—as I changed mine."

"Can you tell us where you were on the night in question?"

"Yes, of course. I was here, in the office until just after seven. I had a dinner meeting with a client at Bistro, just down on Fifty-first. Juna can give you the client's information, if you need it. I left the restaurant about ten-thirty and went home. I caught up on some paperwork for an hour or so, watched the media reports, as I do every night before I turn in. That must have been nearly midnight. Then I went to bed."

"Can anyone verify this?"

"No, not after I left the restaurant, in any case. I took a cab home, but I couldn't tell you the number of the cab. I wouldn't have any reason to break into Sam's house and steal anything, or for God's sake kill Andrea."

"You've had some substance-abuse problems over the years, Mr. Dix."

A muscle twitched in his jaw. "I'm clean, and have been for a number of years. I've been through rehabilitation programs and continue to go to regular meetings. If necessary, I'll submit to a screening, but I'll want legal representation."

"We'll let you know. When's the last time you had contact with Andrea Jacobs?"

"A couple of months, six weeks ago, at least. It seems to me we all went to a jazz club downtown this summer.

Sam and I, Andrea and whoever she was seeing at the time, a couple of other people. It was a few weeks before Sam and I called things off."

"Did you and Ms. Jacobs ever see each other separately?"

"No." His tone took on an edge. "I didn't cheat on Sam, certainly not with one of her friends. And Andrea, as much as she enjoyed men, wouldn't have poached. That's insulting on every level."

"I insult a lot of people, on every level, in my work. Murder doesn't make for nice manners. Thanks for your cooperation, Mr. Dix." Eve rose. "We'll be in touch if there's anything else."

She started for the door, then turned. "By the way, have you read Ms. Gannon's book?"

"Of course. She gave me an advance copy several weeks ago. And I bought one on the day of its release."

"Any theories on the diamonds?"

"Fascinating stuff, isn't it? I think Crew's ex-wife skipped with them and made a really nice life for herself somewhere."

"Could be. Thanks again."

Eve waited until they were riding down to street level. "Impressions, Detective?"

"I just love when you call me that. He's sharp, he's smooth, and he wasn't in a meeting. He had his assistant say so to flip us off, if possible."

"Yeah. People just don't like talking to cops. Why is that? He was prepared," she added, as they stepped out and started across the lobby. "Had his night in question all laid out, didn't even have to remind him of the date. Six days ago, and he doesn't even have to think about it. Rattled it off like a student reciting a school report."

"He still isn't clear for the time of the murder."

"Nope, which is probably why he wanted to flip us off awhile. Let's hit the travel agency next."

Eve supposed under most circumstances Work or Play would've been a cheerful place. The walls were covered with screens where impossibly pretty people romped in exotic locales that probably convinced potential travelers they'd look just as impossibly pretty frolicking half-naked on some tropical beach.

There were a half dozen agents at workstations rather than cubes, and each station was decorated with personal memorabilia: photos, little dolls or amusing paperweights, posters.

All of the agents were female, and the office smelled of girls. Sort of candy-coated sex, to Eve's mind. They were all dressed in fashionable casualwear—or she assumed it was fashionable—even the woman who appeared to be pregnant enough to be carting around three healthy toddlers in her womb.

Just looking at her made Eve jittery.

Even worse were the six pairs of swollen, teary eyes, the occasional broken sob or sniffle.

The room pulsed with estrogen and emotion.

"It's the most horrible thing. The most horrible." The pregnant woman somehow levered herself up from her chair. She had her streaky brown hair pulled back, and her face was wide as the moon and the color of milk chocolate. She laid her hand on the shoulder of one of the other women as she began to cry.

"It might be easier if we go back to my office. This is actually Andrea's station. I've been manning it this morning. I'm Cecily Newberry. I'm, well, the boss."

She led the way to a tiny, tidy adjoining office and shut the door. "The girls are—well, we're a mess. We're just a mess. I honestly didn't believe Nara when she called me this morning, crying and babbling about Andrea. Then I switched on the news channel and got the report. I'm sorry." She braced a hand at the small of her back and lowered herself into a chair. "I have to sit. It feels like a maxibus is parked on my bladder."

"When are you due, Ms. Newberry?" Peabody asked.

"Ten more days." She patted her belly. "It's my second. I don't know what I was thinking, timing this baby so I'd carry it through the summer heat. I came in today—I'd intended to take the next several weeks off. But I came in because . . . I didn't know what else I could do. Should do. Andrea worked here almost since I opened the place. She manages it with me, and was going to take over while I was on maternity."

"She hasn't been in to work for several days. Weren't you concerned?"

"She was taking some leave now. She was actually due back today, when I'd planned to start mine. Oh God." She rubbed at her face. "Usually she'd take advantage of our benefits and go somewhere, but she decided to house-sit for her friend and get her apartment painted, do some shopping, she said, hit a few of the spas and salons around town. I expected to hear from her yesterday or the day before, just to check in with me before we switched over. But I really didn't think anything of it when I didn't. I didn't think at all, to be frank. Between this baby, my little girl at home, the business, my husband's mother deciding now's a dandy time to come stay with us, I've been distracted."

"When's the last time you did talk to her?"

"A couple of weeks. I'm . . . I was very fond of Andrea, and she was wonderful to work with. But we had very different lifestyles. She was single and loved to go out. I'm incredibly married and raising a three-year-old, having another child and running a business. So we didn't see each other often outside of work, or talk often unless it was work-related."

"Has anyone come in asking about her or for her specifically?"

"She has a regular customer base. Most of my girls do. Customers who ask for them specifically when they're planning a trip."

"She'd have a customer list."

"Absolutely. There's probably some legal thing I'm supposed to do before I agree to give that to you, but I'm not going to waste my time or yours. I have all my employees' passcodes. I'll give it to you. You can copy anything you feel might help off her work unit."

"I appreciate your cooperation."

"She was a delightful woman. She made mc laugh, and she did a good job for me. I never knew her to hurt anyone. I'll do whatever I can to help you find who did this to her. She was one of my girls, you know. She was one of mine."

It took an hour to copy the files, search through and document the contents of the workstation and interview the other employees.

Every one of Andrea's coworkers had gone out with her to clubs, bars, parties, with dates, without dates. There was a great deal of weeping but little new to be learned.

Eve could barely wait to get away from the scent of grief and lipdye.

"Start doing a standard run on the names on her

customer base. I'm going to check in with Samantha Gannon and verbally smack this asshole ME around."

"Morris?"

"No, Morris is tanning his fine self on some tropical beach. We caught Duluc. She's slower than a one-legged snail. I'm going to warm up with her, then, if there's time, drop-kick Dickhead," she added, referring to the chief lab tech.

"Boy, that should round out the morning. Then maybe we can have lunch."

"We're dealing with the cleaning service before the morgue and lab. Didn't you have breakfast a couple hours ago?"

"Yeah, but if I start nagging you about lunch now, you'll cave before I get faint from hunger."

"Detectives eat less often than aides."

"I never heard that. You're just saying that to scare me." She trotted on her increasingly uncomfortable shoes after Eve. "Right?"

Chapter 4

Maid In New York was a pared-down, storefront operation that put all its focus and frills into the services. This was explained to Eve with some snippiness by the personnel manager, who reigned in an office even smaller and stingier than Eve's at Central.

"We keep the overhead to a minimum," Ms. Tesky of the sensible bun and shoes informed Eve. "Our clients aren't interested in our offices—and rarely come here in any case—but are concerned about their own offices and homes."

"I can see why," Eve observed, and Tesky's nostrils pinched. It was sort of interesting to watch.

"Our employees are the product, and all are strictly and comprehensively interviewed, tested, screened, trained and must meet the highest of standards in personal appearance, demeanor and skill. Our clients are also screened, to ensure our employees' safety."

"I just bet they are."

"We provide residential and business housekeeping services, in teams, pairs or individually. We use human and droid personnel. We service all of greater New York and New Jersey and will, upon request, arrange for maids to travel with a client who requires or desires approved out-of-town, out-of-country and even off-planet services."

"Right." She wondered how many of the maids were also licensed companions, but it didn't really apply. "I'm interested in the employee or employees who handled Samantha Gannon's residence."

"I see. Do you have a warrant? I consider our personnel and client files confidential."

"I bet you do. I could get a warrant. A little time, a little trouble, but I could get a warrant. But because you made me take that time and that trouble when I'm investigating a murder—a really nasty, messy murder, by the way, that's going to take a whole slew of your mighty maids to tidy up—I'm going to wonder why you slowed me down. I'm going to ask myself, Hey, I wonder what Ms. Testy—"

"Tes-*ky*."

"Right. What she has to hide. I have a suspicious mind, that's why I got to be a lieutenant. So when I get that warrant, and I start wondering those things, I'm going to dig, and I'm going to keep digging, getting my suspicious little finger smears all over your nice tidy files. We'll just have to give INS a heads-up so they can breeze in here and make another big mess, making sure you didn't miss any illegals in all that testing and screening."

The nostrils pinched again, even as a thin breath hooted up them. "Your implication is insulting."

"People keep saying that to me. The fact that I'm

innately suspicious and insulting means I'll probably make a bigger mess than those anal-retentives in INS. Won't I, Detective Peabody?"

"As someone who's cleaned up after you before, sir, I can verify that you will, absolutely, make a bigger mess than anyone. You'll also find something—you always do—that will certainly inconvenience Ms. Tesky and her employer."

"What do they call that? Tit for tat?"

Throughout Eve's recital, Ms. Tesky had turned several interesting colors. She appeared to have settled on fuchsia. "You can't threaten me."

"Threaten? Golly, Peabody, insult, sure, but did I threaten anyone?"

"No, Lieutenant. You're just making conversation, in your own unique style."

"That's what I thought. Just making conversation. So, let's arrange for that warrant, shall we? And since we're taking the time and trouble, let's make it for the financials, and civil and criminal cases or suits brought, as well as those personnel files."

"I find you very disagreeable."

"There you go," Eve said with an easy smile. "Tit for tat one more time."

Tesky spun her chair around to her desk unit, coded in.

"Ms. Gannon's residence is on a twice-monthly schedule, with quarterly extended services, and priority for emergency calls and entertainment requests. She was due for her regular service yesterday."

Several more frown lines dug into Tesky's forehead. "Her maid failed to confirm completed service. That's simply unacceptable."

"Who's the maid?"

"Tina Cobb. She's seen to the Gannon residence for the last eight months."

"Can you check on there if she's missed any other jobs recently?"

"One moment." She called up another program. "All Cobb's jobs were completed and confirmed through Saturday. She had Sunday off. No confirmation of the Gannon residence yesterday. There's a flag by her name today, which means the client notified us she didn't report for work. Scheduling had to replace her."

Ms. Tesky did what Eve assumed anyone named Tesky would. She tsked.

"Give me her home address."

Tina Cobb lived in one of the post–Urban Wars boxes that edged the Bowery. They'd been a temporary fix when buildings had been burned or bombed. The temporary fix had lasted more than a generation. Lewd, creative and often ungrammatical graffiti swirled over the pitted, reconstituted concrete. The windows were riot-barred, and the loiterers on the stoops looked as though they'd be more than happy to burn or bomb the place again, just to break the monotony.

Eve climbed out of her car, scanned the faces, ignored the unmistakable aroma of Zoner. She took out her badge, held it up.

"You can probably guess that's mine," she said, pointing at her vehicle. "What you might not be able to guess is that if anybody messes with it, I'll hunt you down and pop your eyes out with my thumbs."

"Hey." A guy wearing a dingy muscle shirt and a gleaming silver earring flipped her the bird. "Fuck you."

"No, thanks, but it's sweet of you to ask. I'm looking for Tina Cobb."

There were whistles, catcalls, kissy noises. "That's one fiiine piece of ass."

"I'm sure she's delighted you think so. Is she around?"

Muscle Shirt stood up. He poked out his chest and jabbed a finger at Eve's. Fortunately for him, he stopped short of actual contact. "What you want to hassle Tina for? She don't do nothing. Girl works hard, minds her own."

"Who said I was going to hassle her? She might be in trouble. If you're a friend of hers, you'll want to help."

"Didn't say I was a friend. Just said she minds her own. So do I. Whyn't you?"

"Because I get paid to mind other people's own, and you're starting to make me wonder why you can't answer a simple question. In a minute, I'm going to start minding yours instead of Tina Cobb's."

"Cops is all shit."

She bared her teeth in a glittering grin. "Want to test that theory?"

He snorted, shot a glance over his shoulder at his companions as if to let them see he wasn't worried about it. "Too hot to bother," he said, and shrugged his skinny shoulders. "Ain't seen Tina for a couple of days anyway. Don't run a tab on her, do I? Her sister works across the street at the bodega. Whyn't you ask her?"

"I'll do that. Mitts off the car, boys. Pitiful as it is, it's mine."

They walked across the street. Eve assumed the kissing noises and invitations for sexual adventure that came from the stoop were now aimed at her and Peabody. But she let it go. The skinny asshole was right about one thing. It was too hot to bother.

Inside, she noted the girl manning the checkout counter. Short, thin, olive complexion, an odd updo of hair with purple fringes over the ink black.

"I could get us something," Peabody offered. "Something to do with food."

"Go ahead." Eve walked to the counter, waited while the customer in front of her paid for a pack of milk powder and a minuscule box of sugar substitute.

"Help you?" the woman said, without much interest.

"I'm looking for Tina Cobb. You're her sister?"

The dark eyes widened. "What do you want with Tina?"

"I want to talk to her." Eve slipped out her badge.

"I don't know where she is, okay? She wants to take off for a couple days, it's nobody's sweat, is it?"

"Shouldn't be." Eve had run Tina Cobb in the car and knew the sister's name was Essie. "Essie, why don't you take a break?"

"I can't, okay. I can't. I'm working alone today."

"And nobody's in here right now. Did she tell you where she was going?"

"No. Shit." Essie sat down on a high stool. "Oh shit. She's never been in trouble in her life. She spends all the time cleaning up after rich people. Maybe she just wanted some time off." There was fear lurking behind the eyes now. "She maybe went on a trip."

"Was she planning a trip?"

"She's always planning. When she had enough saved she was going to do this, and that, and six million other things. Only she never saved enough for any of it. I don't know where she is. I don't know what to do."

"How long's she been gone?"

"Since Saturday. Saturday night she goes out, doesn't come back since. Sometimes she doesn't come home at night. Sometimes I don't. You get a guy, you want to stay out, you stay, right?"

"Sure. So she's been gone since Saturday?"

"Yeah. She's got Sundays off, so what the hell, you know? But she's never been gone like this without letting me know. I called her work today and asked for her, and they said she didn't show. I probably got her in trouble. I shouldn'ta called her work."

"You haven't reported her missing?"

"Shit, you don't report somebody missing 'cause they don't come home a couple nights. You don't go to the cops for every damn thing. Around here, you don't go to them for nothing."

"She take any of her things?"

"I dunno. Her maid suit's still there, but her red shirt and her black jeans aren't. Her new airsandals neither."

"I want to go inside the apartment, look around."

"She's gonna be pissed at me." Essie scooped up the soft tacos and Pepsis Peabody laid on the counter, did the transaction. "What the hell. She shouldn'ta gone off without saying. I wouldn't do it to her. I gotta close up. I can't take more than fifteen, or I'll get in real trouble."

"That's fine."

It was two tiny rooms with a bump on the living area that served as the kitchen. The sink was about the width and depth of a man's cupped palm. In lieu of the pricier privacy screens, there were manual shades at the windows that did absolutely nothing to cut the street or sky noise.

Eve thought it was like living in a transpo station.

There was a two-seater couch Eve imagined converted to a bed, an ancient and clunky entertainment screen and a single lamp in the shape of a cartoon mouse she suspected one of them had saved from childhood.

Despite its size and sparseness, the apartment was pin neat. And, oddly enough to her mind, smelled as female as the girl-powered travel agency had.

"Bedroom's through there." Essie pointed at the doorway. "Tina won the toss when we moved in, so she has the bedroom and I sleep out here. But it's still pretty tight, you know? So that's why if one of us has a guy, we usually go to his place."

"She have a guy?" Eve asked as Peabody walked toward the bedroom.

"She's been seeing somebody a couple of weeks. His name's Bobby."

"Bobby got a last name?"

"Probably." Essie shrugged. "I don't know it. She's with him, probably. Tina's got this real romantic heart. She falls for a guy, she falls hard."

Eve scanned the bedroom. One narrow bed, neatly made, one child-sized dresser, likely brought from home. There was a pretty little decorative box on it and a cheap vase with fake roses. Eve lifted the top of the box, heard the tinkling tune it played and saw a few pieces of inexpensive jewelry inside.

"We share the closet," Essie said as Peabody poked inside the tiny closet.

"Where'd she meet this Bobby?" Peabody asked her, and moved from the closet into the bathroom.

"I don't know. We live in this box together, but we try to stay out of each other's faces, you know? She just says she met this guy, and he's really cute and sweet and smart. Said he knew all about books and art and shit. She goes for that. She went out to meet him like at an art gallery or something one night."

"You never met him?" Eve asked.

"No. She was always meeting him somewhere. We don't bring guys here much. Jeez, look at this place." She looked around it with the forlorn and resigned expression of a woman who knew it was the best she was going to do. "She was going out to meet him Saturday night, after work and shit. To a play or something. When she didn't come home, I figured she'd stayed at his place. No big. But she doesn't miss work, and she hasn't ever stayed out of touch this long, so I'm starting to worry, you know?"

"Why don't we file a report?" Peabody stepped back out of the bath. "A missing person's report."

"Oh man, you think?" Essie scratched at her bicolored hair. "She comes waltzing in here and finds out I did that, she'll be on my case for a month. We don't have to tell my parents, do we? They'll get all twisted inside out and come running over here hysterical and whatever."

"Have you checked with them? Maybe she went home for a couple days."

"Nah. I mean yeah, I checked. I buzzed my mom and did the hey, how're things, la la la. She said to have Tina call 'cause she likes to hear from her girls. So I know she hasn't seen her. My mom would flip sideways if she thought Tina's shacked up with some guy."

"We'll take care of it. Why don't you give the information to Detective Peabody?" Eve looked at the tidily made bed.

"She's not off with some guy for extended nooky," Eve said when they were back in the car. "Girls like that don't take off without a change of clothes, without taking earrings and their toothbrush. She doesn't miss a day of work in eight months, but she just happens to miss the Gannon job?"

"You think she was in on it?"

Eve thought of the tiny, tidy apartment. The little music box of trinkets. "Not on purpose. I doubt the same can be said for Bobby."

"It's going to be tough to track down some guy named Bobby. No full name, no description."

"He left footprints somewhere. Do a check on Jane Does, any that came in since Saturday night. We're heading down to the morgue anyway. Let's just hope we don't find her there."

"Want your taco?"

Eve unwrapped it on her lap, then decided eating it while she drove was just asking to go through the rest of the day with taco juice on her shirt. She switched to auto, clicked back a couple inches and chowed down.

When the in-dash 'link signaled, she shook her head. "Screen it," she said with a mouthful of mystery meat by-product and sinus-clearing sauce.

"Nadine Furst," Peabody announced.

"Too bad I'm on lunch break." She slurped up Pepsi and ignored the call. "So, a maid from the projects somehow hooks up with some guy named Bobby, who takes her to art galleries and the theater, but he never comes to her place and meets her sister. She's out of touch, missing work, among the missing for three days, but her new boyfriend doesn't call, leave a message, scoot by to see what's up. Nothing."

"He wouldn't if she was with him."

"Point for that. But this girl, who makes her bed like a

Youth Scout, doesn't call in to work sick, doesn't tell her sister she's cozied down in a love nest, doesn't want extra clothes or all the equipment females take on sex safaris. She risks her paycheck, ignores her family, stays in the same outfit? I don't think so."

"You think she's dead."

"I think she had the access code to Gannon's place, and somebody wanted that code. I think if she was alive and well or able, she'd have seen or heard the media reports bombarding the screen about bestselling author Samantha Gannon's recent problem and she'd have gotten to her sister if no one else."

"Three Jane Does last seventy-two," Peabody reported. "Two elderly indigents, no official ID on record. Third's a crispy critter, status pending."

"Where'd they find her?"

"Abandoned lot," Peabody read off her PPC. "Alphabet City. About three hundred Sunday morning. Somebody doused her with gasoline—Jesus, they had some credit to tap on—lit her up. By the time somebody called it in, she was toasted. That's all I've got."

"Who's primary?"

"Hold on. Aha! It's our good pal Baxter, ably assisted by the adorable Officer Trueheart."

"Simplifies. Tag him. See if they can meet us at the morgue."

Eve had to pace her cooling heels in the white-tiled corridor outside the exam room where Duluc completed an autopsy. Morris never made her jump through hoops, she thought. She wouldn't be jumping through them now if Duluc hadn't taken the precaution of locking the exam room doors.

When the buzzer sounded, indicating she was cleared, Eve slammed the doors open, strode through. The stench under the smear of disinfectant made her eyes water, but she fought back the gag reflex and glowered at Duluc.

Unlike Morris, who had both wit and style, Duluc was a stern-minded, by-the-book woman. She wore the clear protective suit over a spotless white lab coat and pale green scrubs. Her hair was completely hidden under a skull cap. Goggles hung around her neck.

She was barely five feet in height, with a chunky build and a face of wide planes. Her skin was the color of roasted chestnuts, and her one good feature—in Eve's opinion—was her hands. They looked as though they could play a mean piano, and were, in fact, greatly skilled at carving cadavers.

Eve jerked her chin at the draped form on an exam table. "That one mine?"

"If you mean is that the remains of the victim of your current investigation, yes, it is."

Duluc's voice always sounded to Eve's ear as if she had a bubble of thick liquid stuck in her throat. As she spoke she washed her hands in a sink. "I told you I'd send through my findings as soon as possible. I don't like being hounded, Lieutenant."

"You get the tox screen?"

Duluc stared at her. "Do you have a particular problem understanding me?"

"No, I understand you just fine. You're stringing me because you're pissed I jumped on you this morning. You're going to have to get over it because she doesn't care we're irritated with each other." She moved toward Andrea. "She just wants us to deal, so we're going to deal."

"Your on-scene was accurate, as far as cause of death. The single throat wound. A keen, smooth-edged blade. Stiletto perhaps. There are no defensive wounds, no other indications of violence. There was no sexual assault or recent sexual activity. Her blood-alcohol was a bit high. I'd estimate she had four vodka martinis with olives. No illegals on the tox. Her last meal was a salad, leafy greens with a lemon dressing, consumed approximately five hours premortem."

"Do you concur that the attacker was behind the victim?"

"From the angle of the wound, yes. Given her height, I'd say he or she is about six feet tall. Average enough for a man, tall for a woman. All of which will be in my official report, delivered to you in the proper fashion. This is not a priority case, Lieutenant, and we are extremely busy."

"They're all priorities. You've got a Jane Doe. Crispy critter, brought in from Alphabet City."

Duluc sighed heavily. "I have no burn victim on my schedule."

"It's on someone's. I need to see the body, and the data."

"Then give your case number to one of the attendants. I have other things to do."

"It's not my case."

"Then you have no need to see the body or the data."

She started to walk by, but Eve grabbed her arm. "Maybe you don't know how this works, Duluc, but I'm a lieutenant in Homicide and can damn well see any body that strikes my fancy. As it happens, Detective Baxter, who's primary, is meeting me here as I believe our respective cases may converge. Just keep pissing on me and I promise you, you'll end up drowning in it."

"I don't like your attitude."

"Wow. Media alert. I need the Jane Doe."

Duluc wrenched away and stalked over to a workstation. She keyed in, brought up data. "The unidentified female burn victim is in Section C, room three, assigned to Foster. She hasn't been examined yet. Backlog."

"You going to clear me?"

"I've done so. Now if you'll excuse me?"

"No problem." She swung back out the doors. How do all these people walk around with sticks up their asses? Eve wondered.

She turned into Section C, gave the door of room three a push and found it secured. "Shit!" She whirled, pointed to an attendant who was sitting in one of the plastic chairs in the corridor, dozing. "You. I'm cleared for this room. Why's it locked?"

"Duluc. She locks every damn thing. Surprised the vendings aren't wired with explosives." He yawned and stretched. "Dallas, right?"

"That's right."

"Getcha in. I was just catching a break. Pulling a double today. Who you coming to see?"

"Jane Doe."

"Little Jane. She's mine."

"You Foster?"

"Yeah. I just finished an unattended. Natural causes. Guy was a hundred and six, and his second ticker conked on him in his sleep. Good way to go if you gotta."

He unlocked the door, led them in. "This is not a good way," he added, gesturing to the charred bones on a table. "I thought this was Bax's case."

"It is. We may have a connected. He's on his way in."

"Okay by me. I haven't gotten to her yet."

He brought up the file, scanned it as he pulled out his protective gear. "Didn't come in until Sunday, and I had the day off—fond, fond memory. You guys get Sundays off?"

"Now and again."

"Something about sleeping in on a Sunday morning, or sleeping off Saturday night until Sunday afternoon. But Monday always comes." He snapped on his cap. "Been backed up since I clocked in Monday morning. Got no flag on here from Bax saying she matches a missing persons. Still little Jane Doe," he said and glanced back toward the body on the table. "No way to print her, obviously. We'll send the dental off for a search."

"What do we know?"

He called up more data on the screen. "Female between twenty-three and twenty-five. Five feet three inches tall, a hundred and twenty pounds. That's approximate from the virtual reconstruct, which is as far as we've got. That's just prelim check-in data."

"You got time to take a look at her now?"

"Sure. Let me set up."

"Want some coffee?"

He looked at her with love. "Oh, Mommy."

Appreciating him, she waved Peabody back and went out to Vending herself.

She ordered three, black.

"Love of my life, we can't keep meeting like this."

She didn't even turn. "Bite me, Baxter."

"I do, nightly, in my dreams. I'll take one of those."

Reminding herself he'd come in at her request, she programmed for a fourth, then glanced back. "Trueheart?"

"I'll have a lemon fizz if it's all the same to you, Lieutenant. Thank you."

He looked like the lemon-fizz type with his clean-cut, boyish face. Adorable, Peabody had called him, and it wasn't possible to deny it. An all-American boy, cute as a button—whatever the hell that meant—in his summer blues.

Beside him, Baxter was slick and smooth and cagey. Good-looking, but with an edge to him. He had a fondness for a well-cut suit and a well-endowed female.

They were good cops, both of them, Eve thought. And tucking the earnest Trueheart in as the smart-ass Baxter's aide had been one of her better ideas.

"To the dead," Baxter said, and tapped his coffee cup lightly to Eve's. "What do you want with our Jane?"

"She might connect to one of mine. Foster's doing her workup right now."

"Let me help you with those, Lieutenant." Trueheart took his fizz and one of the coffees.

Eve briefed them on the way back to the exam room.

"Whether she's your maid or not, somebody wanted her dead real bad," Baxter commented. "Skull cracked, broken bones. Had to be dead, or at least blessedly unconscious, when he lit her up. He didn't kill her where he lit her. It was dump and fry. We coordinated with Missing Persons on the prelim data and came up goose egg. Been canvassing the area all day. Nobody saw anything, heard anything, knew anything. Guy who made the nine-one-one saw the fire from his window but not the source. Statement goes it was too hot to sleep, and he was going to go sit out on the fire escape. Saw the flames, called it in. Call came through at oh-three-sixteen. Fire department responded, arrived on scene at oh-three-twenty—gotta give those guys points for speed. She was still burning."

"Couldn't've lit her up too much earlier."

Foster glanced up as they came in. "Thanks, Lieutenant, just set it down over there. Hey, Bax, hanging low?"

"Low and long, baby, low and long."

Foster continued to run the scanner over the body. "Broken right index finger. That's an old break. Early childhood. Between five and seven. Scanned the teeth already. Running them in the national bank for a match. This one? The skull injury?"

Eve nodded, stepped closer.

"You got severe trauma here. Ubiquitous blunt instrument, most likely. Bat maybe, or a pipe. Skull's fractured. She's got three broken ribs, a fractured tibia, jawbone. Somebody waled on this girl. She was dead before he poured the gas on her. That's a blessing."

"He didn't kill her where he dumped her," Baxter commented. "We found a blood trail from the street. Not a lot of blood. She must've bled a hell of a lot more where he beat her."

"From the angle of the breaks—see on screen here?" Foster nodded toward it, and the enhanced images in blues and reds. "It looks like he hit the leg first. Did that while she was standing. When she went down, he went for the ribs, the face. The skull was the coup de grâce. She was probably unconscious when he bashed her head in."

Did she try to crawl? Eve wondered. Did she cry out in shock and pain and try to crawl away? "To keep her from running," she murmured. "Take the leg out first so she can't run. He doesn't care how much noise she makes. Otherwise, he'd have gone for the head first. It's calculated, calculated to look like rage. But it's not rage. It's cold-blooded. He had to have a place where it wouldn't matter if she screamed. Soundproofed, private. He had to have private transpo to get her to the lot."

The data center beeped, had them all turning.

"Hit the match," Baxter murmured, and he and Eve stepped to the data screen together. "That who you're looking for?"

"Yeah." Eve set her coffee aside and stared into Tina Cobb's smiling face.

Chapter 5

"Book us a conference room. I want to coordinate with Baxter and Trueheart when they get back from Essie Cobb's." Eve stepped into the garage-level elevator at Central.

"Has to be the same killer," Peabody said.

"Nothing has to be. We'll run probabilities. Let's get all current data together into a report and send it to Mira for a profile."

"You want a meet with her?"

When the doors opened, Eve shifted back as cops and civilians piled on. Dr. Charlotte Mira was the best profiler in the city, possibly on the East Coast. But it was early days for a consult. "Not yet."

The car stopped again, and this time rather than deal with the press of bodies and personal aromas, she elbowed her way off to take the glide. "We'll put what we've got together first, run some standards, conference with Baxter and Trueheart. We need a follow-up with Samantha Gannon and a swing by the club."

"A lot of on-the-ass work." Peabody could only be grateful. Her shoes were killing her.

"Get us the room," Eve began as she stepped off the glide. And stopped when she saw Samantha Gannon sitting on a wait bench outside the Homicide division. Beside her, looking camera-ready, and very chatty, was Nadine Furst.

Eve muttered *shit* under her breath, but there wasn't much heat in it.

Nadine fluffed back her streaky blond hair and aimed one of her feline smiles in Eve's direction. "Dallas. Hey, Peabody, look at you! Mag shoes."

"Thanks." She was going to burn them, first chance.

"Shouldn't you be in front of a camera somewhere?" Eve asked.

"There's more to the job than looking pretty on screen. I've just about wrapped an interview with Samantha. A few comments from the primary on the investigation would put a nice cap on the segment."

"Turn off the recorder, Nadine."

For form, Nadine sighed before she deactivated her lapel recorder. "She's so strict," she said to Samantha. "I really appreciate the time, and I'm very sorry about your friend."

"Thank you."

"Dallas, if I could just have one word?"

"Peabody, why don't you show Ms. Gannon into the lounge. I'll be right with you."

Eve waited until they'd moved off, then turned a cool stare toward Nadine.

"Just doing my job." Nadine lifted her hands, palms out for peace.

"Me too."

"Gannon's a hot ticket, Dallas. Her book is this month's cocktail party game. Everybody's playing Where Are the Diamonds? You toss murder in and it's top story, every market. I had vacation plans. Three fun-filled days at the Vineyard, starting tomorrow. I canceled them."

"You were going to make wine?"

"No. Though I'd planned to drink quite a bit. Martha's Vineyard, Dallas. I want out of the city, out of this heat. I want a beach and a long cold adult beverage and a parade of tanned and buff male bodies. So I'm hoping you're going to tell me you're wrapping this one up in a hurry."

"I can't tell you any more than the media liaison would've told you. Pursuing all leads, et cetera and so on. That's it, Nadine. That's really it."

"Yeah, I was afraid of that. Well, there's always a hologram program. I can set it for the Vineyard and spend an hour in fantasyland. I'll be around," she added as she walked away.

Gave up too easy, Eve decided.

She thought about that as she headed off to what the cops called the lounge. It was a room set up for breaks and informal meetings. A scatter of tables, even a skinny, sagging sofa, and several vending machines.

She plugged in a couple of credits and ordered a large bottle of water.

You have selected Aquafree, the natural refreshment, in a twelve-ounce bottle. Aquafree is distilled and bottled in the peaceful and pristine mountains of—

"Jesus, cut the commercial and give me the damn water." She thumped a fist against the machine.

> You are in violation of City Code 20613-A. Any tampering with, any vandalism of this vending unit can result in fine and/or imprisonment.

Even as Eve reared back to kick, Peabody was popping up. "Dallas! Don't! I'll get it. I'll get the water. Go sit down."

"A person ought to be able to get a damn drink of water without the lecture." She flopped down at the table beside Samantha. "Sorry."

"No, that's okay. It's really irritating, isn't it, to get the whole list of ingredients, by-products, caloric intake, whatever. Especially when you're ordering a candy bar or a cupcake."

"Yes!" Finally, Eve thought, someone who got it.

"She has issues with machines all over the city," Peabody commented. "Your water, Lieutenant."

"You pander to them." Eve opened the bottle, drank long and deep. "I appreciate your coming in, Ms. Gannon. We were going to contact you and arrange to speak with you. You've saved us some time."

"Call me Samantha, or Sam, if that's okay. I hoped you'd have something to tell me. Shouldn't I have been talking to the reporter?"

"Free country. Free press." Eve shrugged. "She's okay. Are you planning on staying at the hotel for the time being?"

"I—yes. I thought, as soon as you tell me I can—I'd have my house cleaned. There are specialists, I'm told, who deal with . . . with crime scenes. Cleaning up crime scenes. I don't want to go back until it's dealt with. That's cowardly."

"It's not. It's sensible." That's what she looked like today, Eve thought. A very tired, sensible woman. "I can offer you continued police protection for the short term. You may want to consider hiring private security."

"You don't think it was just a burglary. You think whoever killed Andrea will come after me."

"I don't think there's any point in taking risks. Beyond that, reporters who aren't as polite as Nadine are going to scent you out and hassle you."

"I guess you're right about that. All right, I'll look into it. My grandparents are very upset about all this. I played it down as much as I could, but . . . Hell, you don't pull anything over on them. If I can tell them I've hired a bodyguard and have the police looking out for me, too, it'll go a long way to keeping everyone settled. I'm letting them think it was about Andrea."

Her eyes, very bright, very blue, settled levelly on Eve's. "But I've had time to play this all out in my head. A long night's worth of time, and I don't think that. You don't think that."

"I don't. Ms. Gannon—Samantha—the woman who was assigned to clean your house has been murdered."

"I don't understand. I haven't hired anyone to clean my house yet."

"Your regular cleaning service. Maid In New York assigned Tina Cobb over the last several months to your house."

"She's dead? Murdered? Like Andrea?"

"Did you know her? Personally?"

Without thinking, Samantha picked up Eve's bottle of water, drank. "I don't know what to think. I was just talking about her ten minutes ago, just talking about her with Nadine."

"You told Nadine about Tina Cobb?"

"I mentioned her. Not by name. Just the cleaning service and how I remembered—just when we were talking, I remembered—that I hadn't canceled the service for this week."

No wonder Nadine had given up so easily. She'd already had another line to tug. "Did you know her?"

"Not really. Oh God, I'm sorry," she said, staring at the bottle of water in her hand. She passed it back to Eve.

"No problem. You didn't know Tina Cobb?"

"I met her. I mean, she was in my house, *cleaning* my house," she added as she rubbed her forehead. "Can I have a minute?"

"Sure."

Samantha got up, walked around the room once, started around it again.

"Pulling it together," Peabody murmured. "Calming herself down."

"Yeah. She's got spine. Makes it easier from our end."

After the second circuit, Samantha ordered her own bottle of water, stood patiently until the machine had finished its recital and spat the selection into the slot.

She walked back, opening the bottle as she sat. After one long pull, she nodded at Eve. "Okay. I had to settle down."

"You need more time, it's not a problem."

"No. She always seemed like such a little thing to me. Tina. Young and little, though I guess she wasn't that much younger or smaller than me. I always wondered how she handled all that heavy cleaning. Usually, I'd hole up in my office when she was there, or schedule outside meetings or errands."

She stopped, cleared her throat. "I sort of come from money. Not big mountains of it, but nice comfortable hills. We always had household help. But my place here? It's my first place all my own, and it felt weird having somebody around, even a couple times a month, picking up after me."

She brushed her hands over her hair. "And that is completely beside the point."

"Not completely." Peabody nudged the bottle of water toward Samantha because it seemed she'd forgotten it was there. "It gives us an idea of the dynamics between you."

"We didn't have much of one." She drank again. "I just stayed out of her way. She was very pleasant, very efficient. We might have a brief conversation, but both of us would usually just get to work. Is it because she was in my house? Is she dead because she was in my house?"

"We're looking into that," Eve said. "You told us in your earlier statement that the cleaning service had your access and security codes."

"Yes. They're bonded. They have a top-level reputation. Their employees all go through intense screening. Actually, it's a little scary and nothing I'd want to go through. But for someone like me, who can't always be at home to let a cleaning service into the house, it was ideal. She knew how to get in," Samantha stated. "Someone killed her because she knew how to get in."

"I believe that's true. Did she ever mention a friend—a boyfriend?"

"No. We didn't talk about personal matters. We were polite and easy with each other but not personal."

"Did she ever bring anyone with her? To help her with her work?"

"No. I have a team every three months. The company

sets that up. Otherwise, it was just one maid, twice a month. I live alone, and I have what my mother says is my grandmother's obsession with order. I don't need more help than that, domestically."

"You never noticed, when she came or went, if anyone dropped her off, picked her up?"

"No. I think she took the bus. Once she was late, and she apologized and said her bus got caught in a jam. You haven't told me how she was killed. Was it like Andrea?"

"No."

"But you still think it's a connection. It's too much of a coincidence not to be."

"We're looking carefully at the connection."

"I always wanted to write this book. Always. I'd beg my grandparents to tell me the story, again and again. Until I could play it backward in my mind. I loved picturing how my grandparents met, seeing them sitting at her kitchen table with a pool of diamonds. And how they'd won. It was so satisfying for me to know they'd beaten the odds and won. Lived their lives as they chose to live. That's a real victory, don't you think, living as you choose to live?"

"Yeah." She thought of her badge. She thought of Roarke's empire. "It is."

"The villain of the piece, I suppose you could call him, Alex Crew, he killed. He killed for those shiny stones and, I think, because he could. As much because he could as for the diamonds. He would have killed my grandmother if she hadn't been strong enough, smart enough to best him. That's always been a matter of pride for me, and I wanted to tell that story. Now I have, and two people I know are dead."

"You're not responsible for that."

"I'm telling myself that. Intellectually, I know that. And still, there's a part of me that's separating, and observing. That part that wants very much to tell *this* story. To write down what's happening now. I wonder what that makes me."

"A writer, I'd say," Peabody answered.

Samantha let out a half laugh. "Well, I guess so. I've made a list, everyone I could think of. People I've talked with about the book. Odd communications I've had from readers or people claiming to have known my great-grandfather." She drew a disk out of her bag. The enormous one Eve had noted the day before. "I don't know if it'll help."

"Everything helps. Did Tina Cobb know you'd be out of town?"

"I let the service know, yes. In fact, I remember telling Tina I'd be away and asking her to check the houseplants and my fish. I wasn't sure Andrea would be able to stay, not until just a couple days before I left."

"Did you let the service know you'd have a house sitter?"

"No. That slipped by me. The last few days in New York were insane. I was doing media and appearances here, packing, doing holographic interviews. And it didn't seem important."

Eve rose, extended a hand. "Thanks for coming in. Detective Peabody will arrange for you to be taken back to your hotel."

"Lieutenant. You didn't tell me how Tina Cobb was killed."

"No, I didn't. We'll be in touch."

Samantha watched her walk out, drew a long breath. "I bet she wins, doesn't she? I bet she almost always wins."

"She won't give up. That comes to the same thing."

. . .

Eve sat at her desk, input the data from the Cobb case into a sub file, then updated her files on the Jacobs homicide.

"Computer, analyze data on two current case files and run probability. What is the probability that Andrea Jacobs and Tina Cobb were killed by the same person?"

Beginning analysis . . .

She pushed away from the desk as the computer worked and walked to her skinny window. Sky traffic was relatively light. Tourists looked for cooler spots than stewing Manhattan, she imagined, this time of year. Office drones were busy in their hives. She saw a sky-tram stream by with more than half its seats empty.

Tina Cobb had taken the bus. The sky-tram would've been faster, but that convenience cost. Tina'd been careful with her money then. Saving for a life she'd never have.

Analysis and probability run complete. Probability that Andrea Jacobs and Tina Cobb were murdered by the same person or persons is seventy-eight point eight.

High enough, Eve thought, given the computer's limitations. It would factor in the difference in victim types, the different methodology, geographic location of the murders.

A computer couldn't see what she saw, or feel what she felt.

She turned back as a beep signaled an incoming transmission. The sweepers had been quick, she noted, and sat to read the report.

Fingerprints were Gannon's, Jacobs's, Cobb's. There were no other prints found anywhere in the house. Hair samples found matched Gannon's and the victim's. Eve imagined they'd find some that matched Cobb's.

He'd sealed up, and that wasn't a surprise to her. He'd sealed his hands, his hair. Whether or not he'd planned to kill, he'd planned to leave no trace of himself behind.

If Jacobs hadn't come in, he might have gone through the entire house without leaving a thing out of place. And Samantha would've been none the wiser.

She contacted Maid In New York to check a few details and was adding them to her notes when Peabody came in.

"Gannon had her quarterly clean about four weeks ago," Eve said. "Do you know, the crew's required to wear gloves and hair protectors? Safety goggles, protective jumpsuit. The works. Like a damn sweeper's team. They all but sterilize the damn place, top to bottom."

"I think, maybe, McNab and I could afford something like that. Once we're in the new apartment, it'd be worth it to have somebody sterilize the place three or four times a year. We can get pretty messy when we're both pumping it on the job—and, you know, doing each other."

"Shut up. Just shut up. You're trying to make me twitch."

"I haven't mentioned sex and McNab all day. It was time."

"The point I was making before you stuck the image of you and McNab doing each other in my head, is Gannon's place was polished up bright a few weeks ago and maintained thereafter. There are no prints other than hers, the maid's, Jacobs's. He sealed up before he went in. He's very careful. Meticulous even. But, unless this was a direct hit on Jacobs, he still missed the house-sitter angle. What does that tell you?"

"He probably doesn't know either the vic or Gannon, not

personally. Not enough to be privy to personal arrangements like that. He knew Gannon would be out of town. Could've gotten that from the maid, or from following her media schedule. But he couldn't have gotten the house-sitter angle from the maid or the service because they didn't know."

"He's not inner circle. So we start going outside that circle. And we look for where else Cobb and Gannon and Jacobs connect."

"Baxter and Trueheart are back. We've got conference room three."

"Round them up."

She set up a board in the conference room, pinning up crime-scene photos, victim photos, copies of scene reports and the time line for the Jacobs murder she'd worked up.

She waited while Baxter did the same for his case, and considered, as she programmed a cup of lousy station-house coffee, how to handle the meeting.

Tact might not be her middle name, but she didn't like to step on another cop's toes. Cobb was Baxter's case. Outranking him didn't, in her mind, give her the right to tug it away from him.

She leaned a hip on the conference table as a compromise between standing—taking over—and sitting. "You get anything more out of your vic's sister?"

Baxter shook his head. "Took some time to talk her out of going down to the morgue. No point in her seeing that. She didn't have anything to add to what she told you. She's going to her parents'. Trueheart and I offered to go inform them, or at least go with her. She said she wanted to do it herself. That it would be easier on them if she did. She never met this Bobby character. None of the stoop-sitters or neighbors remember seeing the vic with a guy either. They've got a cheap d and c unit. Trueheart checked it for transmissions."

"She—Tina Cobb," Trueheart began, "sent and received transmissions from an account registered to a Bobby Smith. A quick check indicates the account was opened five weeks ago and closed two days ago. The address listed is bogus. The unit doesn't store transmission over twenty-four hours. If there were 'link trans, to and from, we'd need EDD to dig them out."

"Yippee," Peabody said under her breath and earned a stony stare from Eve.

"You tagging EDD?" Eve asked Baxter.

"Worth a shot. It's probable he used public 'links, but if they can dig out a transmission or two, we might be able to get some sort of geographic. Get a voice print. Get a sense of him."

"Agreed."

"We're going to talk to her coworkers. See if she gabbed about the guy. But from what her sister says, she was keeping him pretty close. Like a big secret. She was only twenty-two, and her record's shiny. Not a smudge."

"She wanted to get married, be a professional mother." Trueheart flushed as all eyes turned to him. "I talked to the sister about her. It, um, I think you can learn about the killer if you know the victim."

"He's my pride and joy," Baxter said with a big grin.

Eve remembered that Trueheart was barely older than the victim they were discussing. And that he'd nearly become a victim himself only a short time before.

The quick glance she exchanged with Baxter told her he was thinking the same thing. Both let it go.

"The theory is the killer used a romantic involvement to lure her." She waited until Baxter nodded. "Your case and ours come together through her. She was Samantha Gannon's maid, and as such had knowledge of the security codes to her residence and knew, intimately, the contents and setup of that residence. She was aware that the owner would be out of town for a two-week period. But she was unaware that there would be a house sitter. Those arrangements were last minute and, as far as we can know, between Jacobs and Gannon."

"Lieutenant." Trueheart raised a hand like a student in the classroom. "It's hard for me to see someone like Tina Cobb betraying security. She worked hard, her employment record's as clean as the rest of it. There isn't a single complaint filed against her on the job. She doesn't seem the type to give out a security code."

"I gotta go with the kid on this one," Baxter confirmed. "I don't see her giving it out willingly."

"You've never been a girl in love," Peabody said to Baxter. "It can make you stupid. You look at the time line, you see that the break-in and Jacobs's murder were prior to Cobb's murder. And, when you calculate the time between her last being seen and time of death, there isn't a lot. He'd been working her for weeks, right? Smoothing her up. It seems to me he'd be more sure she was giving him the straight scoop if it was willing pillow talk or something than if he tried to beat it out of her."

"My pride and joy," Eve said to Baxter and earned a chuckle. "He beats or threatens or tortures, she might lie or just get mixed up. He eases it out of her, it's more secure. But . . . "

She paused while her pride and joy wrinkled her forehead. "He seduces it out, she might talk, or get the guilts and report the lapse to her superior. That's a risk. Either way, if we're right about this connection, he got it out of her. Then after he broke in, killed Jacobs, he had to cover tracks. So he killed Cobb, dumped her. Killed and dumped her in such a way that identification would be delayed long enough for him to tidy up any connection between himself and Cobb."

"What's Gannon got that he wants?" Baxter asked.

"It's more what he thinks she has or has access to. And that's several million in stolen diamonds."

She filled them in and gave them each a disk copy of her file. Without realizing it, she'd straightened and was standing. "The more we find out about this old case, and the stolen gems, the more we know about our current cases. We'll learn more, faster, if we coordinate our time and effort."

"I got no problem with that." Baxter nodded in agreement. "We'll shoot you both copies of our file on Cobb. What angle do you want us to work?"

"Track Bobby. He didn't leave us much, but there's always something. We'll see what EDD can dig out of the vics' 'links."

"Somebody should go through her personal items," Peabody added. "She might've kept mementos. Girls do that. Something from a restaurant where they ate."

"Good one." Baxter winked at her. "The sister said he took Tina to an art gallery and a play. We'll work on that. After all, how many art galleries and theaters are there in New York?" He slapped a hand on Trueheart's shoulder. "Shouldn't take my earnest sidekick more than a couple hundred man-hours to find out."

"Somebody saw them together somewhere," Eve agreed. "Peabody and I will continue to work Jacobs. We pool all information. For homework assignment, read Gannon's book. Let's know all we can know about these diamonds and the people who stole them. Class dismissed. Peabody, you're with me in ten. Baxter? Can I have a minute?"

"Teacher's pet," Baxter said, tapping his heart and winking at Trueheart.

To stall until they were alone, Eve wandered to the board, studied the faces.

"Are you giving him that drone work to keep his ass in the chair?"

"As much as I can," Baxter confirmed. "He's bounced back—Christ, to be that young again. But he's not a hundred percent. I'm keeping him on light duty for now."

"Good. Any problems combining these investigations under me?"

"Look at that face." Baxter lifted his chin toward the ID photo of Tina Cobb. Even the cheap, official image radiated youth and innocence.

"Yeah."

"I play pretty well with others, Dallas. And I want, I really want to find out who turned that into that." He tapped a finger on the crime-scene still of Tina Cobb. "So I got no problem."

"Does it sit right with you if Peabody and I go through your vic's things? Peabody's got an eye for that kind of thing."

"All right."

"You want to take the club where my vic was last seen?"

"Can do."

"Then we'll have a briefing in the morning. Nine hundred."

"Make my world complete and tell me we're having it

at your home office. Where the AutoChef has real pig meat and eggs from chickens that cluck."

"Here—unless I let you know different."

"Spoilsport."

Eve headed back uptown in irritable traffic. A breakdown on Eighth clogged the road for blocks and had what seemed like half of New York breaking the noise pollution codes in order to blast their horns in pitiful and useless protest.

Her own solution was a bit more direct. She hit the sirens, punched into vertical and skimmed the corner to take the crosstown to Tenth.

They were fifteen blocks away when her climate control sputtered and died.

"I hate technology. I hate Maintenance. I hate the goddamn stupid NYPSD budget that sticks me with these pieces-of-shit vehicles."

"There, there, sir," Peabody crooned as she hunkered down to work on the controls manually. "There, there."

After the sweat began to run into her eyes, Peabody gave up. "You know, I could call Maintenance. Yes, we hate them like poison, like rat poison on a cracker," she said quickly. "So I was thinking, I could ask McNab to take a whack at it. He's good with this kind of thing."

"Great, good, fine." Eve rolled down the windows before they suffocated. The stinking, steamy air outside wasn't much of an improvement. "When we finish at Cobb's, you drop me home, take this rolling disaster with you. You can pick me up in the morning."

When she reached the apartment building she considered, actively, the rewards of giving one of the stoop-sitters twenty to steal the damn car. Instead, she decided to hope somebody boosted it while they were inside.

As they started inside, she heard Peabody's quiet whimper. "What?"

"Nothing. I didn't say anything."

"It's those shoes, isn't it? You're limping. Goddamn it, what if we have to pursue some asshole on foot?"

"Maybe they weren't the best choice, but I'm still finding my personal look. There may be some miscues along the way."

"Tomorrow you'd better be in something normal. Something you can walk in."

"Yeah, yeah, yeah." Peabody hunched her shoulders at Eve's glare. "I don't have to say 'sir' all the time because, hey, look, *detective* now. And we're partners and all."

"Not when you're wearing those shoes."

"I was going to burn them when I got home. But now I'm thinking of getting a hatchet and chopping them into tiny, tiny pieces."

Eve knocked on the apartment door. Essie answered. Her eyes were red and swollen, her face splotchy from tears. She simply stared at Eve, saying nothing.

"We appreciate your coming back from your parents to let us go through your sister's things," Eve began. "We're very sorry for your loss and regret having to intrude at this time."

"I'm going to go back and stay with them tonight. I needed to come and get some of my things anyway. I don't want to stay here tonight. I don't know if I'll ever stay here again. I should've called the police right away. As soon as she didn't come home, I should've called."

"It wouldn't have mattered."

"The other cops, the ones who came to tell me? They said I shouldn't go down to see her."

"They're right."

"Why don't you sit down, Essie." Peabody moved in, took her arm and led her to a chair. "You know why we need to go through her things?"

"In case you find something that tells you who did this to her. I don't care what you have to do, as long as you find who did this to her. She never hurt anybody in her whole life. Sometimes she used to piss me off, but your sister's supposed to, right?"

Peabody left her hand on Essie's shoulder another moment. "Mine sure does."

"She never hurt anybody."

"Do you want to stay here while we do this? Or maybe you have a friend in the building. You could go there until we're done."

"I don't want to talk to anybody. Just do what you have to do. I'll be right here."

Eve took the closet, Peabody the dresser. In various pockets, Eve found a tiny bottle of breath freshener, a sample-size tube of lipdye and a mini pocket organizer that turned out to belong to Essie.

"I got something."

"What?"

"They give these little buttons out at the Met." Peabody held up a little red tab. "It's a tradition. You put it on your collar or lapel, and they know you paid for the exhibit. He probably took her there. It's the kind of thing you keep if it's a date."

"The odds of anybody remembering her at the Metropolitan Museum are slim to none, but it's a start."

"She's got a little memento box here. Bus token, candle stub."

"Bag the candle stub. We'll run for prints. Maybe it's from his place."

"Here's a pocket guide for the Guggenheim, and a theater directory. Looks like she printed it out from online. She's circled the Chelsea Playhouse in a little heart. It's from last month," she said as she turned to Eve. "A limited run of *Chips Are Down*. He took her there, Dallas. This is her 'I love Bobby' box."

"Take it in. Take it all in." She moved over to the dented metal stand by the bed, yanked on the single drawer. Inside she found a stash of gummy candy, a small emergency flashlight, sample tubes and packs of hand cream, lotion, perfume, all tucked into a box. And sealed in a protective bag was a carefully folded napkin. On the cheap recycled material, written in sentimental red, was:

Bobby
First Date
July 26, 2059
Ciprioni's

Peabody joined Eve and read over her shoulder. "She must've taken it out to look at every night," she murmured. "Sealed it up so it didn't get dirty or torn."

"Do a run on Ciprioni's."

"I don't have to. It's a restaurant. Italian place down in Little Italy. Inexpensive, good food. Noisy, usually crowded, slow service, terrific pasta."

"He didn't know she was keeping tabs, little tabs like this. He didn't understand her. He didn't get her. He thought he was safe. None of the places we're finding are anywhere near here. Get her away from where she lives, where people she knows might see them. See him. Take her to places where there are lots of people. Who's going to notice them? But she's picking up souvenirs to mark their dates. She left us a nice trail, Peabody."

Chapter 6

After dropping Eve at home, Peabody drove off in the sauna on wheels. And Eve let herself into the blessed cool. The cat thumped down the steps, greeting her with a series of irritated feline growls.

"What, are you standing in for Summerset? Bitch, bitch, bitch." But she squatted down to scrub a hand over his fur. "What the hell do the two of you do around here all day anyway? Never mind. I don't think I want to know."

She checked with the in-house and was told Roarke was not on the premises.

"Jeez." She looked back down at the cat, who was doing his best to claw up her leg. "Kinda weird. Nobody home but you and me. Well . . . I got stuff. You should come." She scooped him up and carted him up the stairs.

It wasn't that she minded being home alone. She just

wasn't used to it. And it was pretty damn quiet, if you bothered to listen.

But she'd fix that. She'd download an audio of Samantha Gannon's book. She could get in a solid workout while she listened to it. Take a swim, loosen up. Grab a shower, take care of some details.

"There's a lot you can get done when nobody's around to distract you," she told Galahad. "I spent most of my life with nobody around anyway, so, you know, no problem."

No problem, she thought. Before Roarke she'd come home to an empty apartment every night. Maybe she'd connect with her pal Mavis, but even if she'd had time to blow off a little steam after the job with the woman who was the blowing-off-steam expert, she'd still come home alone.

She liked alone.

When had she stopped liking alone?

God, it was irritating.

She dumped the cat on her desk, but he complained and bumped his head against her arm. "Okay, okay, give me a minute, will you?" Brushing the bulk of him aside, she picked up the memo cube.

"Hello, Lieutenant." Roarke's voice drifted out. "I thought this would be your first stop. I downloaded an audio of Gannon's book as I couldn't visualize you curling up with the paper version. See you when I get home. I believe there are fresh peaches around. Why don't you have one instead of the candy bar you're thinking about?"

"Think you know me inside out, don't you, smart guy? Thinks he knows me back and forth," she said to the cat. "The annoying part is he does." She put the memo down, picked up the headset. Even as she started to slip it into place, she noted the message light blinking on her desk unit.

She nudged the cat aside again. "Just wait, for God's sake." She ordered up the message and listened once again to Roarke's voice.

"Eve, I'm running late. A few problems that need to be dealt with."

She cocked her head, studied his face on the screen. A little annoyed, she noted. A little rushed. He wasn't the only one who knew his partner.

"If I get through them I'll be home before you get to this in any case. If not, well, soon as possible. You can reach me if you need to. Don't work too hard."

She touched the screen as his image faded. "You either."

She put on the headset, engaged, then much to the cat's relief, headed into the kitchen. The minute she filled his bowl with tuna and set it down for him, he pounced.

Listening to the narrative of the diamond heist, she grabbed a bottle of water, took a peach as an afterthought, then walked through the quiet, empty house and down to the gym.

She stripped down, hanging her weapon harness on a hook, then pulled on a short skinsuit.

She started with stretches, concentrating on the audio and her form. Then she moved to the machine, programming in an obstacle course that pushed her to run, climb, row, cycle on and over various objects and surfaces.

By the time she started on free weights, she'd been introduced to the main players in the book and had a sense of New York and small-town America in the dawn of the century.

Gossip, crime, bad guys, good guys, sex and murder.

The more things changed, she thought, the more they didn't.

She activated the sparring droid for a ten-minute bout and felt limber, energized and virtuous by the time she'd kicked his ass.

She snagged a second bottle of water out of the mini-fridge and, to give herself more time with the book, added a session for flexibility and balance.

She peeled off the skinsuit, tossed it in the laundry chute, then walked naked into the pool house. With the audio still playing in her ear, she dove into the cool blue water. After some lazy laps, she floated her way over to the corner and called for jets.

Her long, blissful sigh echoed off the ceiling.

There was home alone, she thought, and there was home alone.

When her eyes started to droop, she boosted herself out. She pulled on a robe, gathered up her street clothes, her weapon, and took the elevator up to the bedroom before she thought of missed opportunity.

She could have run naked through the house. She could have *danced* naked through the house.

She'd have to hold that little pleasure in reserve.

After a shower and fresh clothes, she went back to her office. She turned off the audio long enough to handle some details, to make new notes.

Top of her list were: Jack O'Hara, Alex Crew, William Young and Jerome Myers. Young and Myers had been dead for more than half a century, with their lives ending before the first act of the drama.

Crew had died in prison, and O'Hara had been in and out of the wind until his death fifteen years ago. So the four men who'd stolen the diamonds were dead. But people rarely got through life without connections. Family, associates, enemies.

A connection to a thief might consider himself entitled to the booty. A kind of reward, an inheritance, a payback. A connection to a thief might know how to gain access to a secured residence.

Blood tells, she thought. People often said that. She, for one, had reason to hope it wasn't true. If it was true, what did that make her, the daughter of a monster and a junkie whore? If it was all a matter of genes, DNA, inherited traits, what chance was there for a child created by two people for the purpose of using her for profit? For whoring her. For raising her like an animal. Worse than an animal.

Locking her in the dark. Alone, nameless. Beating her. Raping her. Twisting her until at the age of eight she would kill to escape.

Blood on her hands. So much blood on her hands.

"Damn it. Damn it, damn it." Eve squeezed her eyes shut and willed the images away before their ghosts could solidify into another waking nightmare.

Blood didn't tell. DNA didn't make us. We made ourselves, if we had any guts we made ourselves.

She pulled her badge out of her pocket, held it like a talisman, like an anchor. We made ourselves, she thought again. And that was that.

She laid her badge on the desk where she could see it if she needed to, then, reengaging the audio, she listened as she ordered runs on the names of her four thieves.

Thinking about coffee, she rose to wander into the kitchen. She toyed with programming a pot, then cut it back to a single cup. One of the candy bars she'd stashed began to call her name. And after all, she'd eaten the damn peach.

She dug it out from under the ice in the freezer bin.

With coffee in one hand, frozen chocolate in the other, she walked back into the office. And nearly into Roarke.

He took one look, raised an eyebrow. "Dinner?"

"Not exactly." He made her feel like a kid stealing treats. And she'd never *been* a kid with treats to steal. "I was just . . . shit." She pulled off the headset. "Working. Taking a little break. What's it to you?"

He laughed, pulled her in for a kiss. "Hello, Lieutenant."

"Hello back. Ignore him," she said when Galahad slithered up to meow and beg. "I fed him already."

"Better, no doubt, than you fed yourself."

"Did you eat?"

"Not yet." He slid a hand around her throat, squeezed lightly. "Give me half that candy."

"It's frozen. You gotta wait it out."

"This then." He took her coffee, smirked at her scowl. "You smell . . . delicious."

When the hand at her throat slid around to cup the nape of her neck, she realized he meant her, not the coffee. "Back up, pal." She jabbed a finger into his chest. "I've got agendas here. Since you haven't eaten, why don't we go try this Italian place I heard about downtown."

When he said nothing, just sipped her coffee, studied her over the rim, she frowned. "What?"

"Nothing. Just making certain you really are my wife. You want to go out to dinner, sit in a restaurant where there are other people."

"We've been out to dinner before. Millions of times. What's the bfd?"

"Mmm-hmm. What does an Italian restaurant downtown have to do with your case?"

"Smarty-pants. Maybe I just heard they have really good lasagna. And maybe I'll tell you the rest on the way because I sort of made reservations. I made them before I realized you'd be this late and might not want to go out. I can check it out tomorrow."

"Is there time for me to have a shower and change out of this bloody suit? It feels as though I was born in it."

"Sure. But I can cancel if you just want to kick back."

"I could use some lasagna, as long as it comes with a great deal of wine."

"Long one, huh?"

"More annoying than long, actually," he told her as she walked with him to the bedroom. "A couple of systemic problems. One in Baltimore, one in Chicago, and both required my personal attention."

She pursed her lips as he undressed for the shower. "You've been to Baltimore and Chicago today?"

"With a quick stop in Philadelphia, since it was handy."

"Did you get a cheese steak?"

"I didn't, no. Time didn't allow for such indulgences. Jets full," he ordered when he stepped into the shower. "Seventy-two degrees."

Even the thought of a shower at that temperature made her shiver. But, somehow, she could still enjoy standing there watching him drench himself in the cold water. "Did you get them fixed? The systemic problems?"

"Bet your gorgeous ass. An engineer, an office manager and two VPs will be seeking other employment. An overworked admin just copped herself a corner office and a new title—along with a nice salary boost—and a young man out of R and D is out celebrating his promotion to project head about now."

"Wow, you've been pretty busy out there, changing lives."

He slicked back that wonderful and wet mane of black

hair. "A little padding of the expense account, that's a time-honored tradition, corporately speaking. I don't mind it. But you don't want to get greedy, and sloppy, and fucking arrogant about it. Or next you know, you're out on your ear and wondering how the hell you're going to afford that condo on Maui and the side dish who likes trinkets that come in Tiffany's little blue boxes."

"Hold it." She stepped back as he walked out of the shower. "Embezzlement? Are you talking embezzlement?"

"That would be Chicago. Baltimore was just ineptitude, which is, somehow, even more annoying."

"Did you have them charged? Chicago?"

He flipped a towel, began to dry off. "I handled it. My way, Lieutenant," he said before she could speak. "I don't call the cops at every bump in the road."

"I keep hearing that lately. Embezzlement's a crime, Roarke."

"Is it now? Well, fancy that." With the towel hooked over his hips, he brushed by her and went to his closet. "They'll pay, you can be sure of that. I imagine they're even now drinking themselves into a sweaty stupor and weeping bitter tears over their respective career suicides. Be lucky to cop a job sweeping up around a desk now much less sitting behind one. Buggering sods."

She thought it over. "The cops would've been easier on them."

He glanced back, his grin fierce and cold. "Undoubtedly."

"I've said it before, I'll say it again. You're a very scary guy."

"So . . ." He pulled on a shirt, buttoned it. "And how was your day, darling Eve?"

"Fill you in on the way."

She told him so that by the time they arrived at the restaurant he was thoroughly briefed.

Peabody, Eve noted, had given an accurate description. The place was packed and noisy and the air smelled amazing. Waitstaff, with white bib aprons over their street clothes, moved at a turtle pace as they carried trays loaded with food to tables or hauled away empty plates.

When waitstaff didn't have to bust ass for tips, Eve had to figure it all came down to the food or the snob factor. From the looks of the process here, and the simplicity of decor, the food must be superior.

Someone crooned over the speakers in what she assumed was Italian, just as she assumed the almost childlike murals that decorated the walls were of Italian locales.

And she noted the stubby candles on each table. Just like the one Tina Cobb had kept among her mementos.

"I booked in your name." She had to raise her voice, aim it toward Roarke's ear to be heard over the din.

"Oh?"

"They were booked solid. Roarke clears a table quicker than Dallas."

"Ah."

"Oh. Ah. Blah blah."

He laughed, pinched her, then turned to the apparently disinterested maître d'. "You've a table for two, under Roarke."

The man was squat, with his ample bulk squeezed into an old-fashioned tuxedo like a soy sausage pumped into a casing. His bored eyes popped wide, and he lurched from his stool station to his feet. When he bowed, Eve expected him to pop out of the tuxedo.

"Yes, yes! Mr. Roarke. Your table is waiting. Best

table in the house." His Italian accent had a definite New York edge. Rome via the Bronx. "Please, come with me. Shoo, shoo." He waved at and jostled waiters and customers alike to clear a path. "I am Gino. Please to tell me if you wish for anything. Anything. Tonight's pasta is spaghetti con polpettone, and the special is rollatini di pollo. You will have wine, yes? A complimentary bottle of our Barolo. It's very fine. Handsome and bold, but not overpowering."

"Sounds perfect. Thank you very much."

"It's nothing. Nothing at all." He snapped his fingers toward a waiter who'd obviously been put on alert. In short order, the wine was displayed, opened, poured and approved. Menus were offered with a flourish, and the staff retreated to hover and largely ignore diners who hoped to be served sometime in the next decade.

"Do you ever get tired of being fawned over?" Eve asked him.

"Let me think." Roarke sipped his wine, leaned back. Smiled. "No."

"Figured." She glanced at the menu. "What's that spaghetti polepot stuff he was talking about?"

"*Polpettone*. Spaghetti and meatballs."

"Really?" She perked up. "Okay, that sets me up." She laid the menu aside. "What are you having?"

"I think I'll try the two-sauce lasagna. You put it in my head, and I can't get it out. We'll have some antipasto to start, or we'll disappoint our hosts."

"Let's keep them happy."

The instant Roarke set down his menu, both the maître d' and the waiter materialized at the table. She let Roarke order, and drew the ID photo of Tina Cobb out of her bag. "Do you recognize this woman?" she asked Gino.

"I'm sorry?"

"She was in here on a date in July. Do you remember seeing her?"

"I'm sorry," he repeated. He looked apologetic, then apoplectic as he glanced at Roarke. "We have so many customers." His brow pearled with sweat; he wrung his hands and stood like a nervous student failing a vital test.

"Just take a look. Maybe you'll remember her coming in. Young, probably spruced up for a date. About five feet three inches, a hundred and twenty pounds. First-date glow on her."

"Ah . . . "

"You could do me a favor," Eve said before the guy dripped into a nerve puddle at her feet. "You could show that to the waitstaff, see if she rings any bells."

"I'd be happy to. *Honored* to, of course. Right away."

"I like it better when they're annoyed or pissed off," Eve decided as he scurried away. "Well, either way, it's a long shot."

"We'll get a good meal out of it. And . . . " He lifted her hand, kissed her knuckles. "I get a date with my wife."

"Place does a hell of a business. How come you don't own it?"

He kept her hand as he sipped his wine. There was no sign of a man who'd bounced from city to city all day, firing embezzlers and incompetents. "Would you like to?"

She only shook her head. "Two dead women. One a means to an end, the other just in the right place at the wrong time. He's not a killer by design. He kills because it's expedient. Wants to reach the goal. To reach it, you have to utilize tools, dispose of obstacles. Sort of like what you did today, only with real blood."

"Hmm" was Roarke's comment.

"What I mean is you're going to get from point A to point B, and if you have to take a side trip and mow over somebody, you do. I mean, he's directed."

"Understood."

"If Jacobs hadn't been there, he wouldn't have had to kill her. If he hadn't had to kill Jacobs, he probably wouldn't have killed Cobb. At least not right away, though I'd lay odds he'd worked out how he'd do it when and if. If he'd found the diamonds—fat chance—or more likely found something that led him to them, he'd have followed the trail."

She grabbed a bread stick, broke it in half, then crunched down. "He doesn't quibble at murder, and must have—because he thinks ahead—he must have considered the possibility of disposing of Samantha Gannon once he had his prize in hand. But he didn't go into her house with murder on the agenda."

"He adjusts. Understands the value of being flexible and of keeping his eye on the ball, so to speak. What you have so far doesn't indicate a man who panics when something alters his game plan. He works with it, and moves on accordingly."

"That's a pretty flattering description."

"Not at all," Roarke disagreed. "As his flexibility and focus are completely amoral and self-serving. As you pointed out, I've had—and have—game plans of my own, and I know, very well, the seductive pull of glittering stones. Cash, however sexy it might be, doesn't hook into you the same way. The light of them, the dazzle and the colors and shapes. There's something primitive about the attraction, something visceral. Despite that, to kill over a handful of sparkles demeans the whole business. To my mind, in any case."

"Stealing them's okay though."

He grinned now, and took the second half of her bread stick. "If you do it right. Once—in another life, of course—I . . . relieved a London bird of a number of her sparkling feathers. She kept them locked away in a vault—in the dark—such a pity. What's the point in locking all those beauties away, after all, where they only wait to shine again? She kept a house in Mayfair, guarded like Buckingham bloody Palace. I did the job solo, just to see if I could."

She knew she shouldn't be amused, but she couldn't help it. "Bet you could."

"You win. Christ, what a rush. I think I was twenty, and still I remember—remember exactly—what it was to take those stones out of the dark and watch them come alive in my hands. They need the light to come alive."

"What did you do with them?"

"Well now, that's another story, Lieutenant." He topped off their wineglasses. "Another story entirely."

The waiter served their antipasto. On his heels the maître d' came hurrying back, pulling a waitress by the arm.

"Tell the signora," he ordered.

"Okay. I think that maybe I waited on her."

"She thinks maybe," Gino echoed. He almost sang it.

"She with a guy?"

"Yeah. Listen, I'm not a hundred percent."

"Is it okay if she sits down a minute?" Eve asked Gino.

"Whatever you like. Anything you like. The antipasto, it's good?"

"It's great."

"And the wine?"

Noting the flicker in Eve's eyes, Roarke shifted. "It's very nice wine. A wonderful choice. I wonder, could we have a chair for . . . "

"I'm Carmen," the waitress told him.

Fortunately there was a chair available as Eve had no doubt Gino would have personally dumped another diner out of one to accommodate Roarke's request.

Though he continued to hover, Eve ignored him and turned to Carmen. "What do you remember?"

"Well." Carmen looked hard at the photo she'd given back to Eve. "Gino said it was a first-date thing. And I think I remember waiting on her—them. She was all nervous and giddy like she didn't get out much, and she looked young enough that I had to card her. I sort of hated to do it because she got all flustered, but it was okay because she was legal. Barely. That's why I sort of remember."

"What about him. What do you remember about him?"

"Um . . . He wasn't as young as her, and he was a lot smoother. Like he'd been around some. He ordered in Italian, casual like. I remember that because some guys do and it's a real show-off deal, and others pull it off. He pulled it off. And he didn't stint on the tip."

"How'd he pay?"

"Cash. I always remember when they pay cash, especially when they don't stiff me."

"Can you describe him?"

"Oh, I don't know. I didn't pay that close. I think he had dark hair. Not too dark. I mean not . . . " She shifted her gaze to Roarke and her eyes skimmed over his hair and would have sighed if they could. "Not black."

"Uh-huh. Carmen." Eve tapped her on the hand to regain her attention. "What about skin color?"

"Oh, well, he was white. But he had a tan. I remember that now. Like he'd had a really good flash or a nice vacation. No, he had light hair! That's right. He had blondish hair because it was a real contrast with the tan. I think.

Anyway. He was really attentive to her, too. Now that I'm thinking, I remember most times I went by he was listening to her, or asking her questions. A lot of guys—hell, most guys—don't listen."

"You said he was older than she was. How much older?"

"Jeez, it's hard to say. To remember. I don't think it was one of those daddy-type things."

"How about build?"

"I don't really know. He was sitting, you know. He wasn't a porker. He just looked normal."

"Piercings, tattoos?"

"Oh wow. Not that I remember. He had a really good wrist unit. I noticed it. She was in the ladies' when I brought out their coffee, and he checked the time. It was really sharp-looking, thin and silvery with a pearly face. What do they call that?"

"Mother-of-pearl?" Roarke suggested.

"Yeah. Yeah, mother-of-pearl. It was one sharp-looking piece. Expensive-looking."

"Would you be willing to work with a police artist?"

"This is a cop thing? Wow. What did they do?"

"It's him I'm interested in. I'd like to arrange for you to come down to Central tomorrow. I can have you transported."

"I guess. Sure. It'd be kind of a kick."

"If you'd give me your information, someone will contact you."

Eve plucked an olive from the plate as Carmen carried her chair away. "I love when long shots pay off." She saw the plates of pasta heading in their direction and struggled not to salivate. "Just give me one minute to set this up."

She pulled out her 'link to call Central and arrange for an artist session. While she listened to the desk sergeant, asked a couple of pithy questions, she twirled pasta on her fork.

She ended the call, stuffed the pasta in her mouth. "Nadine broadcast the connection."

"What?"

"Sorry." She swallowed and repeated the statement more coherently. "Figured she'd make it after talking to Gannon, and that she'd go on air."

"Problem?"

"If it was dicey I'd've stopped her. And to give her credit, she'd have let me. No, it's no problem. He'll catch a broadcast and he'll know we've got lines to tug. Make him think, make him wonder."

She stabbed a meatball, broke off a forkful, wrapped pasta around it. "Bobby Smith, whoever the hell he is, should be doing a lot of thinking tonight."

And he was. He'd come home early from a cocktail party that had bored him to death. The same people, the same conversations, the same ennui. There was never anything new.

Of course, he had a great deal new to talk about. But he hardly thought his recent activities were cocktail conversation.

He'd switched on the screen. Before he'd gone out he'd programmed his entertainment unit to record any mention of various key words: Gannon, Jacobs—as that had turned out to be her name—Cobb. Sweet little Tina. And sure enough, there'd been an extended report by the delicious Nadine Furst on 75 that had combined all of those key words.

So, they'd made the connection. He hadn't expected the police to make it quite that quickly. Not that it mattered.

He changed into lounging pants, a silk robe. He poured himself a brandy and fixed a small plate of fruit and cheese, so that he could be comfortable while he viewed the report again.

Settled on the sofa in the media room of his two-level apartment on Park Avenue, he nibbled on Brie and tart green grapes while Nadine relayed the story again.

Nothing to link him to the naive little maid, he concluded. He'd been careful. There'd been a few transmissions, true, but all to the account he'd created for that purpose, and sent or received from a public unit. He'd always taken her places where they were absorbed by a crowd. And when he'd decided he needed to kill her, he'd taken her to the building on Avenue B.

His father's company was renovating that property. It was untenanted, and though there had been some blood—actually, considerable blood—he'd tidied up. Even if he'd missed a spot or two, crews of carpenters and plumbers would hardly notice a new stain or two among the old.

No, there was nothing to connect a silly maid from the projects to the well-educated, socially advanced and cultured son of one of the city's top businessmen.

Nothing to connect him to the earnest and struggling young artist Bobby Smith.

The artist angle had been brilliant—naturally. He could draw competently enough, and he'd charmed the naive and foolish Tina with a little sketch of her face.

Of course, he'd had to ride a *bus* to create the "chance" meeting. Hideous ordeal. He had no idea how people tolerated such experiences, but imagined those who did neither knew nor deserved any better.

After that, it was all so simple. She'd fallen in love with him. He'd hardly had to expend any effort there. A few cheap dates, a few kisses and soulful looks, and he'd had his entrée into Gannon's house.

He'd had only to moon around her, to go with her one morning—claiming as he met her at the bus stop near the town house that he hadn't been able to sleep thinking of her.

Oh, how she'd blushed and fluttered and strolled with him right to Gannon's front door.

He'd watched her code in—memorized the sequence, then, ignoring her halfhearted and whispered protests, had nipped in behind her, stealing another kiss.

Oh Bobby, you can't. *If Miz Gannon comes down, I could get in trouble. I could get fired. You have to go.*

But she'd giggled, as if they were children pulling a prank, as she shooed at him.

So simple then to watch her quickly code into the alarm. So simple.

Not as simple, he admitted now, not nearly as simple for him to walk out again and leave her waving after him. For a moment, just one hot moment, he'd considered killing her then. Just bashing in that smiling, *ordinary* face and being done with it. Imagined going upstairs, rooting Gannon out and beating the location of the diamonds out of her.

Beating her until she told him everything, *everything* she hadn't put in her ridiculous book.

But that hadn't been the plan. The very careful plan.

Then again, he thought with a shrug, plans changed. And so he'd gotten away with murder. Twice.

After toasting himself, he sipped brandy.

The police could speculate all they liked, they'd never connect him, a man like him, with someone as common as Tina Cobb. And Bobby Smith? A figment, a ghost, a puff of smoke.

He wasn't any closer to the diamonds, but he would be. Oh, he would be. And at least he wasn't, by God, *bored*.

Samantha Gannon was the key. He'd read her book countless times after the first shocked reading, when he'd found so many of his own family secrets spread out on the page. It amazed him, astounded him, infuriated him.

Why hadn't he been told there were millions of dollars—*millions*—tucked away somewhere? Diamonds that belonged, by right, to him.

Dear old Dad had left that little detail out of the telling.

He wanted them. He would have them. It really was that simple.

With them he could, he would, break away from his father and his tedious work ethic. Away from the boredom, the sameness of his circle of friends.

He would be, as his grandfather had been, unique.

Stretching out, he called up another program and watched the series of interviews he'd recorded. In each, Samantha was articulate, bright, attractive. For that precise reason he hadn't attempted to contact her directly.

No, the dim-witted, stars-in-her-eyes Tina had been a much safer, much smarter move.

Still, he was really looking forward to getting to know Samantha better. Much more intimately.

Chapter 7

Eve woke, as usual, to find Roarke up before her, already dressed and settled into the sitting area of the bedroom with coffee, the cat and the morning stock reports on screen.

He was, she saw through one bleary eye, eating what looked like fresh melon and manually keying in codes, figures or state secrets, for all she knew, on a 'link pad.

She gave a grunt as way of good morning and stumbled off to the bathroom.

As she closed the door, she heard Roarke address the cat. "Not at her best before coffee, is she?"

By the time she came out, he'd switched the screen to news, added the audio and was doctoring up a bagel. She nipped it out of his hand, stole his coffee and carried them both to her closet.

"You're as bad as the cat," he complained.

"But faster. I've got a morning briefing. Did you catch a weather report?"

"Hot."

"Bitching hot or just regular hot?"

"It's September in New York, Eve. Guess."

Resigned, she pulled out whatever looked less likely to plaster itself against her skin after five minutes outside.

"Oh, I've a bit of information on the diamonds for you. I did some poking around yesterday."

"You did?" She glanced around, half expecting him to tell her the shirt didn't go with the pants, or the jacket didn't suit the shirt. But it seemed she'd lucked out and grabbed pieces that met his standards. "I didn't think you'd have time with all that ass-kicking."

"That did eat up considerable time and effort. But I carved out a little time between bloodbaths. I've just put it together for you this morning, while you were getting a little more beauty sleep."

"Is that a dig?"

"Darling, how is telling you you're beautiful a dig?"

Her answer was a snort as she strapped on her weapon.

"That jacket looks well on you."

She eyed him warily as she adjusted her weapon harness under the shoulder. "But?"

"No buts."

It was tan, though she imagined he'd call it something else. Like pumpernickel. She never understood why people had to assign strange names to colors.

"My lovely urban warrior."

"Cut it out. What did you get?"

"Precious little, really." He tapped the disk he'd set on the table. "The insurance company paid out for the quarter of them and the investigator's fee of five percent on the rest. So it was a heavy loss. Could've been considerably worse, but insurance companies tend to take a dim view on multimillion-dollar payouts."

"It's their gamble," she said with a shrug. "Don't play if you don't wanna pay."

"Indeed. They did a hard press on O'Hara's daughter, but couldn't squeeze anything out. Added to that, she was the one to find or help the investigator find what there was to recover, and she was instrumental in nailing Crew for the police."

"Yeah, I got that far. Tell me what I don't know."

"They pushed at the inside man's family, associates, at his coworkers. Came up empty there, but watched them for years. Any one of them had upped their lifestyle without having, say, won the lottery, they'd have been hauled in. But they could never find Crew's ex-wife or his son."

"He had a kid?" And she kicked herself for not going back in and checking the runs after they'd returned home the night before.

"He did, apparently. Though it's not in Gannon's book. He was married, divorced and had a son who'd have been just shy of seven when the heist went down. I couldn't find anything on her with a standard starting six months after the divorce."

Interest piqued, she walked back to the sitting area. "She went under?"

"She went under, the way it looks, and stayed there."

He'd gotten another bagel while he spoke, and more coffee. Now he sat again. "I could track her, if you like. It'd take a bit more than a standard, and some time as we're going back half a century. I wouldn't mind it. It's the sort of thing I find entertaining."

"Why isn't it in the book?"

"I imagine you'll ask Samantha just that."

"Damn right. It's a thread." She considered it as she disbursed her equipment in various pockets: communicator, memo book, 'link, restraints. "If you've got time, great. I'll pass it to Feeney. EDD ought to be able to sniff out a woman and a kid. We've got better toys for that than they did fifty years ago."

She thought of the Electronic Detective Division's captain, her former partner. "I bet it's the sort of thing that gets him off, too. Peabody's picking me up." She checked her wrist unit. "Pretty much now. I'll tag Feeney, see if he's got some time."

She scooped up the disk. "The ex–Mrs. Crew's data on here?"

"Naturally." He heard the signal from the gate and, after a quick check, cleared Peabody through. "I'll walk you down."

"You going to be in the city today?"

"That's my plan." He skimmed a hand over her hair as they started down the steps, then stopped when she turned her head and smiled at him. "What's that about?"

"Maybe I just think you're pretty. Or it could be I'm remembering other uses for stairs. Or maybe, just maybe, it's because I know there's no bony-assed, droid-brained puss face waiting down there to curl his lip at me on my way out."

"You miss him."

The sound she made was the vocal equivalent of a sneer. "Please. You must need a pill."

"You do. You miss the little routine, the dance of it."

"Oh ick. Now you've got this picture in my head of

Summerset dancing. It's horrible. He's wearing one of those . . . " She made brushing motions at her hips.

"Tutus?"

"Yeah, that's it."

"Thanks very much for putting that in *my* head."

"Love to share. Know what? You really are pretty." She stopped at the bottom of the steps, grabbed two handfuls of his hair and jerked his head toward hers for a long, smoldering kiss.

"Well, that put other images entirely in my head," he managed when she released him.

"Me too. Good for us." Satisfied, she strode to the door, pulled it open.

Her brow knit when she saw Peabody along with the young EDD ace McNab climbing out of opposite sides of her pea-green police unit. They looked like . . . She didn't know what the hell they looked like.

She was used to seeing McNab, Central's top fashion plate, in something eye-searing and strange, so the shiny chili-pepper pants with their dozen pockets and the electric-blue tank shirt covered with—ha-ha—pictures of chili peppers didn't give her more than a moment's pause. Neither did the hip-length vest in hot red, or the blue air boots that climbed up to his knobby knees.

That was just McNab, with his shiny gold hair slicked back in a long, sleek tail, his narrow and oddly attractive face half covered by red sunshades with mirrored blue lenses and a dozen or so silver spikes glinting at his ears.

But her aide—no, partner now, she had to remember that—was a different story. She wore skinpants that stopped abruptly mid-calf and were the color of . . . mold, Eve decided. The mold that grew on cheese you'd forgotten you stuck in the back of the fridge. She wore some sort of drapey, blousy number of the same color that looked like it had been slept in for a couple of weeks, and a shit-colored jacket that hung to her knees. Rather than the fancy shoes she'd suffered through the day before, she'd opted for some sort of sandal deal that seemed to be made of rope tied into knots by a crazed Youth Scout. There were a lot of chains and pendants and strange-colored stones hanging around her neck and from her ears.

"What are you supposed to be, some upscale street peddler from a Third World country and her pet monkey?"

"This is a nod to my Free-Ager upbringing. And it's comfortable. All natural fabrics." Peabody adjusted her sunshades with their tiny round lenses. "Mostly."

"I think she looks hot," McNab said, giving Peabody a quick squeeze. "Sort of medieval."

"You think tree bark looks hot," Eve tossed back.

"Yeah. Makes me think of the forest. She-body running naked through the forest."

Peabody elbowed him, but she chuckled. "I'm searching for my detective look," she told Roarke. "It's a work in progress."

"I think you look charming."

"Oh shut *up*" was Eve's response as Peabody's cheeks pinked in pleasure. "You fix that heap?" she asked McNab.

"There's good news and bad news. Bad news is that's a piece of crap with a faulty comp system, which makes it about the same as every other police-issue on the streets. Good news is I'm a fricking genius and got her up and running with some spare parts I keep around. She'll hold until you get lucky and wreck it or some asshole who doesn't know better boosts it."

"Thanks. Backseat," she ordered. "Behind the driver.

I'm afraid if I keep catching sight of you in the rearview I'll go blind." She turned to Roarke. "Later."

"I'll look forward to it. Hey." He caught her chin in his hand before she could walk away, then, ignoring her wince, brushed his lips lightly over hers. "Be careful with my cop."

Peabody sighed as she slid into the car. "I just love the way he says that. 'My cop.' " She scooted around to face McNab. "You never call me that."

"It doesn't work when you're a cop, too."

"Yeah, and you don't have the accent anyway. But you're cute." She pursed her lips at him.

"And you're my absolutely female She-body."

"Stop it, stop it, stop it! The neurons in my head are popping." Eve slapped her safety harness in place. "There will be no gooey talk in this vehicle. There will be no gooey talk within ten yards of my person. This is my official ban on gooey talk, and violators will be beaten unconscious with a lead pipe."

"You don't have a lead pipe," Peabody pointed out.

"I'll get one." She slid her eyes over as she drove toward the gates. "Why do you wear something that's wrinkled all to shit?"

"It's the natural state of the natural fabric. My sister wove this material."

"Well, why didn't she smooth it out or something while she was at it? And I can't believe how much time I waste these days discussing your wardrobe."

"Yeah. It's kind of frosty." Her smile turned to a frown as she looked down at her legs. "Do you think these pants make my calves look fat?"

"I can't hear you because something just burst in my brain and my ears are filled with blood."

"In that case, McNab and I will return to our rudely interrupted gooey talk." She yipped when Eve snaked out a hand and twisted her earlobe. "Jeez. Just checking."

Eve considered it a testament to her astounding self-control that she didn't kill either one of them on the way to Central. To keep her record clean, she strode away from them in the garage, nabbing the elevator alone. She had no doubt they'd have to exchange sloppy words or kisses before each separated to check in with their squad.

And judging by the sleepy, satisfied look in Peabody's eye when she strolled in, Eve assumed there'd been some groping added to the lip locks.

It didn't bear thinking about.

"Briefing in fifteen," Eve said briskly. "I have some new data and need to skim over it. I want to bring Feeney in, if he can manage it. To pursue one angle, we're going to need a person search that goes back over fifty years."

Peabody sobered. "The diamonds. We're looking for one of the thieves? Aren't they all dead?"

"Records would indicate. We're looking for the ex-wife and son of Alex Crew. They went into the wind shortly after the divorce and weren't mentioned in Gannon's book. I want to know why."

"Do you want me to contact Feeney?"

"I'll do that. You contact Gannon, schedule a meeting with her."

"Yes, sir."

After loading the disk Roarke had given her and getting coffee, Eve called Feeney's office in EDD.

His familiar, droopy face came on screen. "Seventy-two," he said before she could speak, "and I'm outta here."

She'd forgotten he had vacation coming up and juggled

the time factor in with her other internal data. "Got time for a person search before you clock out with your sunscreen and party hat?"

"Didn't say I wasn't on the job until. Besides, you need a person search, I can put one of my boys on it." All his department were boys to Feeney, regardless of chromosomes.

"I'm looking for brilliance on this one, so I'm asking you to see to it personally."

"How much butter you got to slather on me to grease me up for it? I've got a lot of *i*'s to dot before I take off."

"It involves multiple homicides, a shitload of diamonds and a vanishing act going back over half a century. But if you're too busy packing your hula skirt, I can order up a couple of drones."

"Hula skirt's the wife's." He drew air in and out his nose. "Fifty years?"

"Plus a few. I've got a briefing down here in about ten."

"The one you hooked McNab for?"

"That's the one."

He pulled on his lips, scratched his chin. "I'll be there."

"Thanks." She cut off, then opened Roarke's file to familiarize herself with the data. While it played, she made copies, added them to the packs she'd already put together for the team, made up another for Feeney.

And thought fondly of the days when Peabody would've done all the grunt work.

As a result, she was the last one in the conference room.

"Detective Peabody, brief Captain Feeney on the investigation to date."

Peabody blinked. "Huh?"

"All those things in your ears clogging your hearing? Summarize the case, Detective, and bring Captain Feeney up to speed."

"Yes, sir."

Her voice squeaked a bit, and she stumbled over the initial data, but Eve was pleased Peabody found her rhythm. It would be a while yet before she had the stones to lead a team, but she had a good, agile mind and, once she got past the nerves, a straightforward and cohesive method of relaying data.

"Thank you, Detective." Eve waited while Feeney finished up making notes. "Baxter, anything from the club on Jacobs?"

"No leads. She was a regular. Came in solo or with a date, with a group. Night in question it was solo, and that's how she left. Hit the dance floor, had some drinks, chatted up a couple guys. Bartender knows she left alone because she talked to him over the last drink. Told him she was in a dry spell. Nobody she met lately did it for her. We got some names, and we'll check them out today, but it looks like a bust."

"Well, tie it up. Pursuant to the information gathered re Cobb, I flashed her picture around the restaurant Ciprioni's, where it's believed she had a date with the man we know as Bobby Smith."

"You went to Ciprioni's?" Peabody exclaimed.

"I needed to eat, I needed to follow up the lead. Two birds."

"Other people like Italian food," Peabody whined.

Eve ignored her. "I found the waitress who had their table in July. She remembers Cobb, and I've set her up with a police artist to try to jog her memory a little more on her description of Cobb's date. We can check the museums, galleries, theaters we believe they visited. Somebody might remember them."

"We'll take it," Baxter told her. "We've knocked down a few already."

"Good. Now that the media's announced the possible connection between these murders, our quarry is aware, almost certainly aware, we've made the link and are investigating concurrently. I don't see this as a deterrent to the investigation."

She waited a beat. "In your packs you'll find data relating to Alex Crew, one of the diamond thieves, and the only one of the four who demonstrated violent behavior. My source related that Crew had an ex-wife and a son. Both of these individuals vanished between the divorce and the heist. I want to find them."

"Crew might have killed them," Peabody suggested.

"Yes, I've considered that. He didn't have any problem killing one of his partners, or attempting murder on another partner's daughter. He'd done some time previously and was suspected of other crimes. He was into the life. Killing an ex wouldn't have been beyond his pathology. Neither would harming or killing a child. His child."

Fathers did, she thought. Fathers could be monsters as easily as anyone else.

"Dead or alive, I want to find them. We have their birth names, and their locations prior to their disappearance. Peabody and I will talk to Gannon this morning." She cocked a brow at Peabody.

"Eleven hundred at the Rembrandt."

"It's possible she has more information on them gathered through her family or her research for her book. I also want her reasoning for leaving them out of that book when others are named. Feeney, you're on the search?"

"On it."

"Ah . . . Roarke has offered to assist, if necessary, as civilian consultant. As he gathered the current data for me, he has an interest in following through."

"Never a problem for me to use the boy. I'll tag him."

"McNab, I want anything you can get me off Cobb's d and c, her 'links. Gannon's and Jacobs's communications equipment are already in-house. Check with the officer assigned to clearing those units."

"You got it."

"I've urged Gannon to consider private security, and she appears to be amenable. We'll keep a man on her as long as the budget allows. This perpetrator is very specific in his goal. Very specific in his targets. Both victims connected to Gannon. If he feels she's in his way, or has information he wants, he won't hesitate to try for her. At this point, we have nothing that leads to him but a fifty-year-old crime. Let's get more."

On the way back to the division, Eve watched idly as two plainclothes muscled along a restrained woman who weighed in at about three hundred pounds and was flinging out an impressive array of obscenities. Since both cops had facial cuts and bruises, Eve assumed the prisoner had flung more than curses before they'd cuffed her.

God, she loved the job.

"Peabody, my office."

She led the way in, closed the door, which had Peabody sending it a puzzled look. Then she programmed two cups of coffee, gestured to a chair.

"Am I in trouble?"

"No."

"I know I didn't handle the briefing very well. It threw me a minute, that's all, to do the stand-up. I—"

"You did fine. You want to work on focusing on the

data instead of yourself. Self-conscious cops don't lead teams. Neither do cops who second-guess themselves every two minutes. You earned the shield, Peabody, now you have to use it. But that's not what this is about."

"The clothes are . . . " She trailed off at Eve's stony stare. "Self-conscious again. Putting it away. What is this about, then?"

"I work after shift a lot. Regularly. Go back out into the field to tug on a lead, work up various scenarios or do 'link or comp work in my home office. Bounce the case off Roarke. It's how I work. Are you going to have a problem with me not hooking you in every time I do?"

"Well, no. Well . . . I guess I'm trying to find the partner rhythm. Maybe you are, too."

"Maybe I am. It's not because I'm flipping you off. Let's get that clear. I live the job, Peabody. I breathe it and I eat it and I sleep with it. I don't recommend it."

"It works for you."

"Yeah, it works for me. There are reasons it works for me. My reasons. They're not yours."

She looked down into her coffee and thought of the long line of victims, and they all led back to herself, a child, bleeding and broken in a freezing hotel room in Dallas.

"I can't do this any other way. I won't do this any other way. I need what this gives me. You don't need the same thing. That doesn't make you less of a cop. And when I go out on my own on something, I'm not thinking you're less of a cop."

"I can't always put it away either."

"None of us can. And those who can't find a way to deal with that burnout get mean, get drunk or off themselves. You've got ways to deal. You've got family and outside interests. And shit, I'll say it this once, you've got McNab."

Peabody's lips curved. "That must've hurt."

"Some."

"I love him. It's weird, but I love him."

Eve met her eyes, a brief but steady acknowledgment. "Yeah, I get that."

"And it does make a difference. And I get what you're saying, too. I can't always put it away, but sometimes I have to. So I do. I probably won't ever be able to spin it around in my head the way you do, but that's okay. I'm probably still going to bitch some when I find out you went out without me."

"Understood. We're all right then?"

"We're all right."

"Then get out of my office so I can get some work done before we see Gannon."

She wrangled for a consult with Mira and after some heated negotiations with the doctor's admin, was given a thirty-minute during lunch break at Central's infamous Eatery. Eve couldn't figure out why anyone with Mira's class would suffer the Eatery's indignities, but she didn't argue.

She managed, with considerable footwork, to delay her report to Commander Whitney until late that afternoon.

Another call included threats of doubtful anatomical possibility and a bribe of box seats at a Mets game. The combination netted her the promise from the chief lab tech of a full report on both cases by fourteen hundred.

Considering her 'link work a job well done, she grabbed her files, signaled Peabody and went into the field.

• • •

Peabody fisted her hands on her hips. "This is returning to the scene of the crime way, way after the fact."

"We didn't commit a crime, so technically we're not returning." Eve ignored the people who trooped or stalked around her as she stood at the corner of Fifth and Forty-seventh. "I just wanted a look at the place."

"Got hit pretty hard in the Urban Wars," Peabody commented. "Easy target, I guess. Conspicuous consumption. The haves and have-nots. All that fancy jewelry showcased while the economy took a nosedive, illegals were sold on the street like soy dogs and guns were strapped on like fashion accessories."

She edged closer to one of the displays. "Shiny."

"So three guys walk in, do a little switch-and-grab with the fourth, and walk out with pockets full of diamonds. Nobody's prepared for it as the inside guy's long-term, trusted, considered above reproach."

Eve studied the window displays as she spoke, and the people who stopped to huddle at them, dreaming over that shine. Gold and silver—metals; rubies and emeralds, and diamonds bright as the sun—stones. Since they couldn't be consumed for fuel, didn't keep you warm in the winter, it was tough for her to relate to the pull.

Yet she wore a circle of gold on her finger and a bright, glittering diamond on a chain under her shirt. Symbols, she thought. Just symbols. But she'd fight for them, wouldn't she?

"Inside man has to walk out, too," she went on, "practically on their heels, and go straight under. Finger's going to point at him, he knows that going in. But he wants what he wants and he tosses everything else away for it.

And gets taken out before he can pat himself on the back. Crew did him, so Crew had to know how to get to him. Not only his location, but how to lure him out."

She looked up, as a tourist might, to the upper floors. No people glides on a building like this. There wouldn't have been any early century either, she mused. It had been rehabbed and rebuilt after the wars but was, essentially, the same as the history image she'd studied.

And leading down from the corner it dominated were shop after shop, display after display of body adornments. This single crosstown block held millions in merchandise. It was a wonder it wasn't hit on a daily basis.

"They didn't even bother to take out the security cams," she commented. "In and out and no sweat. But the cops would've ID'd them eventually. Every one of them had a sheet but the inside guy, and his gambling problem would've flagged him. So they were just going to stay under, keep the stones tucked away, wait for the air to cool. Then poof. You know why it might've worked?"

"The investigation would have focused, at least initially, on the inside man. They'd figure he cracked up, planned and executed. He's gone, diamonds are gone. They move on him."

"Yeah, while the rest of them scatter and wait it out. Crew was smart to eliminate him, but he went off when he didn't dispose of the body. Smarter, much smarter to dump the guy in the river so the cops waste time and resources looking for a dead man. Didn't think it through all the way, because he wanted what he wanted, too. Once he had it, he just wanted more. That's why he ended up dying in prison. This guy, our guy, he's a little smarter."

She studied a group of three women who stopped by a display window to make ooohing noises and exclamations.

Yeah, the stuff was shiny and sparkly. She wasn't entirely sure why people wanted to shine and sparkle, but they did—and had since the dawn.

"But he's just as obsessed," Peabody commented. "Crew was obsessed with the diamonds, I think. That's what I get from the book. He had to have all of them. He couldn't settle for his cut, no matter what it took. I think this guy's the same in that area. Obsessed. Even possessed, in a way. Like they were—the diamonds—cursed."

"They're carbon-based stones, Peabody. Inanimate objects." Unconsciously she rubbed a finger over the tear-shaped diamond she wore on a chain under her shirt. "They don't do anything but sit there."

Peabody looked back in the window. "Shiny," she said again with her eyes unfocused and her jaw slack.

Despite herself, Eve laughed. "Let's get out of this heat and go see Gannon."

Chapter 8

The Rembrandt, Eve discovered, was one of those small, exclusive, European-style hotels snuggled into New York almost like a secret. No sky-reaching towers or mile-wide lobby, no gilt-encased entrance. Instead it was a lovely old building she assumed had once been a high-dollar residence in a style that murmured elegant discretion.

Rather than her usual snarling match with a doorman, this one trotted over in his sedate navy blue uniform and cap to greet her with a respectful nod.

"Welcome to the Rembrandt. Will you be checking in, madam?"

"No." She flashed her badge, but his polite manner took some of the fun out of it. "I'm here to see a guest."

"Shall I arrange parking for you during your visit?"

"No, you should leave this vehicle exactly where I've put it."

"Of course," he said without a wince or a gasp, and sucked the rest of the wind from her sails. "Enjoy your visit at the Rembrandt, Lieutenant. My name's Malcolm if you need any assistance while you're here."

"Yeah. Well. Thanks." His manner took her off-guard enough to have her break her own firm policy. She pulled out ten credits and handed it to him.

"Thank you very much." He was at the door before her, sweeping it open.

The lobby was small and furnished like someone's very tasteful parlor with deeply cushioned chairs and gleaming wood, glossy marble, paintings that might have been original work. There were flowers, but rather than the twenty-foot arrangements Eve often found a little scary, there were small, attractive bouquets arranged on various tables.

Instead of a check-in counter with a platoon of uniformed, toothy clerks, there was a woman at an antique desk.

With security in mind, Eve scanned the area and spotted four discreetly placed cameras. So that was something.

"Welcome to the Rembrandt." The woman, slender, dressed in pale peach, with her short shock of hair streaked blond and black, rose. "How may I assist you?"

"I'm here to see Samantha Gannon. What room is she in?"

"One moment." The woman sat back down, scanned the screen on her desk unit. She looked up at Eve with an apologetic smile. "I'm sorry. We have no guest by that name."

The words were hardly out of her mouth when two men

stepped out of a side door. Eve tagged them as security, and noted by stance that they were armed.

"Good. I'm on the job." She directed this to the men as she held up her right hand. "Dallas, Lieutenant, Homicide. My partner. Peabody, Detective. IDs coming."

She reached for her badge with two fingers and kept her eyes on the security team. "Your security's better than it looks at first glance."

"We're very protective of our guests," the woman answered, and took Eve's badge to scan it, then Peabody's. "These are in order," she said, and nodded to the two men. "Ms. Gannon is expecting you. I'll just ring her room and let her know you're here."

"Fine. What do they load you with?" Eve nodded toward security, and one of them flipped aside his jacket to reveal a multi-action, mid-range hand stunner in a quick-release side holster. "That oughta do it."

"Ms. Gannon's ready for you, Lieutenant. She's on four. Your officer is in the alcove by the elevator. He'll show you her room."

"Appreciate it." She walked to the two-bank elevator with Peabody. "She showed sense picking a place like this. Solid security, probably the kind of service that gives you everything you want five minutes before you ask for it."

They stepped on, and Peabody ordered the fourth floor. "How much you think it costs for a night here?"

"I don't know that stuff. I don't know why people don't just stay home in the first place. No matter how snazzy the joint, there's always some stranger next door when you're in a hotel. Probably another one over your head, the other under your feet. Then there's bell service and housekeeping and other people coming in and out all the damn time."

"You sure know how to take the romance out of it."

The uniform was waiting when they stepped off. "Lieutenant." He hesitated, looked pained.

"You've got a problem asking me for an ID check, Officer? How do you know I didn't get on at two, blast Dallas and Peabody between the eyes, dump their lifeless bodies and ride the rest of the way up intending to blast you, then get to the subject?"

"Yes, sir." He took their IDs, used his hand scanner. "She's in four-oh-four, Lieutenant."

"Anyone attempt entrance since your shift began?"

"Both housekeeping and room service, both ordered by subject, both checked before given access. And Roarke, who was cleared at lobby level, by subject and by myself."

"Roarke."

"Yes, sir. He's been with subject for the past fifteen minutes."

"Hmm. Stand down, Officer. Take ten."

"Yes, sir. Thank you, sir."

"Are you going to be pissed at him?" Peabody asked. "Roarke, I mean."

"I don't know yet." Eve rang the bell and was satisfied by the slight wait that told her Samantha made use of the security peep.

There were circles under Samantha's eyes, and a pallor that spoke of sleepless nights. She appeared to have dressed carefully though, in dark pants and a white tailored shirt. There were tiny square hoops at her ears and a thin matching bracelet on her wrist.

"Lieutenant. Detective. I think you know each other,"

she added, gesturing to where Roarke sat, sipping what smelled like excellent coffee. "I didn't put it together. You, my publisher. I knew the connection, of course, but with everything . . . with everything, it just didn't input."

"You get around," Eve said to Roarke.

"As much as possible. I wanted to check on one of our valued authors, and convince her to accept security. I believe you recommended private security in this matter, Lieutenant."

"I did." Eve nodded. "It's a good idea. If he's providing it," she told Samantha, "you'll have the best."

"I didn't take any convincing. I want to live a long and happy life, and I'll take whatever help I can get to make sure of it. Do you want coffee? Anything?"

"It's real coffee?"

"She has a weakness." Roarke smiled. "She married me for the coffee."

Some of the bloom came back into Samantha's cheeks. "I could write a hell of a book about the two of you. Glamour, sex, murder, the cop and the gazillionaire."

"No," they said together, and Roarke laughed.

"I don't think so. I'll deal with the coffee, Samantha. Why don't you sit down? You're tired."

"And it shows." Samantha sat, sighed and let Roarke go into the kitchen area for more coffee and cups. "I can't sleep. I can work. I can put my head into the work, but when I stop, I can't sleep. I want to be home, and I can't stand the thought of being home. I'm tired of myself. I'm alive, I'm well and whole, and others aren't, and I keep spiraling into self-pity anyway."

"You should give yourself a break."

"Dallas is right," Peabody put in. "You were up and running a couple of weeks, come home to something that would put a lot of people under. You've been hit with everything all at once. A little self-pity doesn't hurt. You should take a tranq and check out for eight or ten hours."

"I hate tranqs."

"There you take hands with the lieutenant." Roarke came in with a tray. "She won't take them voluntarily either." He set the coffee down. "Do you want me out of your way?"

Eve studied him. "You're not in it yet. I'll let you know when you are."

"You never fail."

"Samantha, why did you leave out Alex Crew's family connections in your book?"

"Connections?" Samantha leaned forward for her coffee and, Eve noted, avoided eye contact.

"Specifically Crew's ex-wife and son. You give considerable details regarding Myers's family and what they dealt with after his death. You speak at great length of William Young and your own family. And though you feature Crew prominently, there's no mention of a wife or a child."

"How do you know he had a wife and child?"

"I'm asking the questions. You didn't miss those details in your research. Why aren't they in the book?"

"You put me in a difficult position." Samantha held the coffee, stirring, stirring, long after the minute sprinkle of sugar she'd added would have dissolved. "I made a promise. I couldn't and wouldn't have written the book without my family's blessing. Most specifically without my grandparents' permission. And I promised them I'd leave Crew's son out of it."

As if realizing what her hand was doing, she tapped the spoon on the rim of her cup, then set it aside. "He was only a little boy when this happened. My grandmother felt—still feels—that his mother was trying to protect him from Crew. Hide him from Crew."

"Why did she think that?"

After setting her untasted coffee down, Samantha dragged her fingers through her hair. "I'm not free to talk about it. I swore I wouldn't write about it, or talk about it in interviews. No." She held up her hands before Eve could speak. "I know what you're going to say, and you're absolutely right. These are not ordinary circumstances. This is murder."

"Then answer the question."

"I need to make a call. I need to speak with my grandmother, which is going to start another round of demands, debates and worry with her and my grandfather. Another reason I'm not sleeping."

She pressed her fingers to her eyes before dropping them into her lap. "They want me to come to Maryland, stay with them, or they threaten to descend on me here. It's tough going to keep them from calling my parents and sibs. I'm holding them off, and I'm gratefully accepting Roarke's offer for security on them until this is resolved. Until it is, I'm staying here. I think it's important that I see this through, that I deal in my way with what's happening now just as they did in theirs with what happened then."

"Part of dealing is giving the primary any and all data that may pertain to this investigation."

"Yes, you're right again. Just let me call, speak to her first. We don't break promises in my family. It's like a religion to my grandmother. I'll go in the bedroom, call her now, if you can just wait a few minutes."

"Go ahead."

"Admirable," Roarke said when she'd gone. "To set such store by your word, particularly to family when for some reason the more intimate you are, the easier a promise is to break. Or at least bend to circumstance."

"Her great-grandfather broke a lot of promises," Eve reflected. "Jack O'Hara broke a lot of promises, to Laine and Laine's mother. So Samantha's grandmother wanted to end the cycle. You don't intend to keep your word, even when it's hard, you don't give it. You have to respect that."

She glanced toward the bedroom, back at him. "Offering to take care of her security, and the Maryland Gannons', is classy. But you could've sent a lackey to handle it."

"I wanted to meet her. She struck a chord with you, and I wanted to see why. I do."

When Samantha came out of the bedroom a few minutes later, she was teary-eyed. "I'm sorry. I hate worrying her. Worrying them. I'm going to have to go down to Maryland and put their minds at ease very soon."

She sat, took a bracing sip of coffee. "Judith and Westley Crew," she began. She gave them the foundation data she had, and at one point went to get some of her own notes to refresh her memory.

"So you see, when my grandfather tracked her and found Crew had been there, he believed he might've given the child something that held the diamonds. A portion of them, in any case. It was a safe place to keep them while he went about his work."

"He would've had half of them, or access to half of them, at that time?" Eve made her own notes.

"Yes. With what was recovered in the safe-deposit box, that left a quarter of the diamonds among the missing. Crew's ex-wife and son were gone. Everything indicated, to my grandmother at least, that she'd been hiding from Crew. The change of names, the quiet job, the middle-class neighborhood. Then the way she packed up and left—sold everything she could or gave it away and just got out. It seemed she was running again because he'd found her. Or more, to my grandmother's mind, the boy. Just a little boy, you see, and his mother was trying to protect him from a man she'd come to know was dangerous and obsessive. If you look at Crew's background and criminal record, his pattern of behavior, she was right to be afraid."

"She might have taken off because she had a few million in diamonds in her possession," Eve pointed out.

"Yes. But my grandparents didn't believe, and I don't believe, that a man like Crew would have given them to her, would have told her. Used her, yes, and the boy, but not given her that kind of power. *He* needed to be in charge. He would've found them again when he wanted to. I've no doubt he threatened the woman and would have discarded or disposed of her when his son was older. Old enough to be of more interest and use to Crew. My grandfather let it go, let the remaining diamonds go, let them go. Because my grandmother asked it of him."

"She'd once been a young child," Roarke said with a nod, "who'd had to be uprooted or moved about, who'd never had a settled home or the security that comes with it. And like Crew's ex, her mother had made a choice—to separate herself from the man and shield her child."

"Yes. Yes. The bulk of the diamonds were back where they belonged. And they were, as my grandmother is fond of saying, only things, after all. The boy and his mother were finally safe. If they'd pursued it, and I have no doubt my grandfather could have tracked them down, they'd have been pulled into the mess. The young boy would have had everything his father had done pushed in his face, would very likely have ended up a national news story himself. His life might have been damaged or severely changed by this one thing. So they told no one."

She leaned forward. "Lieutenant, they withheld information. It was probably illegal for them to withhold it. But they did it for the best possible reason. They would have gained more. Five percent more of over seven million, if they'd tracked her down. They didn't, and the world's managed to sputter along without those particular stones."

Samantha wasn't just defending herself and her grandparents, Eve noted. She was defending a woman and child she'd never met. "I'm not interested in dragging your grandparents into this. But I am interested in finding Judith and Westley Crew. The diamonds don't mean squat to me, Samantha. I'm not Robbery, I'm Homicide. Two women are dead, you may very well be a target. The motive for this comes from the diamonds, and that's my interest in them. Someone else can do the research and dig up the fact that Crew had a wife and child. This could make them targets."

"Well, my God." As it struck home, Samantha squeezed her eyes shut. "I never thought of it. Never considered it."

"Or the person who killed Andrea Jacobs and Tina Cobb may be connected to Crew. It may be his son, who's decided he wants to get back what he feels belonged to his father."

"We always assumed . . . Everything my grandparents found out about Judith showed, clearly showed, she was doing everything she could to give her son a normal life.

We assumed she succeeded. Just because his father was a murderer, a thief, a son of a bitch, doesn't mean the child took on his image. I don't believe we work that way, Lieutenant. That we're genetically fated. Do you?"

"No." She glanced at Roarke. "No, I don't. But I do believe, whatever their parentage, some people are just born bad."

"What a happy thought," Roarke murmured.

"Not finished. However we're born, we end up making choices. Right ones, wrong ones. I need to find Westley Crew and determine what choices he made. This needs to be closed out, Samantha. It needs to end."

"They'll never forgive themselves. If somehow this has come full circle and struck out at me, my grandparents will never forgive themselves for making the choice they made all those years ago."

"I hope they're smarter than that," Roarke said. "They made a choice, for a child they didn't even know. If that child made choices as a man, it's on him. What we do with our lives always is."

They left together, with Eve bouncing the new information in her head until she formed patterns. "I need you to find them," she said to Roarke.

"Understood."

"Coincidence happens, but mostly it's bullshit. I'm not buying that some guy read Gannon's book and got a hard-on for missing diamonds and decided to kill a couple of women in order to find them. He's got an investment in them, a connection to them. The book set it off, but the connection goes further back. How long before the book came out did the hype for it start?"

"I'll find out. There will also be a list of some sort of people, reviewers, accounts and so forth, that were sent advance copies. You have to add word of mouth to that, I'm afraid. People the editorial staff, publicity and others might have spoken to."

"We've got this great book coming out," Peabody began. "It's about this diamond heist right here in New York."

"Exactly so. The man you're looking for might have heard of it over drinks somewhere. Might have an acquaintance or attended a party with one of the editors, a reviewer, someone in sales who spoke about it."

"Won't that be fun to wade through? Get me the list," she repeated as they stepped out into the lobby. "And let me know who you put on her, security-wise. I want my people to know your people. Oh, and I need two box seats, Mets game."

"Personal use or bribe?"

"Bribe. Please, you know I'm a Yankees fan."

"What was I thinking. How do you want them?"

"Just send the authorization to Dickhead at the lab. Berenski. Thanks. I gotta book."

"Kiss me goodbye."

"I already kissed you goodbye this morning. Twice."

"Third time lucky." He planted his lips firmly on hers. "I'll be in touch, Lieutenant." He strolled out. Even before he hit the sidewalk a sleek black car pulled up to the curb, and a driver hopped out to open the door.

Like magic, Eve thought.

"I'd like to be in touch with him. Anytime. Anywhere. Any way."

Eve turned her head slowly. "Did you say something, Peabody?"

"Who, sir, me, sir? Nope. Absolutely not."

"Good."

• • •

She took the meeting with Mira next while Peabody ate lunch at her desk and updated the file. As far as food went, Eve figured Peabody had the better end of the stick.

The Eatery was always crowded, always noisy, no matter what the time of day. It made Eve think of a public school cafeteria, except the food was even worse and most of the people chowing down were armed.

Mira was there ahead of her and had a booth. She'd either gotten very lucky, Eve thought, or had used some clout to order one up earlier. Either way, a booth was a big step up from one of the tiny four-tops crammed together, or the counter service, where cop asses hung over the stingy stools.

Mira wasn't a cop—technically—and sure as hell didn't look like one. She didn't, to Eve's mind, look like a criminologist, a doctor or a psychiatrist either. Though she was all of those.

What she looked like was a pretty, well-dressed woman who might be seen browsing the high-end shops along Madison.

She might've bought the suit in one of them. Surely only the very brave or very stylish would wear that lemon-foam shade in a city like New York, where grime just sprang up off the asphalt and clung to any available surface like a leech to flesh.

But the suit was spotless and looked cool and fresh. It set off the highlights in Mira's soft brown hair and made her eyes seem bluer. She wore a trio of long, thin, gold ropes with it where stones of a deeper yellow glinted like little pieces of sunlight.

She was drinking something out of a tall glass that looked as frosty as her suit, and smiled over the rim as Eve slid into the booth across from her.

"You look hot and harried. You should have one of these."

"What is it?"

"Delicious." Without waiting for Eve's assent, Mira ordered one from the comp menu bolted to the side of the booth. "How are you otherwise?"

"Okay." It always took Eve a moment to adjust when small talk was involved. And with Mira it wasn't exactly small talk. People made that when they didn't give a damn one way or the other, and mostly, she assumed, to hear their own voices. Mira cared. "Good. Summerset's vacationing far, far away. Cheers me right up."

"He made a quick recovery from his injuries."

"He was still a little wobbly on the one pin, but yeah."

"And how is our newest detective?"

"She likes to sneak her badge out and grin at it a lot yet. And she manages to work the word 'detective' into a sentence several times a day. She's dressing really weird. Throws me off. Otherwise, she's jetting along with it."

Eve glanced at the drink that slid out of the serving slot. It did look pretty good. She took one cautious sip. "It tastes like your suit. Cool and summery and a little tart." She thought it over. "That probably sounded wrong."

"No." With a laugh, Mira sat back. "Thank you. A color like this? Completely impractical. That's why I couldn't resist it. I was just admiring your jacket, and how that wonderful shade of toast looks on you. It would turn my complexion muddy. And I just can't wear separates with the same panache as you."

"Separates?"

It took Mira a moment to realize such a basic fashion

word baffled her favorite cop. "Jacket, pants, whatever, sold individually rather than as part of a unit, as a suit would be."

"Hah. Separates. How about that. And I always thought they were, you know, jacket, pants, whatever."

"My God, I would *love* to go shopping with you." This time Mira's laugh flowed over the cranky noises of the Eatery. "And you look as if I've just stabbed you with my fork under the table. One day I'll rope you into it, but for now rather than ruin your appetite, why don't I ask you how Mavis is doing?"

"Good." Though Eve wasn't sure talking about pregnancy was any less of an appetite blower than shopping. "You wouldn't know she was, ah, cooking anything in there if she didn't advertise it. She and Leonardo might rent blimp space. He's designing her all kinds of pregnant-chick clothes, but I can't really tell the difference."

"Give them all my best. I know you want to get to business. Why don't we order first? I'm having a Greek salad. You can usually trust those here."

"Yeah, that's fine."

Mira ordered two from the menu. "Do you know I remember bits and pieces about the robbery at the Exchange? It was very big news at the time."

"How? You're too young."

"Now *that* has set me up for the day. Actually, I was only, what . . . oh, how depressing. I'd've been about four, I suppose. But my uncle happened to be dating a woman who had a booth in the Exchange. She was a jewelry designer and was there, on the main floor, when the robbery happened. I remember hearing my parents talk about it, and when I was a bit older I developed such an interest in crime that I looked up the details. The family connection, however distant, added to the excitement for me."

"Is she still around? The designer?"

"I have no idea. It didn't work out between her and my uncle. I do know that she didn't know a thing until security shut the place down. She didn't know the inside man. At least that's what I got from my uncle when I asked him about it later. I could get you her name, I'm sure, if you want to try to track her down."

"I might, but it's probably the wrong direction. At least at this point. Tell me about the killer."

"Well. The act, the murders themselves, aren't his priority. They're a by-product. His victims and his methods are different, each suiting his needs at the time. He would be most interested in his own needs. The fact that they were both women, even attractive, isn't important. I doubt he has a spouse or serious relationship as either would interfere with his self-absorption. There was nothing sexual, despite his romancing of Tina Cobb, and that romancing was not only a means to an end but on his own terms."

"Taking her places he preferred in order to show off his superior intellect and taste."

"Yes. There was nothing personal in either murder. He sees the big picture, from his own narrow view. Cobb could be utilized and exploited, and so she was. He plans and considers, so it follows that he knew he could kill her when her use to him ended. He knew her, set out to know her. He knew her face, the touch of her hand, the sound of her voice, may have been intimate with her physically if it moved him toward his goal, but there would be no personal connection for him."

"He destroyed her face."

"Yes, but not out of rage, not out of personal emotion. Out of self-preservation. Both murders were a result of his need to protect himself. He will remove, destroy, eliminate anything or anyone who gets in the way of his goal or his own personal safety."

"There was violence in his elimination of Cobb."

"Yes."

"He hurt her. To extract information?"

"Possibly, yes. More likely to attempt to mislead the police, to make them think it was a crime of passion. It may have been both. He would have considered. He has time to consider. He took Cobb to crowded places, away from her own aegis. But his choices reflect a certain style. Art, theater, a trendy restaurant."

"Reflecting his aegis."

"He would want to be comfortable, yes." The first salad plate slid out, and Mira set it in front of Eve. "He entered Gannon's home when he knew she was out. He was careful to shut down the security, to take the disks. To protect himself. He brought a weapon—though he believed the house empty, he brought the knife. He prepares for eventualities, takes detours when necessary. He didn't attempt to make the break-in and murder appear to be a burglary gone wrong by taking away valuables."

"Because it had already been done? Because Alex Crew used that method with Laine Tavish?"

Mira took the second plate, smiled. "It reflects a powerful ego, doesn't it? 'I won't repeat, I'll create.' And a respect for art and antiques. He didn't vandalize, didn't destroy the artwork, the valuable furniture. He'd consider such a thing beneath him. He has knowledge of such things, likely owns such things himself. Certainly he aspires to. But if it was only aspiration, he would have taken what appealed to his sense of aesthetic or avarice. He's very focused."

"He's educated? Cultured?"

"Art galleries, museums, West Village theater?" Mira shrugged a shoulder. "He could have taken the girl to Coney Island, to Times Square, to a dozen places a young man of her same sphere might take a girl on a date. But he didn't."

"Because, like stealing art pieces or electronics, it would be beneath him to munch on a soy dog in Coney Island."

"Mmm." Mira nibbled on salad. "He isn't looking for glory, fame or attention. He isn't looking for sex or even wealth in the traditional sense. He's looking for something very specific."

"Alex Crew had a son."

Mira's brows winged up. "Did he?"

"A kid at the time this all went down."

She filled Mira in, then let the doctor absorb the new data while they ate.

"I see what you're considering. The son hears of the book, or reads it, and learns one of his father's former partners' ancestors is right here in New York. That she has enough information for a book, and very likely has more. That she may very well have access to the diamonds. But why, if he's known of them all this time, hasn't he tried to find them, or get to the Gannons before?"

"Maybe he didn't know the whole story until the book. Maybe he didn't know the connection." Eve waved with her fork. "Anyway, that's for me to figure out. What I want is your opinion. Does it follow pattern, profile, that the person I'm after is Crew's son?"

"It could give him what he'd consider a proprietary

right to them. They were his father's property, so to speak. But if his father brought them to him when he was a child—"

"It wasn't in the book," Eve reminded her. "And we can't know what Crew did or didn't do or say or take when he paid that last visit."

"All right. From what we know of Crew, he felt entitled to the entire booty, and killed for it. They were an obsession for him, one he pursued even though he had enough to ensure he'd live well for the rest of his life. It's possible the son is working with the same obsession, the same view."

"My gut tells me it comes from Crew."

"And your gut is usually right. Does it trouble you to take that line, Eve? To play the sins of the father in your head?"

"Yeah." She could say it here, to Mira. "Some."

"Heredity can be a strong pull. Heredity and early environment together, an almost irresistible pull. Those who break it, who make their own despite it, are very strong."

"Maybe." Eve leaned forward. No one around them would listen, but she leaned closer, lowered her voice. "You know, you can just sink down, you can sink and say it's somebody else's fault you're down there in the piss and the shit of the world. But it's just an excuse. The lawyers, the shrinks, the doctors and social reformers can say, 'Oh, it's not her fault, she's not responsible. Look where she came from. Look what he did to her. She's traumatized. She's damaged.' "

Mira laid a hand over Eve's. She knew she was thinking of herself, the child, and what the woman might have become. "But?"

"The cops, we know that the victims, the ones who are

broken or shattered or dead . . . or dead, they need somebody to stand up for them, to say, 'Goddamn it, it *is* your fault. You did this, and you have to pay for it, no matter if your mother beat you or your father . . . No matter what, you don't have the right to damage the next guy.' "

Mira gave Eve's hand a squeeze. "And that's why you are."

"Yeah. That's why I am."

Chapter 9

Eve viewed a session in the lab with Dickie Berenski as she did a dental checkup. You had to do it, and if you were lucky it wouldn't be as bad as you imagined. But it was usually worse.

And like the dental techs in her experience, Dickhead exhibited a smarmy, self-righteous satisfaction when it got worse.

She swung into the lab with Peabody and pretended not to notice several techs slide looks in her direction, then get busy elsewhere.

When she didn't see a sign of Dickie, she cornered the first tech who couldn't skitter away fast enough. "Where's Berenski?"

"Um. Office?"

She didn't think she deserved the quaking voice or the frozen rictus of a smile. It had been months since she'd threatened a lab tech. Besides, they should know it was physically impossible for her to put a man's internal organs on display by turning him inside out.

She crossed the main lab, over the white floors, around the white stations manned by people in white coats. Only the machines and the vials and tubes filled with substances best not considered had color.

All in all, she thought she'd rather work in the morgue.

She walked into Dickie's office without knocking. He was kicked back at his desk, feet propped up as he sucked on a grape-colored ice pop.

"You got the box seats?" he asked.

"You'll get them when I get my results."

"I got something for you." He pushed away from the desk, started out, then stopped to study Peabody. "That you in there, Peabody? Where's the uniform?"

Delighted with the opportunity, she pulled out her badge. "I made detective."

"No shit? Nice going. Liked the way you filled out a uniform though."

He hopped onto his stool and began to ride it up and down his long white counter as he ordered up files, keyed in codes with his spider-quick fingers. "You got some of this already. No illegals in either vic. Vic one—that's Jacobs—had a blood-alcohol level of point oh-eight. She was feeling pretty happy. Got her last meal. No recent nooky. Fibers on her shoes match the crime-scene carpet. Couple others here she probably picked up in the cab on the way home."

His fingers danced; the screens revolved with color and shapes. "Got a couple hair samples, but says here she was clubbing prior to getting dead. Coulda picked those up in the club. If any of them are from the killer, we'll match 'em when you nab 'im.

"Now we've reconstructed the wound—used her ID photo and some others to create an image of her at time of death."

He brought it up so Eve could look at Andrea Jacobs as she had been, on screen. A pretty woman in a fancy dress, with a gash at her throat.

"Using our techno-magic, we can pretty well determine the size and shape of your murder weapon."

Eve studied the split-screen image of a long, smooth blade, and the specs beneath it that gave her width and length.

"Good. That's good, Dickie."

"You're working with the best. We concur with the investigator and the ME re the positioning of vic at time of the death blow. Came from behind. Yanked her by the hair. We got some of her hair from the scene that substantiates the scenario. Unless one of those stray hairs came from the perp, and I'm not putting money on that, we got nothing from him. Nada. He was sealed up tight.

"Now vic two—Cobb—different ball game. You sure you're looking at the same guy?"

"I'm sure."

"Your call. Smashed her up. Pipe, bat, metal, wood. Can't tell you 'cause we got nothing to work with there but the shape of the breaks in the bones. Look for something long, smooth and about two inches in diameter. Probably weighted. Leg shot took her down, rib shot kept her down. But then it gets interesting."

Shifting to another screen, he brought up the picture of Cobb's charred skull. "You see the busted cheekbone, and . . . " He revolved the image. "Your classic busted-in skull. Setting her on fire took care of most of the trace, but we got some that adhered to the bone fragments—face and head."

"What kind of trace?"

"It's a sealer." He split the screen. A series of jagged shapes in cool blues came on. "A fire-retardant. Smart guy missed that step. Professional-grade. Brand name's Flame Guard. Harry Homemaker can get it, but mostly it's used by contractors. You seal subflooring or walls with it."

"Subflooring. Before the finished deal goes down?"

"Yep. She had trace in the facial and head wounds. He lit her up, but this shit didn't burn. Truth in advertising for once. Didn't seal the bone, though, so it wasn't wet when she made contact. Little tacky maybe in spots but not wet."

Eve bent down closer, caught a whiff of grape from Dickhead. "She picked up the trace, cheekbone hitting the floor or the wall. Then again with the skull. No trace in the leg or rib wounds because of her clothes. There was blood when she hit, when she crawled. Might've helped pick up the trace. Splinters maybe, splinters from the boards she hit, adhere to the broken bones."

"You're the detective. But a girl that size, hit like that, she'd go down hard. So yeah, it could happen. We got our trace, so it did happen. It left a mess behind, too."

"Yeah." And that was a factor. "Shoot all of this to my office. Not half bad, Dickie."

"Hey, Dallas!" He called after her as she started out. "Take me out to the ball game."

"They're on their way. Peabody." She scooped at her hair as she lined up new data. "Let's do a run on the sealant. See what else we can find out. He could've used his own place for it. Could have. But he doesn't seem like the type to soil his own nest. Professional-grade," she mumbled. "He could have a place being rehabbed. Or access to a building under construction or being remodeled. Let's start on construction sites near the dump site. He didn't pick that empty lot out of a hat. He doesn't pick anything out of a hat."

Following that line, she called Roarke. By the time he came on, she was already in her car and headed back to Central. "Lieutenant. You have a gleam in your eye."

"Might've caught a break. Do you have anything going up or getting a face-lift in Alphabet City?"

"Rehabbing a midsized apartment complex. And . . . There are a couple of small businesses being changed over. I'd have to check to get you specifics."

"Do that. Shoot them to my office. Know of anything else? A competitor, associate, whatever?"

"Why don't I find out?"

"Appreciate it."

"Wait, wait." He held up a hand, well aware she'd have cut him off without another word. "There's a bit of progress on the search. Not enough to dance about, and Feeney and I are both tied up with other matters for the next part of the day. We've agreed to put in some time this evening, at our place."

"Good." She turned into Central's underground garage. "See you."

"I gotta ask." Peabody braced as Eve shot into her narrow parking slot, then let out a breath when there was no impact. "When you see his face come on screen, all sexy and gorgeous with that, you know, *mouth,* do you ever just want to pant like a dog?"

"Jesus, Peabody."

"Just wondering."

"Stomp out the hormones and keep your mind in the game. I've got Whitney." She looked at the time. "Shit. Now. I wanted to see if we've had any luck with the artist rendering."

"I can do that. If there's anything, I'll bring it up."

"That works."

"See how handy it is to have a detective for a partner?"

"I should've known you'd find a way to work it in."

They separated, and Eve rode the miserably crowded elevator another three floors before she bailed and switched to the glide for the rest of the trip to Commander Whitney's office.

Whitney suited his rank. He was a commanding man with a powerful build and a steely mind. The lines dug around his eyes and mouth only added to the image of leadership, and the toll it took on the man.

His skin was dark, and his hair had sprinkles of gray, like dashes of salt. He sat at his desk, surrounded by his com unit, his data center, disk files and the framed holos of his wife and family.

Eve respected the man, the rank and what he'd accomplished. And secretly marveled he'd kept his sanity between the job and a wife who lived to socialize.

"Commander, I apologize for being late. I was detained at the lab."

He brushed that away with one of his huge hands. "Progress?"

"Sir. My case and Detective Baxter's connect through Samantha Gannon."

"So I see from the files."

"Further information has come to light after a follow-up

interview with Gannon this morning. We're pursuing the possibility that Alex Crew's son or another connection or descendant may be involved in the current cases."

She sat only because he pointed to a chair. She preferred giving her orals standing. She relayed the details of the morning interview.

"Captain Feeney is handling the search personally," she continued. "I haven't yet spoken with him this afternoon, but have word there's been some progress in that area."

"The son would be in his sixties. A bit old to have interested a girl of Cobb's age."

"Some are attracted to older men for their experience, their stability. And he may have passed as younger." Though she doubted it. "More likely, he has a partner he used to get to Cobb. If this link holds, Commander, there are numerous possibilities. Judith Crew may have remarried, had another child, and that child may have learned of the diamonds and Gannon. Westley Crew may have children, and have passed his father's story to them, much as Gannon was passed the family legend. But it's someone with a proprietary interest. I feel certain of it, and Mira's profile concurs. I hope to have an artist rendering shortly.

"We got a break through the lab. There was trace of a fire-retardant substance on Cobb. A sealant, professional-grade. We'll run it down and concentrate on buildings near the dump site. He's been very careful, Commander, and this was a big mistake. One I don't believe he would have made if he had applied the sealant himself. Why kill her on or around flame-retardant material when you plan to light her up? It's too basic a mistake for this guy. Once we find the crime scene, we're a big step closer to finding him."

"Then find it." He shifted when his interoffice 'link signaled. "Yes."

"Commander, Detectives Peabody and Yancy."

"Send them in."

"Commander, Lieutenant." Peabody angled over so Yancy, the Ident artist, could precede her. "We thought it would be more expedient if Detective Yancy reported to both of you at once."

"Wish I had more." He handed out printouts and a disk. "I worked with the witness for three hours. I think I got her close, but I'm not passing out cigars. You can only lead them so far," he explained, and studied the printout image Eve held. "And you can tell when they're just making things up, or mixing them up, or just going along so you'll finish and let them go."

Eve stared at the rendering and tried to see a resemblance to Alex Crew. Maybe, maybe around the eyes. Or maybe she just wanted to see it.

But this was no sixty-year-old man.

"She tried," Yancy continued. "Really gave it her best shot. If we'd gotten to her closer to the time she saw the guy, I think we could've nailed it down. But a lot of time's passed, and she sees dozens of men at her tables every day. Once we got to a certain point, she was just tossing in features at random."

"Hypnosis could juggle her memory."

"I tried that," he said to Eve. "Mentioned it to her, and she freaked. No way, no how. Added to that, she caught a media report on the murder, and she's freaked about that. This is going to be the best we get."

"But is it him?" Eve demanded.

Yancy puffed out his cheeks, then deflated them. "I'd say we're on, as far as the skin tone, the hair, the basic shape of the face. Eyes, the shape's close, but I wouldn't bank on color. She thought age-wise, late twenties, early thirties, then admitted that was because of the age of the girl. She bounced to thirties, back to twenties, then maybe older, maybe younger. She figures rich because he had an expensive wrist unit, paid in cash and added a substantial tip. And some of that played into her description." He jerked a shoulder. "Smooth complexion, smooth manner."

"Is it close enough to give it to the media, get some play?"

"Sorta stings the pride, but I wouldn't. You gotta call it, Lieutenant, but my sense is we're off. I think a cop, a trained observer, might be able to make him from this, but not a civilian. Sorry I couldn't dunk it for you."

"That's okay. You probably got us closer than anybody else could. We'll run this through an ID program, see if we get any hits."

"You're going to want to set for at least a thirty-percent adjustment." Yancy shook his head at his own work. "With that, you're going to get a few thousand hits, citywide alone."

"It's a start. Thanks, Yancy. Commander, I'd like to get moving on this."

"Keep me in the loop."

Back in her office, she pinned a copy of the artist rendering to her board. At her desk she cobbled her notes together into a report, then read it over to see the steps and stages.

She would leave the person search to Feeney, the electronic excavation to McNab. She sent a memo to Baxter detailing the new data and included a copy of Yancy's sketch.

While Peabody worked to nail down the sealant, Eve looked at construction sites. Her 'link signaled an incoming through the data port, and switching over, she brought up a list of all properties with current construction or rehab licenses in a ten-block radius of the dump site.

Roarke was not only quick, she thought, but he got the gist without anyone having to spell it out.

She separated them into tenanted and untenanted.

Empty, she thought. Privacy. Hadn't he waited until he believed the Gannon house was empty? There was little enough pattern, so she'd try this one on for size.

Empty buildings first.

Taking them, she broke them down a second time into construction and rehab.

Had to lure her in. Smarter to lure her rather than force or debilitate. She's young and foolish, but she's a girly girl, too. Would that type want to tromp around a construction site, even to make a date happy?

She rose, paced. Probably. What did she know about that kind of thing? Young girls in love, or who believed they were in love, probably did all sorts of things that went against type.

She'd never been a young girl in love. A few lust bouts along the way, but that was a different thing. She knew that much seeing as love had sucker punched her and dumped her right into Roarke's lap. And didn't she slick herself up from time to time, fiddling with enhancements and hair, draping on fancy duds, because he liked it?

Yeah, love could easily make you go against type.

But what about the killer? No reason for him to go against type. He wasn't in love. He hadn't been in lust, either. And his type liked to impress, show off. He liked to be comfortable and in charge. He liked to plan things out with an eye toward his own goals, his own ego, his self-preservation.

A rehab with some fancy touches. A place he knew he wouldn't be disturbed. Where he wouldn't be questioned if caught on the premises. Where he could, again, deal with any security features.

She sent the data to her home unit, printed out her lists, then went into the bull pen to get Peabody. "With me."

"I'm running down the sealant."

"Run it down in transit."

"Where are we going?" Peabody demanded as she scrambled to gather her work disk, files, jacket.

"To look at buildings. To talk to guys with power tools."

"Hot damn!"

The first stop was a small theater originally constructed in the early twentieth century. Her badge got them through to the foreman. Though he bitched about workload and schedule, he took them through. The lobby floors were the original marble, and apparently a point of pride for the foreman. The theater section was bare particleboard on the floor and as yet unsealed. The walls were old plaster.

Still, she went through the entire building, using her scope to look for blood traces.

They suffered through late-afternoon traffic en route to the next stop.

"The sealant, professional-grade, can be purchased wholesale or retail in five-, ten- and twenty-five-gallon tubs." Peabody read the data off her PPC. "Or you can, with a contractor's license, purchase it in powder form and mix it yourself. Residential-grade comes in one- or five-gallon tubs. No powder available. I've got the suppliers."

"You'll need to hit those. We'll want a list of individuals and companies who've bought the sealant so we can cross-check them with the construction crews on these sites."

"Going to take a while."

"He's not going anywhere. He's right here." She scanned the street. "Thinking of his next move."

He let himself into his apartment and immediately ordered the house droid to bring him a gin and tonic. It was so annoying to have to spend half the damn day in an office doing absolutely nothing that could possibly interest him.

But the old man was tying up the purse strings, demanding he show more interest in the company.

Your legacy, son. What bullshit! His legacy was several million in Russian whites.

He couldn't care less about the company. As soon as he was able, as soon as he had what was his, by right, he'd tell the old man to fuck himself.

It would be a fine day.

But meanwhile he had to placate and coddle and pretend to be the good son.

He stripped down, letting his clothes fall as he went, and lowered himself into the one-man lap pool built into the penthouse's recreation area.

The fact that the company he despised and deplored paid for the penthouse, the clothes, the droid, never made a scratch on the surface of his ego.

He reached up a hand for the g and t, then simply sprawled in the cool water.

He had to get to Gannon now. He'd considered and rejected the idea of going to Maryland and just beating the information he needed out of the old couple. It could come back on him in too many ways.

As it stood now, they could have no clue. He could be an obsessed fan, or a lover of the maid's who'd been in league with her to burgle the Gannon residence. He could be anyone at all.

But if he went to Maryland he might be seen, or traced. He would hardly blend well in some silly small town. If he killed Samantha Gannon's grandparents, even the most dim-witted of cops might work their way back to the diamonds as the cause.

If he could get to Gannon herself . . . It was so damn *frustrating* to discover she'd vanished. None of the careful probes he'd sent out had netted him a single clue to her whereabouts.

But she had to surface sometime. She had to come home sooner or later.

If he had all the time in the world, he could wait her out. But he couldn't tolerate dragging himself into that stupid office much longer, dealing with the idiotic working class or paying lip service to his pathetic parents. All the while knowing everything he wanted, everything he deserved, was just beyond his reach.

He sipped the drink with one arm braced on the pool's edge to anchor him. "Screen on," he said idly, then scanned the news channels for any updates.

Nothing new, he saw with satisfaction. He couldn't understand the mind-set of those who fed on media, on what they perceived as the glory. A true criminal gained all the satisfaction necessary by succeeding at his work, in secret.

He liked being a true criminal, and liked—very much—raising the bar on his own exploits.

He smiled to himself as he looked around the room at the shelves and displays of antique toys and games. The cars, the trucks, the figures. He'd stolen some of them, simply for the buzz. The same way he sometimes stole a tie or a shirt.

Just to see if he could.

He'd stolen from friends and relatives for the same reason, and long before he'd known he came by the habit . . . honestly. That thievery was in his blood. Who'd have believed it looking at his parents?

But then, he'd gotten his interest in the toy collection from his father, and it had served him well. If his fellow collector and acquaintance Chad Dix hadn't bitched to him about his girlfriend, about the book she was writing that was taking all her time and attention, he wouldn't have known about the diamonds, the connection, as soon as he had.

He might never have read the book. It wasn't the sort of thing he did with his time, after all. But it had been a simple matter to pry Dix for more details, then to wheedle the advance copy from him.

He finished off the drink, and though he wanted another, denied himself. A clear head was important.

He set the glass aside, did a few laps. When he pulled himself out of the pool, the empty glass was gone and a towel and robe were laid out. He had a party to attend that evening. He had a party of some sort to attend every evening. And he found it ironic that he'd actually met Samantha Gannon a few times at various affairs. How odd he'd had no interest in her, had assumed they had nothing in common.

He'd never had more in common with a woman.

He might have to take the time and the trouble to

pursue her romantically, which would certainly be considerably less *lowering* than his brief association with Tina Cobb. No more his type, when it came to that. Not from what he'd observed of her, in any case.

Full of herself, he thought as he began to dress. Attractive enough, certainly, but one of those brainy, single-minded females who either irritated or bored him so quickly.

From what he'd been told of her by Chad, she was good in bed, but entirely too absorbed with her own needs and wants outside the sheets.

Still, unless he could figure out a more efficient, more direct way to the diamonds, he would have to spend some quality time with Jack O'Hara's great-granddaughter.

In the meantime, he thought as he flicked a finger over the scoop of a clever scale-model backhoe, he thought it might be time for a heart-to-heart with dear old dad.

Chapter 10

There was a headache simmering like a hot stew behind her eyes by the time Eve got home. She'd only managed to hit three sites. Construction workers, she learned, called it a day long before cops did. She'd gotten nothing from the ones she'd managed to survey but the headache from the clatter of tools, the blasts of music, the calls of workers all echoing in empty or near-empty buildings.

Added to that was the hassle of cajoling, browbeating or begging suppliers for their customer lists. If she never visited another building-supply warehouse or outlet in this lifetime, she would die a happy woman.

She wanted a shower, a ten-minute nap and a gallon of ice water.

Since she'd pulled up behind Feeney's vehicle, she didn't bother to check the in-house. Roarke would be upstairs with him, in the office or the computer lab, playing their e-geek games. Since the cat didn't come out to greet her, she assumed he was with them.

She scotched the idea of ten minutes with her eyes shut. She couldn't quite bring herself to get horizontal with another cop in the house, especially if the cop was on the clock. It would be too embarrassing if she got caught. She compromised with an extra ten minutes in the shower and felt justified when the headache backed off to threatening.

She traded in the day's separates—she was going to remember that one—for a T-shirt and jeans. She thought about going barefoot, but there was that cop-in-the-house factor, and bare feet always made her feel partially naked.

She went for tennis shoes.

Since she felt nearly human again, she stopped by the computer lab on her way to her office.

Roarke and Feeney were manning individual stations. Roarke had his sleeves rolled up and his hair tied back, as was his habit when he settled into serious work. Feeney's short-sleeved shirt looked as if he'd mashed it into a ball and bounced it a few times before putting it on that morning. It also showed off his bony elbows. She wondered why she found them endearing.

She must be seriously tired.

There were screens up with data zipping across them too quickly for her eye to read. The men tossed comments or questions at each other in the geek language she'd never been able to decipher.

"You guys got anything for me in regular English?"

They both looked over their shoulders in her direction, and she was struck how two men who couldn't have been more different in appearance could have identical looks in their eyes.

A kind of nerdy distraction.

"Making some headway." Feeney reached into the bag of sugared nuts on his work counter. "Going back a ways."

"You look . . . fresh, Lieutenant," Roarke commented.

"I didn't a few minutes ago. Grabbed a shower." She moved into the room as she studied the screens. "What's running?"

Roarke's smile spread slowly. "If we tried to explain, your eyes would glaze over. This one here might be a little more straightforward." He gestured her closer so she could see the split screen working with a photo of Judith Crew on one side and a blur of images running on the other.

"Trying for a face match?"

"We dug up her driver's license from before the divorce," Feeney explained. "Got another run going over there from the license she used when the insurance guy located her. Different name, and she'd changed her hair, lost weight. Computer's kicking out possible matches. We're moving from those dates forward."

"Then we're using a morph program on yet another unit," Roarke continued. "Searching for a match on what the computer thinks she looks like now."

"The civilian thinks if the image was close, we'd have matched by now."

"I do, yes."

Feeney shrugged, nibbled nuts. "Lot of people in the world. Lots of women in that age group. And she could be living off-planet."

"She could be dead," Eve added. "Or she could have evaded standard IDing. She could be, shit, living in a grass shack on some uncharted island, weaving mats."

"Or had facial restructuring."

"Kids today." Feeney blew out an aggrieved breath. "No faith."

"What about the son?"

"Working a morph on that, too. We've hit some possibles. Doing a secondary on them. And our boy here's looking for the money."

Eve looked away from the screens. The rapid movements were bringing back the headache. "What money?"

"She sold the house in Ohio," Roarke reminded her. "It takes a bit of time for the settlement, the payoff. The bank or the realtor would have had to send the check to her, or make an e-transfer per instructions. In the name she was using at the time, unless she authorized it to be paid to another party."

"You can find out stuff like that? From that long ago?"

"If you're persistent. She was a careful woman. She authorized the settlement check to be transferred electronically to her lawyer, at that time, then sent to another law firm in Tucson."

"Tucson?"

"Arizona, darling."

"I know where Tucson is." More or less. "How do you know this?"

"I have my ways."

She narrowed her eyes when Feeney looked up at the ceiling. "You lied, you bribed and you broke any number of privacy laws."

"And this is the thanks I get. She was in Tucson, from

what I can find, less than a month in early 2004. Long enough to pick up the check, deposit it in a local bank. My educated guess would be, she used that point and those funds to change identities once again, then moved to another location."

"We're narrowing it down. Once the matches are complete, we'll take a hard look at the hits." Feeney rubbed his temple. "I need a break."

"Why don't you go down, have a swim, a beer?" Roarke suggested. "We'll see what we've got in another half hour."

"That's a plan I can get behind. You got anything for us, kid?"

Nobody but Feeney ever called her "kid." "I'll bring you up to date after you take a thirty," Eve told him. "I need to set a few things up in my office."

"Meet you there then."

"I could use a beer myself," Eve commented when Feeney walked out.

"A break seems to be in order." Roarke ran a finger down the back of her hand, then tugged it closer to nibble.

She knew that move.

"Don't even start sniffing at me."

"Too late. What is this scent? All over your skin?"

"I don't know." Warily, she lifted her shoulder, sniffed at it herself. Smelled like soap to her. "Whatever was in the shower." She gave her hand a little yank, but made the mistake of glancing around in case Feeney was still nearby. The instant of distraction gave him the opening to hook a foot around hers, tip her off balance and into his lap.

"Jesus, cut it *out*!" Her voice was a fierce and frantic whisper. On the mortification scale, getting caught snuggled in Roarke's lap hit the top three, even above getting caught napping or barefoot by another cop. "I'm on the clock. Feeney's right here."

"I don't see Feeney." He was already nuzzling his way along her neck toward her ear. "And as an expert consultant, civilian, I'm entitled to a recreational break. I've decided I prefer adult activity to adult beverage."

Little demons of lust began to dance along her skin. "You can't even think I'm going to mess around with you in the computer lab. Feeney could come back in here."

"Adds to the excitement. Yes, yes." He chuckled as he nipped at a spot—his personal favorite—just under her jaw. "Sick and perverted. And though I'd wager Feeney suspects we have occasional sex, we'll take our recreational break elsewhere."

"I've got work to do, Roarke, and . . . Hey! Hands!"

"Why, yes, those are indeed my hands." Laughing now, he cupped them under her and levered out of the chair. "I want my thirty," he said, and carted her toward the elevator.

"The way you're going, you'll be done in five."

"Bet."

She struggled against a laugh of her own and put up a token struggle by clamping a hand on the opening of the elevator. "I can't just go off and get naked with Feeney in the house. It's too weird. And if he comes back and—"

"You know, I suspect Feeney gets naked with Mrs. Feeney, and this is probably how they had their little Feeneys."

"Oh my God!" Her hand trembled, went limp, and her face paled considerably. "That's just despicable, the dirtiest of dirty fighting to shove that one into my head."

Because he wanted to keep her unbalanced, he reached

behind her and keyed in the bedroom rather than using audio command. "Whatever works. Now you're too weak to hold me off."

"Don't count on it."

"Do you remember the first time we made love?" He touched his lips to hers as he said it, changing tactics with a gentle brush.

"I have a vague recollection."

"We rode up in the elevator like this and couldn't keep our hands off each other, couldn't get to each other quick enough. I was mad for you. I wanted you more than I wanted to keep breathing. I still do." He deepened the kiss as the elevator doors opened. "It's never going to change."

"I don't want it to change." She combed her fingers through his hair, shoving the band away so all that thick, soft black slid through her fingers. "You're so damn good at this." She pressed her lips to his throat. "But not quite good enough to have me doing this with the door open. Feeney could, you know, wander in. I can't focus."

"We'll fix that." With her legs hooked around his waist, her arms around his neck and her lips beginning to lay a hot line over his skin, he went to the door. He closed it. Locked it. "Better?"

"I'm not sure. Maybe you should remind me how we did this the first time again."

"I believe, if memory serves, it went something like this." He spun her around, trapping her between the wall and his body. And his mouth was fever hot on hers.

She felt the need, instant and primal, slice through her. It was like being cleaved in two—the woman she'd been before him, the woman she'd discovered with him.

She could be what she was, and he understood her. She

could be what she'd become, and he cherished her. And the wanting each other, through all the changes, all the discoveries, never abated.

She let him ravish her, and felt the power in surrender. It pumped and swelled inside her as she slid down his body. Her hands were as busy as his, her mouth as impatient as they dragged each other toward the bed.

They stumbled up the platform, and remembering, she laughed. "We were in a hurry then, too."

They fell on the bed in a tangle of limbs, then rolled as they struggled to strip away clothes, to take and devour. Before, that first time, it had been in the dark. Groping and grasping and desperation in the dark. Now they were in the light that spilled through the windows, through the sky window over the bed, but the desperation was the same.

It ached in her like a wound that would never quite heal.

She'd been a mass and a maze of demands then, too, he remembered. All heat and motion, driving him toward frenzy so that he'd burned to ram himself into her and batter them both toward release.

But he'd wanted more. Even then, he'd wanted more of her. And for her. He gripped her hands, drawing her arms over her head, and she arched, pressing center to center until his pulse was a pounding of jungle drums.

"Inside me." Her eyes were blurred and dark. "I want you inside me. Hard. Fast."

"Wait." He knew what it would be now, where they would take each other, and control was a thin and slippery wire. He cuffed her wrists with one hand. If she touched him now, that wire would snap.

But he could touch her. God, he needed to touch her, to watch her, to feel her body gather and quake from the assault of pleasure. Her skin was damp when he ran his free hand down her. The moan trembled from her lips, then broke with a hoarse cry as he used those clever fingers on her.

He watched those blurry eyes go blind, felt the scramble of her pulse in the wrists he held and heard her release a sob in the air before she went pliant. Wax melted in the heat.

Again, was all he could think as his mouth came down on hers, fierce and frantic. Again and again and again.

Then her arms were free and banded around him, and her hips pistoned up. He was inside her as she'd demanded. Hard and fast.

She knew, with the part of her brain that could still reason, that he'd gone over, gone where he could so often send her. Somewhere beyond the civilized and sensible, where there were only sensations fueled by needs. She wanted him there with her, where control was impossible and pleasure saturated both mind and body.

As her own system quivered toward that last leap, she heard his breath catch, as if on a pain. Wrapping around him, she gave herself over. "Now," she said, and pulled him with her.

She stretched under him, curled and uncurled her toes. She felt, Eve discovered, pretty damn good. "Okay." She gave Roarke a noisy slap on the ass. "Recreational break's over."

"Christ. Christ Jesus."

"Come on, you've had your thirty."

"I'm sure you're wrong. I'm sure I have five or six minutes left. And if I don't, I'm having them anyway."

"Off." She gave his butt another slap, then a pinch.

When neither budged him, she shifted her knee over, and up.

"Son of a bitch." That moved him. "Mind the merchandise."

"You mind it. I've already used it." She was smart enough to roll over and away before he could retaliate. She landed on her feet, rolled up to the balls, back to the heels. "Man, I'm revved."

He stayed where he was, flat on his back, and eyed her. Long, lean, naked, with her skin glowing from the energetic recreational break.

"You look it." Then he smiled, slyly. "I wonder if Feeney's finished his swim."

The color drained out of her cheeks. "Oh jeez, oh, *shit*!" She made a dive for her clothes. "He'll know. He'll just know, and then we'll have to avoid looking at each other while we pretend he doesn't know. Damn it."

Roarke was laughing as she dashed with her bundle of clothes into the bath.

Feeney beat her into her office, and that made her wince. But she strode in briskly and moved straight to her desk to set up files.

"Where were you?"

"Just, ah, you know . . . dealing with a couple things."

"I thought you were gonna . . . " He trailed off with a sound she recognized as embarrassed horror not quite suppressed. She could feel her skin heat and kept her attention trained on her computer as if it might leap off the desk and grab her by the throat.

"I think I'll—um—" His voice cracked a bit. She didn't glance over but she could *feel* him looking frantically around the room. "Get some coffee."

"Coffee's good. That'd be good."

When she heard him escape to the kitchen, she rubbed her hands over her face. "Might as well be wearing a sign," she muttered. " 'Just Got Laid.' "

She set up her disks, her case board, then shot Roarke a vicious glare when he strolled in. "I don't want that look on your face," she hissed.

"Which look?"

"You know which look. Wipe it off."

Relaxed, amused, he sat on the corner of her desk. When Feeney walked in, he could see the fading flush. Feeney cleared his throat, very deliberately, then set the second mug of coffee he carried on the desk. "Didn't zap you one," he said to Roarke.

"It's all right. I'm fine for now. How was your swim?"

"Fine. Good." He rubbed a hand over the drying sproings of ginger and silver hair. "Good and fine."

He turned away to study the board.

Weren't they a pair? Roarke thought, two veteran cops who've waded through blood and madness. But put a bit of sex on the table between them, and they're fidgety as virgins at an orgy.

"I'm going to bring you both up to date," Eve began. "Then I'll work on my angles while you work on yours. You see the artist's sketch on the board, and on screen."

She picked up a laser pointer, aimed it toward the wall screen. "Detective Yancy did the Ident, but isn't confident enough in this rendering for us to pass it to the media. But I think it gives us some basics. Coloring and basic facial structure, in any case."

"Looks, what," Feeney asked, "range of thirty?"

"Yeah. Even if Crew's son has spent the better part of a fortune on face work and sculpting, I don't think a guy in his sixties is going to look this young. And the witness never put him over forty. We may be looking for a family connection, or a young friend, protégé. We have to pursue the connection. It's the most logical, given pattern and profile."

"Yeah, and it opens it up instead of narrowing it down," Feeney commented.

"We caught a break on narrowing it."

Eve told them about the trace evidence, and her fieldwork to date attempting to find the location of the Cobb crime scene.

"It's the first trace he's left. When we nail this down, we'll have another link toward identifying this creep. He chose the place, so he knows the place. He knew he could get in, do what he wanted to do in private and clean it up enough to have the crime undetected."

"Yeah." Feeney nodded agreement. "Had to splash some blood around. He cleaned up, or there'd be a report. A construction crew's not going to strap on tool belts with blood all over the damn place."

"Which means he had to spend time doing so. Again in private. Had to have transpo, had to know there was a handy dump site and access to the flammable."

"Probably didn't seal up for that one," Feeney commented. "Why bother?"

"Not an efficient use of his time," Eve agreed. "He's going to burn the body and destroy any possible trace to him, or so he believed. Why bother to avoid any trace on the scene as long as it's reasonably cleaned? Particularly if he had some legitimate reasons for being there."

"Could own the place, work or live in it."

"Could be a building or construction inspector," Roarke put in. "Though if he is, it wouldn't have been bright of him to forget about the fire sealant."

"You got the data I asked for, the properties being built or rehabbed in that area. Is what you sent me the whole shot?"

"It is, yes. But that doesn't take into account ones that are under the table. Small jobs," he explained. "A private home or apartment where the owner might decide to do some work, or hires a contractor who's willing to forgo the permits and fees and work off the books."

Eve visualized the map of her investigation suddenly crisscrossed with hundreds of dead ends and detours. "I'm not going to worry about side deals until we exhaust the legitimate ones. Sticking with that, don't they sometimes use gas on construction sites?"

"For some of the vehicles and machines." Roarke nodded. "As it's inconvenient to transport it from one of the stations outside the city, you might use a storage compartment on-site or nearby. You've a fee to pay for that as well."

"Then we follow that down, too."

"Bureaucrats in Permits and Licensing are going to make you jump through hoops," Feeney reminded her.

"I'll deal with it."

"You're going to need to put the arm on these guys, get the warrants and assorted paperwork and other bullshit. We get lucky with the matches, you'll cut back on that." Feeney considered, pulled on his nose. "But you got a lot to wade through one way or the other. I can put my leave off a few days, until this is closed."

"Leave?" She frowned at him until she remembered his scheduled vacation. "Crap. I forgot all about it. When are you going?"

"Got two more days on the clock, but I can juggle some things around."

She was tempted to take him up on it. But she paced it off, heaved out a breath. "Yeah, fine, you do that and your wife will eat both our livers for breakfast. Raw."

"She's a cop's wife. She knows how it goes." But there wasn't much conviction behind his words.

"Bet she's already packed."

Feeney offered a hangdog smile. "Been packed damn near a week now."

"Well, I'm not facing her wrath. Besides, you've already juggled enough to give me this much time. We can handle the rest of it."

He looked back at the board, as she did. "I don't like leaving a case hanging."

"I've got McNab and this guy." She jerked a thumb toward Roarke. "If we don't wrap it before you have to go, we'll keep you in the loop. Long distance. Can you give me a couple more hours tonight?"

"No problem. Look, why don't I get back to it, see if I can work some magic?"

"Do that. I'll see if I can wrangle some warrants. Okay with you if we brief here tomorrow, oh-eight hundred?"

"Only if it comes with breakfast."

"I'll be right along," Roarke told him, and waited until he was alone with Eve. "I can save you time with the red tape. A little time on the unregistered, and I can have a list of permits for you."

She jammed her hands into her pockets as she studied her murder board, as she looked at the faces of the dead. Roarke's unregistered equipment would blind the unblinking eye of CompuGuard. No one would know he'd hacked into secured areas and nipped out data with his skilled hands.

"I can't justify it for this. I can't shortcut this just to save myself a little time and a lot of aggravation. Gannon's secure. To my knowledge she's the only one who might be in immediate jeopardy from this guy. I'll play it by the book."

He stepped up behind her, rubbed her shoulders as they both looked at the images of Jacobs and Cobb. Before and after.

"When you don't play it by the book, when you do take that shortcut, it's always for them, Eve. It's never for yourself."

"It's not supposed to be for me. Or about me."

"If it wasn't for you, or about you, in some sense, you wouldn't be able to go on day after day, facing this and caring, day after day. And if you didn't, who would pick up the standard for people like Andrea Jacobs and Tina Cobb and carry it into the battle?"

"Some other cop," she said.

"There is no other like you." He pressed his lips to the top of her head. "There's no other who understands them, the victims and those who victimize them, quite like you. Seeing that, knowing that, well, it's made an honest man out of me, hasn't it?"

She turned now to look him straight in the eye. "You made yourself."

She knew he thought of his mother, of what he'd learned only a short time before, and she knew he suffered. She couldn't stand for Roarke's dead as she did for those of strangers. She couldn't help him find justice for the woman he never knew existed, for the woman who'd loved him and died at the brutal hand of his own father.

"If I could go back," she said slowly, "if there was a

way to twist time and go back, I'd do everything I could to bring him down and put him away for what he did. I wish I could stand for her, for you."

"We can't change history, can we? Not for my mother, not for ourselves. If we could, you're the only one in this world I would trust with it. The only one who might make me stand back and let the law do what the law does." He traced his finger down the dent in her chin. "So, Lieutenant, whenever you do take one of those shortcuts, you should remember there are those of us who depend on you who don't give a rat's ass about the book."

"Maybe not. But I do. Go help Feeney. Get me something I can use so we can make him pay for what he did to them."

She sat alone when he'd gone, her coffee forgotten and her gaze on the murder board. She saw herself in each of the victims. In Andrea Jacobs, struck down and abandoned. In Tina Cobb, robbed of her own identity and discarded.

But she'd come back from those things. She'd been created from those things. No, you couldn't change history, she thought. But you could sure as hell use it.

Chapter 11

She lost track of time when she worked alone. Eve supposed, if pressed on the subject, she lost track of time when she worked with others, too.

But there was something soothing about sitting in or pacing around her office by herself, letting the data and the speculations bump around in her head with only the computer's bland voice for company.

When her 'link beeped, she jerked out of a half trance and realized the only light in the room was from her various screens.

"Dallas. What?"

"Hey, Lieutenant." McNab's young, pretty face popped on screen. She could see the slice of pizza in his hand. Hell, since she could all but smell the pepperoni, it occurred to her she'd missed dinner. "Were you asleep or something?"

She could feel her embarrassment scale rising just because another cop had tagged her when she'd been drifting off. "No, I wasn't asleep. I'm working."

"In the dark?"

"What do you want, McNab?" She knew what she wanted. She wanted his pizza.

"Okay. I put in some OT on the 'links and d and c's." He took a bite of pizza. Eve was forced to swallow her own saliva. "Lemme tell you, these dink units are tougher than the pricey ones. Memory's for shit, and the broadband—"

"Don't walk me down that path, McNab. Bottom-line it."

"Sure. Sorry."

He licked—the bastard actually licked sauce from his thumb.

"I got locations on two of the transmissions we believe the killer sent Cobb. One of them matches the location of an aborted trans sent to the Gannon residence and picked up by the answering program on the night of Jacobs's murder."

"Where?"

"The location that hit both is a public 'link in Grand Central. The other, generated from a cyber club downtown. Oh, and there's a second aborted to the Gannon residence, ten minutes after the first, from another public three blocks from her residence."

Public places, public access. Phony accounts. Careful, careful, careful. "You with Peabody?"

"Yeah. She's in the other room."

"Why don't you check out the club? See if you can pinpoint the unit he used. Maybe you can get us a better description."

"No problem."

"We're going to brief at my home office, eight hundred hours."

His mouth might've been full of pizza, but she recognized a groan when she heard one. Served him right for eating on her empty stomach.

"You get anything hot, I want to hear right away. No matter what time it is. That's good work on the 'links."

"I am the wizard. You guys got any of that real bacon?"

She cut him off. Sitting back in the blue-shadowed dark, she thought about diamonds and pizza and murder.

"Lieutenant."

"Hmm?"

"Lights on, twenty-five percent." Even in the dimness, Roarke watched her blink like an owl. "You need to eat."

"McNab had pizza. It broke my focus." She rubbed her tired eyes. "Where's Feeney?"

"I sent him home, not without a struggle. His wife called. I think she's going into a low-level state of panic that he's going to do what he suggested to you earlier and postpone this family trip."

"I won't let him. You got anything for me?"

"The first stage of matching's done on Judith Crew, nearly so on the boy. Once that's done we'll . . . " He remembered who he was talking to and edited out the techno jargon. "Essentially, we'll cross-match and reference the two sets. If she kept her son with her until he came of age—and it certainly seems she'd do so—we should be able to locate that match, or matches."

He cocked his head at her. "Is it going to be pizza for you, then?"

"I would give you five hundred credits for a slice of pepperoni pizza."

He sneered. "Please, Lieutenant. I can't be bought."

"I will give you the sexual favor of your choice at the next possible opportunity."

"Done."

"Cheap date."

"You don't know the sexual favor I have in mind. Did you get your warrants?" he called out as he went into the kitchen.

"Yeah. Jesus, I had to tap-dance until my toes fell off, but I'm getting them. And McNab's pinned locations on transmissions. He and Peabody are going to check out a cyber club tonight where one was zipped to Cobb."

"Tonight?"

"They're young, able and afraid of me."

"So am I." He brought her in a plateful of bubbling pizza and a large glass of red wine.

"Where's yours?"

"I had something with Feeney in the lab, and foolishly assumed you'd feed yourself."

"You've already eaten and you still fixed me dinner?" She scooped up pizza, singed her fingertips. "Wow, you're like my body slave."

"Those roles will be reversed when I collect my payment. I think it may involve costumes."

"Get out." She snorted, bit into the pizza and burned her tongue. It was great. "He made a call to both Cobb and Gannon from a port in Grand Central. Called Gannon's place the night he killed Jacobs—twice, two locations. Just covering his bases, sounds like. Gets her answering program on both aborts, confirms the all clear. Goes over."

She washed down pizza with wine and knew God was in His heaven.

"Could've walked from there, that's how I'd've done it. Better than a cab. Safer."

"And allows him to case the neighborhood," Roarke added.

"Then he gets there, gets inside. Maybe he's smart enough to do a room-by-room check of the house first. Can't be too careful. Then he goes upstairs to get started, and before you know it, the house sitter comes in. All that care, all that trouble, and for what?"

"Pissed him off."

Eve nodded, drank some more wine, considered the second slice of pizza. Why the hell not? "I'm thinking, yeah. Had to piss him off. You know he could've gotten out. Or he could've debilitated her, restrained her. But she'd ruined his plans. She'd become the fly in his soup. So he killed her. But he wasn't in a rage when he did it. Controlled, careful. But not as smart as he thinks. What if she knows something? He didn't take that leap in logic."

"He struck out, coldly, but didn't take the time to completely calm himself." Roarke nodded. "He had to improvise. We could assume he's not at his best when he hasn't been able to script the play and follow the cues."

"Yeah, I can see inside his head, but it's not helping." She tossed the slice of pizza down and stared at the artist's image she kept on screen. "If I've structured this investigation right, I know what he wants. I know what he'll do to get it. I even know, if we're following the same logic, that his next step would be to go after Samantha Gannon or one of her family. To buddy up with them if he calculates it's worth the time and effort, to threaten, torture, kill, if it's not. Whatever it takes to get the diamonds or information leading to them out of her."

"But he can't get to her, or them."

"No, I got them covered. And maybe that's part of the problem. Why it's stalled."

"If you use her as bait, you could lure him out."

With the wineglass cupped in her hand, Eve tipped back, closed her eyes. "She'd do it, too. I can see that in her. She'd do it because it's a way to end it, and because it makes a good story, and because she's gutsy. Not stupidly, but gutsy enough to go for this. Just like her grandma."

"Gutsy enough, because she'd trust you to look out for her."

Eve shrugged a shoulder. "I don't like to use civilians as bait. I could put a cop in her place. We can fix one up to look enough like her to pass."

"He'd have studied her. He might see through it."

"Might. Hell, he might even know her. Anyway, I'm too tall. Peabody's the wrong body type."

"A droid could be fashioned."

"Droids only do what they're programmed to do." And she never fully trusted machines. "Bait needs to be able to think. There's someone else he might go for."

"Judith Crew."

"Yeah. If she's still alive, he might try for her. Or the son. If neither one of them is a part of this, he might push those buttons. There's nobody else left from back then, nobody with direct knowledge of what went down, and how. He can't even be sure they exist."

"Eat."

Distracted, she looked down at the pizza. Because it was there, she picked it up, bit in, chewed. "It's a kind of fantasy. Now that I see he's younger than I assumed, it makes more sense to me. It's a treasure hunt. He wants them because he feels he's entitled to them, and because they're valuable, but also because they're shiny," she added, thinking of Peabody outside the display windows at Fifth and Forty-seventh.

"You talked me into swimming around that reef off the island. Remember? You said not to wear my pendant deal. Not only because, hey, big fat diamonds can get lost in the ocean, but because I shouldn't wear anything shiny in there. Barracudas get hyped up when something shines and gleams in the water and can take great big, nasty bites out of you."

"So you have a barracuda on a treasure hunt."

Yeah, she liked bouncing a case off Roarke, Eve thought. You didn't have to tell him anything twice, and half the time didn't have to tell him the first time.

"I don't know where this is taking me, but let's play it out. He wants them because he feels entitled, because they're valuable and because they're shiny. This tells me he's spoiled, greedy and childish. And mean. The way a bully's mean. He killed not only because it was expedient but because he could. Because they were weaker and he had the advantage. He hurt Cobb because there was time to, and he was probably bored by her. This is how I see him. I don't know what it gets me."

"Recognition. Keep going."

"I think he's used to getting what he wants. Taking it if it isn't given. Maybe he's stolen before. There was probably a safer way to get information, but he chose this way. It's more exciting to take something that isn't yours in the dark than to bargain for it in the light."

"I certainly used to think so."

"Then you grew up."

"Well, in my way. There's a thrill about the dark, Eve. Once you've experienced it, it's difficult to resist."

"Why did you? Resist."

"I wanted something else. More." He took her wine for a sip. "I'd built my way toward it, with the occasional and often recreational side step. Then I wanted you. There's nothing in the dark I could want as I want you."

"He doesn't have anyone. He doesn't love. He doesn't want anyone. It's things he craves. Shiny things that gleam in the dark. They're shinier, Roarke, because they already have blood on them. And I think, I'm damn sure, some of that blood runs in him. They're more valuable to him, more important to him, because of the blood."

She rolled her shoulders. "Yeah, I'll recognize him. I'll know him when I see him. But none of this gets me any closer to where he is."

"Why don't you get some rest?"

She shook her head. "I want to look at the matches."

Steven Whittier sipped Earl Grey out of his favorite red mug. He claimed it added to the flavor, a statement that caused his wife, who preferred using the antique Meissen, to act annoyed. Still, she loved him as much for his everyman ways as she did for his sturdiness, dependability and humor.

The match between them—the builder and the society princess—had initially baffled and flustered her family. Patricia was vintage wine and caviar, and Steve was beer and soy dogs. But she'd dug in her fashionable heels and ignored her family's dire predictions. Thirty-two years later, everyone had forgotten those predictions except Steve and Pat.

Every year on their anniversary, they tapped glasses to the toast of "It'll never last." After which, they would laugh like children pulling one over on a bunch of grown-ups.

They'd built a good life, and even his early detractors

had been forced to admit Steve Whittier had brains and ambition, and had managed to use both to provide Pat with a lifestyle they could accept.

From childhood he'd known what he wanted to do. To create or re-create buildings. He'd wanted to dig in his roots, as he'd never been able to do as a child, and provide places for others to do the same.

He'd structured Whittier Construction from the ground up, through his own sweat and desire, his mother's unbending belief in him—then Pat's. In the thirty-three years since he'd begun with a three-man crew and a mobile office out of his own truck, he'd cemented his foundation and added story after story onto the building of his dream.

Now, though he had managers and foremen and designers on his payroll, he still made it a habit to roll up his sleeves on every job site, to spend his day traveling from one to another or burrowing in to pick up his tools like any laborer.

There was little that made him happier than the ring and the buzz of a building being created, or improved.

His only disappointment was that Whittier had not yet become Whittier and Son. He still had hopes that it would, though Trevor had no interest in or talent for the hands-on of building.

He wanted to believe—needed to believe—that Trevor would settle down soon, would come to see the value of honest work. He worried about the boy.

They hadn't raised him to be shallow and lazy, or to expect the world handed to him on a platter. Even now, Trevor was required to report to the main offices four days a week, and to put in a day's work at his desk.

Well, half a day, Steve amended. Somehow, it was never more than half a day.

Not that he got anything done in that amount of time, Steve thought as he blew on his steaming tea. They would have to have another talk about it. The boy was paid a good salary, and a good day's work was expected. The problem, of course, or part of it, was the trust funds and glittery gifts from his mother's side of the family. The boy took the easy route no matter how often his parents had struggled to redirect him.

Given too much, too easily, Steve thought as he looked around his cozy den. But some of the fault was his own, Steve admitted. He'd expected too much, pinned too many hopes on his son. Who knew better than he how terrifying and debilitating it could be for a boy to have his father's shadow looming everywhere?

Pat was right, he thought. They should back off a bit, give Trevor more room. It might mean taking a clip out of the family strings and setting him loose. It was hard to think of doing so, of pushing Trevor out of the nest and watching him struggle to cross the wire of adulthood without the net they'd always provided. But if the business wasn't what he wanted for himself, then he should be nudged out of it. He couldn't continue to simply clock time and draw pay.

Still, he hesitated to do so. Not only out of love, for God knew, he loved his son, but out of fear the boy would simply turn to his maternal grandparents and live, all too happily, off their largess.

Sipping his tea, he studied the room his wife laughingly called Steve's Cave. He had a desk there as he more often than not preferred to hunker down in that room rather than the big, airy office downtown or his own well-appointed, well-equipped office in the house. He liked the deep colors of this room, and the shelves filled with his boyhood toys—the trucks and machines and tools he'd routinely asked for at birthdays and Christmastime.

He liked his photographs, not only of Pat and Trevor, of his mother, but of himself with his crews, with his buildings, with his trucks and machines and tools he'd worked with as an adult.

And he liked the quiet. When the privacy screens were on, the windows and the doors were shut, it might very well be a cave instead of one of the many rooms in a three-level house.

He glanced up at the ceiling, knowing if he didn't go up to the bedroom shortly, his wife would roll over in bed, find him gone, then drag herself up to search him out.

He should go up, spare her that. But he poured a second mug of tea and lingered in the soft light and quiet. And nearly dozed off.

The buzzer on his security panel made him jolt. His first reaction was annoyance. But when he blinked his eyes clear and looked at the view screen, the image of his son brought him a quick rush of pleasure.

He rose out of his wide leather chair, a man of slightly less than average height, with the bare beginnings of a potbelly. His arms and legs were well muscled, and hard as brick. His eyes were a faded blue with webs of lines fanning out from them. Though it had gone stone gray, he still had most of his hair.

He looked his age, and eschewed any thought of face or body sculpting. He liked to say he'd earned the lines and gray hair honestly. A statement, he knew, that caused his fashionable and youth-conscious son to wince.

He supposed if he'd ever been as handsome as Trevor,

he might have been a bit more vain. The boy was a picture, Steve thought. Tall and trim, tanned and golden.

And he worked at it, Steve thought with a little twinge. The boy spent a fortune on wardrobe, on salons and spas and consultants.

He shook off the thought as he reached the door. It didn't do any good to poke at the boy over things that didn't matter. And since Trevor rarely visited, he didn't want to spoil things.

He opened the door and smiled. "Well, this is a surprise! Come on in." He gave Trevor's back three easy pats as Trevor walked past him and into the entrance hall.

"What're you doing out this time of night?"

Deliberately, Trevor turned his wrist to check the time on the luminous mother-of-pearl face of his wrist unit. "It's barely eleven."

"Is it? I was dozing off in my den." Steve shook his head. "Your mother's already gone up to bed. I'll go get her."

"No, don't bother." Trevor waved him off. "You've changed the security again."

"Once a month. Better safe than sorry. I'll give you the new codes." He was about to suggest they go into the den, share the pot of tea, but Trevor was already moving into the more formal living room. And helping himself from the liquor cabinet.

"It's good to see you. What're you doing out and about and all dressed up?"

The casual jacket, regardless of label and price, was hardly what Trevor considered *dressed up*. But it was certainly a step up from his father's choice of Mets T-shirt and baggy khakis.

"I've just come from a party. Dead bore." Trevor took the snifter of brandy—at least the old man stocked decent liquor—swirling it as he sprawled into a chair. "Cousin Marcus was there with his irritating wife. All they could do was talk and talk and talk about that baby they made. As if they were the first to procreate."

"New parents tend to be wrapped up." Though he'd have preferred his tea, Steve poured a brandy to be sociable. "Your mother and I, we bored the ears off everyone who couldn't run and hide for months after you were born. You'll do the same when it's your turn."

"I don't think there's any danger of that as I'm not the least bit interested in making something that drools and smells and demands every minute of your time."

Steve continued to smile, though the tone, and sentiment, set his teeth on edge. "Once you meet the right woman, you'll probably change your mind."

"There is no right woman. But there are any number of tolerable ones."

"I hate hearing you sound so cynical and hard."

"Honest," Trevor corrected. "I live in the world as it is."

Steve let out a sigh. "Maybe you need to begin to. It must be meant to be that you came by tonight. I was thinking of you before you did. About where you're going with your life, and why."

Trevor shrugged. "You've never understood or approved of my life because it doesn't mirror yours. Steve Whittier, man of the people, who built himself from nothing. Literally. You know, you should sell your life story. Look how well the Gannon woman has done with her family memoirs."

Steve set his snifter down, and for the first time since Trevor had come in, there was a warning edge in his tone. "No one is to know about any of that. I made that clear to you, Trevor. I told you because I felt you had a right to know, and that if, somehow, through that book's publication the connection was made to your grandmother, to me, to you, you'd be prepared. It's a shameful part of our family history, painful to your grandmother. And to me."

"It hardly affects Grandma. She's out of it ninety percent of the time." Trevor circled a finger at his ear.

Genuine anger brought a red flush to Steve's face. "I don't ever want to hear you make light of her condition. Or to shrug off everything she did to keep me safe and whole. You wouldn't be here, swilling brandy and sneering, if it wasn't for her."

"Or him." Trevor inclined his head. "He had a part in making you, after all."

"Biology doesn't make a father. I explained to you what he was. A thief and a murderer."

"A successful one, until the Gannons. Come on now." Trevor shifted, leaned forward, the brandy snifter cupped between his knees. "Don't you find him fascinating, at least? He was a man who made his own rules, lived his life on his own terms and took what he wanted."

"Took what he wanted, no matter what it cost anyone else. Who so terrorized my mother she spent years running from him. Even after he died in prison, she kept looking over her shoulder. I know, whatever the doctors say, I *know* it was him and all those years of fear and worry that made her ill."

"Face it, Dad, it's a mental defect, and very likely genetic. You or I could be next. Best to live it up before we end up drooling in some glorified asylum."

"She's your grandmother, and you *will* show respect for her."

"But not for him? Blood's blood, isn't it? Tell me about him." He settled back again.

"I've told you all you need to know."

"You said you kept moving from place to place. A few months, a year, and you'd be packing up again. He must've contacted her, or you. Come to see you. Otherwise why would she keep running?"

"He always found us. Until they caught him, he always found us. I didn't know he'd been caught, not till months afterward. I didn't know he'd died for more than a year. She tried to protect me, but I was curious. Curious children have a way of finding things out."

Don't they just? Trevor thought. "You must've wondered about the diamonds."

"Why should I?"

"His last big job? Please, you must've wondered, and being a curious child . . . "

"I didn't think about them. I only thought of how he made her feel. How he made me feel the last time I saw him."

"When was that?"

"He came to our house in Columbus. We had a nice house there, a nice neighborhood. I was happy. And he came, late at night. I knew when I heard my mother's voice, and his, I knew we'd have to leave. I had a friend right next door. God, I can't remember his name. I thought he was the best friend I'd ever have, and that I'd never see him again. And well, I didn't."

Boo-hoo, Trevor thought in disgust, but he kept his tone light and friendly. "It wasn't easy for you, or Grandma. How old were you?"

"Seven, I think. About seven. It's difficult to be sure. One of the things my mother did to hide us was change my birth date. Different names, a year or two added or taken away on our ages. I was nearly eighteen when we stuck with Whittier. He'd been dead for years, and I told her I needed to stay one person now. I needed to start my life. So we kept it, and I know she worried herself sick because of that."

Paranoid old bat, Trevor thought. "Why do you suppose he came to see you there and then? Wouldn't that have been around the time of the heist? The diamonds?"

"Keeping tabs on me, tormenting her. I can still hear him telling her he could find her wherever she ran, that he could take me from her whenever he wanted. I can still hear her crying."

"But to come then." Trevor pushed. "Of all times. It could hardly have been a coincidence. He must have wanted something. Told you something, or told her."

"Why does this matter?"

He'd plotted it out carefully. Just because he found his father foolish didn't mean he didn't know how the man worked. "I've given this a lot of thought since you first told me. I don't mean to argue with you, but I suppose it's upset me to realize, at this point in my life, what's in my blood."

"He's nothing to you. Nothing to us."

"That's just not true, Dad." Sorrowfully, Trevor shook his head. "Didn't you ever want to close the circle? For yourself, and for her? For your mother? There are still millions of dollars of those diamonds out there, and he had them. Your father had them."

"They got nearly all of them back."

"*Nearly?* A full quarter was never recovered. If we could piece things back together, if we could find them, we could close that circle. We could work a way to give them back, through this writer—this Samantha Gannon."

"Find the diamonds, after over fifty years?" Steve

would have laughed, but Trevor was so earnest, and he himself so touched that his son would think about closing that circle. "I don't see how that's possible."

"Aren't you the one who tells me constantly that anything's possible if you're willing to work for it? This is something I want to do. I feel strongly about it. I need you to help me put it back together. To remember exactly what happened the last time he came to see you, to remember exactly what happened next. Did he ever contact you from prison? You or my grandmother? Did he ever give you anything, send you anything, tell you anything?"

"Steve?"

Steve looked over as he heard his wife's voice. "Let's put this away for now," he said quietly. "Your mother knows all about this, but I don't like dragging it out. Down here, Pat. Trevor's dropped by."

"Trevor? Oh, I'll be right down."

"We need to talk about this," Trevor insisted.

"We will." Steve gave his son a nod and an approving smile. "We will, and I'll try to remember anything that may help. I'm proud of you, Trevor, proud of you for thinking about trying to find a way to make things right. I don't know if it can be, but knowing you want to try means the world to me. I'm ashamed I never thought of it myself. That I never thought beyond putting it all away and starting fresh instead of cleaning the slate."

Trevor kept his annoyance behind a pleasant mask as he heard his mother hurrying downstairs. "I haven't been able to think of much else for weeks."

He left an hour later and strolled along in the steamy heat rather than hail a cab. He could count on his father to line up details. Steve Whittier was hell on details. But the visit had already given him his next move. He'd play concerned grandson the very next day and go see his grandmother in the loony bin.

About the time Trevor Whittier was crossing the park, Eve stifled a yawn. She wanted another hit of coffee, but knew that would mean getting through Roarke. He had a habit of knowing when her ass was dragging before she did.

"Three potentials on the woman, twice that on the kid." She scratched her scalp, hard, to get the blood moving.

"If we discount the rest of the first-level matches."

"I'm discounting them. The computer likes these picks, so we go with them. Let's move on the kid—man now. See if anything looks good."

She shot those six images on screen and began to scan the attached data. "Well, well, lookie here. Steven James Whittier, East Side address. Owns and runs his own building company. That's a nice pop for me."

"I know him."

She looked around sharply. "You know this guy?"

"Mostly in that vague professional sense, though I've met his wife a number of times at various charity functions. His company has a solid rep, and so does he. Blue-collar him, meets blue-blood her. He does good work."

"Check the lists from the job sites you got earlier. Let's see if Whittier's got anything going in or around Alphabet City."

Roarke brought up the file, then leaned back in his chair. "I should learn not to question your instincts."

"Rehab on Avenue B. Five-story building, three sections." She pursed her lips, made a popping sound. "More than enough to take a closer look. See there, he's got a son. One son, Trevor, age twenty-nine. Let's get that image."

Roarke did the tech, and they studied Trevor Whittier's face together. "Not as close on the artist rendering as I'd like, but it's not a total bust. Let's see what else we can find out about Trevor."

"You can't do anything about him tonight. It's nearly one in the morning. Unless you think you can build a case strong enough with this to go over and scoop him up and into a cage, you're going to bed. I'll set the computer to gather data while you get a few hours' sleep."

"I could go wake him up, hassle him." She considered. "But that would just be for fun. And it would give him a chance to whine for a lawyer. It can wait." She pushed to her feet.

"Until morning. We'll check out this job site, see if we can nail it to the trace from Cobb's body. I need to approach Whittier and find his mother, interview her, too. They might be in on this. This Trevor feels the best to me. Smarter to wait to move on him until I have it all lined up."

"While it lines up, you lie down."

She'd have argued, but her eyes were starting to throb. "Nag, nag, nag. I'll just contact the team and tell them we're going to brief at seven hundred instead of eight."

"You can do that in the morning. It's easier, and more humane."

"Yeah, but it's more fun to do it now," she protested as he took her hand and pulled her out of the room. "This way I get to wake them up so they have to work at getting back to sleep. The other way, I just get them out of bed a little early."

"You're a mean one, Lieutenant."

"Yeah. So?"

Chapter 12

While she slept it all played in her head. Father to son, murder and greed, blood gleaming on sparkling stones. There were legacies you couldn't escape, no matter how fast or how far you ran.

She could see herself, a child, with no mother to panic or protect. No one to hide her or stand as a shield. She could see herself—she could always see herself—alone in a freezing room with the light washed red from the sign blinking, blinking, blinking from the building next door.

She could taste her fear when he came in, that bright, metallic flavor. As if there was already blood in her throat. Hot blood against the chill.

Children shouldn't fear their fathers. She knew that now, in some part of her restless brain, she knew that. But the child knew nothing but fear.

There had been no one to stop him, no one to fight for her when his hand had slashed out like a snake. No one to protect her when he'd torn at her, torn into her. There'd been no one to hear her scream, to beg him to stop.

Not again, not again. Please, please, not again.

She'd had no one to run to when the bone in her arm had snapped like a twig broken under a careless foot. She'd had only herself, and the knife.

She could feel the blood flooding over her hands, her face, and the way his body had jerked when she'd hacked that blade into his flesh. She could see herself smeared with it, coated with it, dripping with it, like an animal at the kill. And even in sleep, she knew the madness of that animal, the utter lack of humanity.

The sounds she made were vile. Even after he was dead, the sounds she made were vile.

She struggled, jabbing, jabbing, jabbing.

"Come back. Oh God, baby, come back."

Panic and protection. Someone to hear, to help. Through the madness of memory, she heard Roarke's voice, scented him and curled up tight in the arms he'd wrapped around her.

"Can't." Couldn't shake it off. There was so much blood.

"We're here. We're both right here. I've got you." He pressed his lips to her hair, her cheek. "Let it go, Eve. Let it go now."

"I'm cold. I'm so cold."

He rubbed his hands over her back, her arms, too afraid to leave her even for the time it would take to get up for a blanket. "Hold on to me."

He lifted her into his lap, rocking her as he would a

child. And the shudders that racked her gradually eased. Her breathing steadied.

"I'm okay." She let her head fall limply on his shoulder. "Sorry." But when he didn't loosen his hold, when he continued to rock, she closed her eyes, tried to drift into the comfort he needed as much as she.

Still, she saw what she'd been, what she'd done. What she'd become in that horrible room in Dallas. Roarke could see it. He lived it with her through her nightmares.

Burrowing against him, she stared off into the dark again and wondered if she could bear the shame if anyone else caught a glimpse of how Eve Dallas had come to be.

Peabody loved briefings at Eve's home office. However serious the business, there was always an informal atmosphere when you added food. And a breakfast meeting not only meant real coffee, but real eggs, real meat and all manner of sticky, sugary pastries.

And she could justify the extra calories because it was work-related fuel. There was, in her opinion, no downside to the current situation.

They were all loaded in—Feeney, McNab, Trueheart, Baxter, Dallas, even Roarke. And boy, oh boy, a look at Roarke in the morning was as delicious a jolt to the system as the strong black coffee sweetened with honest-to-God sugar.

It was hardly a wonder the lieutenant was so slim. She had to burn up the calories just looking at him. Considering that, Peabody snatched a couple extra slices of bacon and calculated she might actually *lose* weight during the briefing.

It was a pretty good deal.

"Updates are in your packs," Eve began, and Peabody divided her attention between her plate and her partner.

Eve leaned on the corner of her desk, coffee in one hand, laser pointer in the other. "Feeney and our civilian made some progress last night, as did McNab. McNab, give the team your data."

He had to swallow, fast and hard, a mouthful of Danish. "Sir. My area deals with the 'links and d and c's from both vics."

He ran through it, pinpointing transmission locations, with considerable comp-jock code. The jargon, and the questions and comments Feeney tossed him in the same idiom gave Eve time to finish her coffee and contemplate another cup.

"You'll scout those locations this morning," Eve put in when there was a short lull. "With these images. Screen One. This is Steven Whittier. Current data leads us to believe he is the son of Alex Crew. On Screen Two you see Trevor Whittier, son of Steven Whittier and likely the grandson of Crew. Given accumulated data and the profile, he fits. Steven Whittier is the founder and current owner of Whittier Construction."

"That's a nice little pop," Baxter commented.

"Bigger and louder one as we've determined Whittier Construction is the contractor on a major rehab job, building on Avenue B. The company is licensed for four gasoline storage facilities. None of the other potential matches have as many links as this. Steven Whittier's official data states his father is deceased. His mother . . ."

She split the screen and brought up the image of a woman known as Janine Strokes Whittier. "Currently residing at Leisure Gardens, a retirement and care facility on Long Island, where Whittier senior has a second home. She's in the right age group, has the right racial profile and matches the computer morphs."

"Will we bring the Whittiers in to interview, Lieutenant?" Peabody asked.

"Not at this time. We've got circumstantial and supposition. It's good circumstantial and supposition, but it's not enough to push the PA for a warrant. It's not enough to arrest, much less convict. So we get more."

"Trueheart and I can take the images, toss in a couple more and show them to the waitress. She picks out one of these guys," Baxter said, "we've got more."

"Do it. McNab, find me somebody at the transmission sources who remembers seeing one or both of these men. Feeney, I need you to dig back. If Janine and Steven Whittier went by other names previous to this, I want them."

"You'll get them," he told her, and scooped up a mouthful of eggs.

"Peabody and I will head to this job site first, match the trace and do a sweep. If Cobb was killed there, there'll be blood. I want witnesses, I want physical evidence. We lock it down, then we pull them in. Roarke, I'm counting on your security to keep Samantha Gannon and her family safe under wraps until we nail this."

"It's done."

"Sir." Like any well-disciplined student, Trueheart raised his hand. "Detective Baxter and I could go by the hotel and show Ms. Gannon the images. She might recognize one or both of these men. If so, it could give us another link."

"That's good thinking, Trueheart. Do the legwork. Let's build this case tight." She glanced toward the board, and the victims. "Nobody else is going to die over a bunch of fucking rocks."

When the team began to disperse, Roarke ran a fingertip along Eve's shoulder. "A moment, Lieutenant?"

"Half a moment." With her mind on dovetailing points of the investigation, she trailed after him into his office.

He closed the door, then, cupping his hands under her elbows, lifted her to the toes of her boots and took her mouth in a short and heated kiss.

"Jeez!" She dropped back to the flat of her feet with a thud. "What is *wrong* with you?"

"Had to get that out of my system. Something about watching you take command just gets me started."

"Watching grass grow gets you started." She turned toward the door, but he slapped a hand on it. "Do the words 'obstruction of justice' ring a bell?"

"Several. And though a quick bout of obstruction might be entertaining, that's not what I had in mind. I have some things to deal with this morning, but some of the day can be shuffled around."

"If Feeney wants you on board for the e-work, that's between you and him."

"He has his teeth in it now. I don't imagine he needs me to chew through the rest. But you might want me along when you speak to Steven Whittier."

"Why?"

"Because he knows me. And from what I know of him, he couldn't have had a part in what was done to those women. Not knowingly."

"People can do a lot of things that are out of character when they're blinded by bright, shiny stones."

"Agreed. Another reason you might want me along. I know a bit about that sort of thing." He drew the chain from under her shirt so the teardrop diamond he'd once given her sparkled between them. "I've known people who've killed for them. I'll know if he has. They're just things to you. You wear this for me. That's its only value to you."

He smiled a little as he slid it under her shirt again. "If I'd given you a hunk of quartz, it would mean the same."

"He may not have done it for the diamonds, not directly, but to protect himself and his family. Samantha Gannon knows things about him that aren't in the book. Things no one outside that group formed a half century ago knows. Who he is, who he comes from. People kill for that, too."

"Is this line of thinking what brought on your nightmare?"

"I don't know. Maybe this line of thinking came out of it. On the surface, Whittier's built a good, decent life. But it's often what's under the surface that drives people. He has a lot to lose if it comes out—who his father was, what he did, that Steven Whittier is a figment."

"Is that what you think?" He touched her, a hand to her cheek, a cheek pale from a restless night. "Because the name was given to him along the way instead of at the beginning, it isn't real?"

"It's not what I think, it's what he thinks that matters."

Now he framed her face. "You know who you are, Eve."

"Most of the time." She lifted a hand, laid it on his wrist. "You want to come along because of the nightmare. You'd already worked it out that I was making correlations with myself on this. I won't deny I have, but it doesn't get in the way of the job."

"I didn't think it would."

"I'll think about it. I'll contact you and let you know." She turned toward the door, then back. "Thanks."

"You're welcome."

• • •

The building on Avenue B was a beauty. Or as she was told by the cooperative job foreman, the three buildings being turned into one multipurpose complex was a beauty. The old brick had already been blasted clean of grime and soot and graffiti so the color glowed muted rose.

She doubted that would last long.

The lines were clean and straight, with the beauty in the simplicity of form.

"Damn shame the way it was let go" was foreman Hinkey's opinion as he walked them inside the entrance of the middle building. "Useta be apartments and such, and the basic structures held up. But, jeemaneze, you shoulda seen the guts of the place. Torn to shit and back. Wood rotted out, floors sagging, plumbing out of the freaking Ice Age. You had your cracked drywall and your busted windows. Some people just got no respect for buildings, you know?"

"Guess not. You lock the place down tight when the crew's not here?"

"Damn straight. You got your vandals and your looters and your sidewalk sleepers, your assholes looking for a place to screw around or deal." He shook his head, adorned with a dusty Whittier gimme cap. "We got a lot of equipment in here, not to mention the supplies. Steve—Mr. Whittier—he don't stint on security. He runs a class operation."

She didn't know about class, but she knew about noise. Inside there was plenty of it.

"Lot of space," she commented.

"Five floors, three buildings. You got round about eighteen thousand square, not counting rooftop area. Gonna be a mix of residential and business. Keeping as much of the original structures and features we can salvage, and we'll install new where we can't, keeping the original style."

"Yeah. This much space, three buildings, there's a lot of ways in and out. A lot to cover."

"We got a central security system, and individual backups on each building."

"Who's got the codes?"

"Ah, that'd be Steve, myself, head carpenter, assistant foreman and the security company."

"You can give those names to my partner. We'd like to look around."

"You going any farther than this, you gotta have your hard hat and goggles. That's the law."

"No problem." Eve took the canary-yellow construction hat and the safety glasses. "Can you show me where you've used the flame sealant?"

"Damn near all the subflooring's been sealed." He scratched his chin. "You want, we can start here, work our way through. But I'm telling you, nobody coulda gotten in here after hours."

"It's my job to check it out, Hinkey."

"Gotta do what you gotta." He jerked a thumb and began to wind his way around equipment. "This here's commercial space. Probably lease it to a restaurant. This here floor's been sealed up. Had to rip out what was left of the original. New flooring's not installed yet, just the sub and seal."

Eve took the scanner out of her field kit and ran a standard for blood trace. Gauging the size of the building, the time it would take to scan each area of flooring, she straightened from her crouch.

"Can you do me a favor, Hinkey? How about you get

somebody to take my partner through the next building while you and I go through this one? We'll hit the third after that. Save us all some time and trouble."

"Whatever you want." He took a two-way off his belt. "Yo, Carmine. Need you floor one, building two."

They divided into teams, and Eve moved from area to area on the first floor. After a while she was able, for the most part, to tune out the noise. Buzzing and whirling, the sucking of compressors and the smack of air guns.

The voices of the crew came in a variety of accents. Brooklyn and Queens, Hispanic and street jive. She filtered it out, along with the music each section selected as background tunes. Trash rock, tinny country, salsa, rap.

Because he was giving her time and no hassle, she listened to Hinkey's running commentary on the job progress and details with half an ear.

He droned on about climate controls, inspections, electrical and filter systems, walls, trims, labor, plumbing. Her brain was jammed with it by the time they hit the second floor.

He nattered on about windows, framing, stopped off to chew out a laborer and to consult with another crew member on specs. It gave Eve hope she'd shake him off, but he caught up with her before she made it to the third level.

"Apartments up here. Give people a decent place to live. Fact is, my daughter's getting married next spring. She and the guy, they've already put in for this unit right here."

Eve glanced over in time to see him look a bit baffled and sentimental. "Be nice for them, I guess. And I know the place is built good. Solid." He rapped a hand on the wall. "None of that toothpick-and-glue shit some of these places use when they slap one of these old buildings back together. Steve, he takes pride."

"You worked for him long?"

"Seventeen years this October. He ain't no fly-by-night. Knows his buildings, too. Works side by side with you in a crunch."

She found a few drops of blood, discounted it as she had in other areas. Not enough. And you put a bunch of people together with a bunch of tools, a little blood was going to spill.

"He spend much time on this job?"

"Oh yeah. Biggest we've had. Worked his ass off to get this bid, and he's by here every day."

He walked with her out of the unit, down the hall formed by studded walls.

"How about his son?"

"What about him?"

"He put in time?"

Hinkey snorted derisively, then caught himself. "Works in the office."

Eve paused. "You don't like him much."

"Not for me to say, one way or the other." Hinkey lifted a beefy shoulder. "I'll just say he don't take after his old man, not that I see."

"So he doesn't come around."

"Been here once or twice, maybe. Doesn't take much interest. Suit-and-tie type, you know?"

"Yeah, I know." She stepped over a stack of some sort of lumber product. "Would he have the access codes?"

"Don't see why he would."

"Boss's son."

Hinkey's shrug was his response.

Her ears were ringing, her head pounding by the time

they hit the fourth floor. She decided she'd have asked for ear protectors if she'd known how bad it would get. It seemed to her that the tools had gone to scream level here. She eyed, with some respect, a large, toothy saw run by a man who looked to weigh in at a hundred pounds flat.

She gave it a wide berth, flipped on the scanner.

And hit the mother lode.

"What the fuck is that—beg pardon."

"It's a hell of a lot of blood, Hinkey." She ran the scanner over the floor, revealing a bright blue pattern along the floor, splattered on the wall. "One of your men cut off an appendage with that saw up here?"

"Jesus Christ, no. Lieutenant, I don't see how that could be blood."

But she could. Just as she could see the smear of it running down the hall. Where Tina Cobb had tried to crawl.

He'd walked through it, she noted, squatting down for a better look. He'd left some prints, and wasn't that handy?

So had Cobb, she saw. Handprints, bloodied. Tried to pull herself up the wall, used it for support and pressed her hand there, there.

He'd taken his time with her, Eve was sure of it. He'd let her crawl, limp, stumble the entire length of the fourth-floor corridor before he delivered the death blow.

"Can't be blood." Hinkey stared at the blue, shaking his head slowly from side to side. "We'd've seen it. Jeezopetes, you couldn'ta missed it."

"I need this area cleared. I've got to ask you to get your crew out of this building. This is a crime scene." She took out her communicator. "Peabody? I've found her. Fourth floor."

"I've gotta . . . I gotta call the boss."

"You do that, Hinkey. Tell him to be available, at his home, in an hour." Eve turned to him, felt a pang of sympathy as she saw the horror in his eyes. "Get your crew out of this building and call Whittier. I want to talk to him."

In under an hour, the construction noise had been replaced by cop noise. Though she didn't have much hope of picking up more evidential trace, she had a team of sweepers spread throughout the building. A crime-scene unit took images of the hand- and footprints, and with their tech magic extracted microscopic blood traces for DNA match.

She'd already matched the index fingerprint on the wall to the prints on file for Tina Cobb.

"I know you're going to say it's just cop work, Dallas, just step-by-step investigation, but it's just short of miraculous we were able to nail this scene."

Peabody studied the blood patterns, boldly blue under the scanners set on tripods.

"Another few weeks, maybe days, they'd have set the floor, covered the walls. He picked a good spot for this."

"Nobody to see her, hear her," Eve stated. "Easy enough to get her inside, dozens of reasons he could've used. There's plenty of pipe for the murder weapon, tarps to wrap her body in to transport it. He'd get the gas first. Have that in the transfer vehicle. He got in here, he could access the gas. We'll follow up there. There'll be records of what's stored or purchased through the Whittier account."

"I'll get on that."

"Do it on the way. Let's go see Whittier."

• • •

She didn't want him on scene, not yet. She wanted this first contact in his home, where a man felt most comfortable. And where a man, guilty or innocent, tended to feel most uneasy when confronted with a badge.

She didn't want him surrounded by his employees and friends.

He opened the door himself, and she saw a sleepless night on his face that was layered over now with what might have been shock and worry.

He extended a hand to her in what she took as the automatic manners of a man raised to be polite. "Lieutenant Dallas? Steve Whittier. I don't know what to think, what to say. I'm not taking this in. Hinkey thinks there's been some mistake, and I'm inclined to agree. I'd like to get down to the site and—"

"I can't allow that, at this time. Can we come in?"

"What? Oh, yes. Sorry. Excuse me. Ah . . . " He gestured, stepped back. "We should sit down." He scrubbed a hand over his face. "Somewhere. In here, I think. My wife's out, but I expect her back soon. I don't want her to walk in on this. I'd rather try to tell her . . . Well."

He walked them into his den, held out his hands to chairs. "Would you like something? Something to drink?"

"No. Mr. Whittier, I'm going to record this interview. And I'm going to give you your rights."

"My . . . " He sank into a chair. "Give me a minute, will you? Am I a suspect in something? Should I . . . Do I need a lawyer?"

"You have a right to a lawyer or a representative at any time during this process. What I want is to get a statement from you, Mr. Whittier. To ask you some questions." She set a recorder in plain view on the table and recited the revised Miranda. "Do you understand your rights and obligations in this matter?"

"Yes, I guess I do. That's about all I do understand."

"Can you tell me where you were on the night of September sixteenth?"

"I don't know. Probably here at home. I need to check my book."

He rose to go to the desk for a sleek little day calendar. "Well, I'm wrong about that. Pat and I had dinner out with friends. I remember now. We met at about seven-thirty at the Mermaid. It's a seafood place on First Avenue between Seventy-first and -second. We had drinks first, then took the table about eight. Didn't get home until around midnight."

"The names of the people you were with?"

"James and Keira Sutherland."

"And after midnight?"

"I'm sorry?"

"After midnight, Mr. Whittier, what did you do?"

"We went to bed. My wife and I went to bed." He flushed when he said it, and the expression reminded her of Feeney's embarrassment when he'd realized what she and Roarke had been up to on their recreational break.

She deduced Whittier and wife had indulged in some recreation before sleep.

"How about the night of September fourteenth?"

"I don't understand this." He muttered it, but checked his book. "I don't have anything down. A Thursday, a Thursday," he said, closing his eyes. "I think we were home, but I'd have to ask Pat. She remembers these things better than I do. We tend to stay home most evenings. It's too hot to go out."

He was a lamb, she thought, innocent as a lamb, just

as he'd been at seven. She'd have bet the bank on it. "Do you know a Tina Cobb?"

"I don't think . . . the name's a little familiar—one of those things you think you've heard somewhere. I'm sorry. Lieutenant Dallas, if you could just tell me what's going on, exactly what's . . . " He trailed off.

Eve saw on his face the minute the name clicked for him. And seeing it, she knew she'd been right in betting the bank. This man had had no part in splattering the girl's blood.

"Oh my sweet Jesus. The girl who was burned, burned in the lot a few blocks from the site. You're here about her."

Eve reached in her bag, just as the bell rang at the door. Roarke, she thought. She'd made the right choice in contacting him after all. Not to help her determine Whittier's involvement, but to give the man someone familiar in the room when she pushed him about his son.

"My partner will get the door," she said, and took Tina's photo out of the bag. "Do you recognize this woman, Mr. Whittier?"

"God, yes, oh God. From the media reports. I saw her on the reports. She was hardly more than a child. You think she was killed in my building, but I don't understand. She was found burned to death in that lot."

"She wasn't killed there."

"You can't expect me to believe anyone on my crew would have a part in something like this." He glanced up, confusion running over his face as he got to his feet. "Roarke?"

"Steve."

"Roarke is a civilian consultant in this investigation," Eve explained. "Do you have any objection to his presence here at this time?"

"No. I don't—"

"Who has the security codes to your building on Avenue B?"

"Ah. God." Steve pressed a hand to his head a moment. "I have them, and the security company, of course. Hinkey, ah . . . can't think straight. Yule, Gainer. That should be it."

"Your wife?"

"Pat?" He smiled weakly. "No. No point in that."

"Your son?"

"No." But his eyes went blank. "No. Trevor doesn't work on sites."

"But he's been to that building?"

"Yes. I don't like the implication here, Lieutenant. I don't like it at all."

"Is your son aware that his grandfather was Alex Crew?"

Every ounce of color drained from Steve's cheeks. "I believe I'd like that lawyer now."

"That's your choice." Standing as shield, Eve thought. Instinct. A father protecting his son. "More difficult to keep certain facts out of the media once the lawyers come into it, of course. Difficult to keep your connection to Alex Crew and events that transpired fifty years ago out of the public stream. I assume you'd prefer if certain details of your past remained private, Mr. Whittier."

"What does this have to do with Alex Crew?"

"What would you do to keep your parentage private, Mr. Whittier?"

"Nearly anything. Nearly. The fact of it, the fear of it has ruined my mother's health. If this is exposed, it might kill her."

"Samantha Gannon's book exposed quite a bit."

"It didn't make the connection. And my mother doesn't know about the book. I can control, somewhat, what she hears about. She needs to be protected from those memories, Lieutenant. She's never hurt anyone, and she doesn't deserve to be put on display. She's not well."

"I've no intention of doing that. I don't want to have to speak to her, to force her to speak to me about any of this."

"You want to shield your mother," Roarke said quietly. "As she shielded you. But there are prices to be paid, Steve, just as she paid them in her day. You'll have to speak for her."

"What can I tell you? For God's sake, I was a child the last time I saw him. He died in prison. He's nothing to do with me, with any of us. We *made* this life."

"Did the diamonds pay for it?" Eve wondered, and his head snapped around, insult plain on his face.

"They did not. Even if I knew where they were, I wouldn't have touched them. I used nothing of his, want nothing of his."

"Your son knows about them."

"That doesn't make him a killer! That doesn't mean he'd kill some poor girl. You're talking about my *son*."

"Could he have gotten access to the security codes?"

"I didn't give him the codes. You're asking me to implicate my son. My child."

"I'm asking you for the truth. I'm asking you to help me close the door your father opened all those years ago."

"Close the circle," Steve mumbled and buried his face in his hands. "God. God."

"What did Alex Crew bring you that night? What did he bring to the house in Columbus?"

"What?" With a half laugh, Steve shook his head. "A

toy. Just a toy." He gestured to the shelves, and the antique toys. "He gave me a scale-model bulldozer. I didn't want it. I was afraid of him, but I took it because I was more afraid not to. Then he sent me upstairs. I don't know what he said to my mother in the next few minutes, other than his usual threats. I know I heard her crying for an hour after he left. Then we were packing."

"Do you still have the toy?"

"I keep it to remind me what he was, what I overcame thanks to my mother's sacrifices. Ironic really. A bulldozer. I like to think I razed and buried the past." He looked over to the shelves, then, frowning, rose. "It should be here. I can't remember moving it. Odd."

Antique toys, Eve mused while Whittier searched. Gannon's ex had antique toys in his office and an advance copy of the book.

"Does your son collect this sort of thing, too?"

"Yes, it's the one thing Trevor and I shared. He's more interested in collector's values, more serious about it than I from that standpoint. It's not here."

He turned, his face was sheet-white now and seemed to have fallen in on itself. "It doesn't mean anything. I must have misplaced it. It's just a toy."

Chapter 13

"Could it have been moved?" Eve studied the shelves. She had a vague sort of idea what a bulldozer looked like. Her knowledge of machines was more finely tuned to urban style. The maxibuses that belched up and down the avenues, the airjacks that tore up the streets in the most inconvenient places at the most inconvenient times, the droning street-cleaning units, the clanking recycler trucks.

But she recognized models of old-fashioned pickup trucks and service vans, and a shiny red tractor, not unlike the one she'd seen on Roarke's aunt's farm recently.

There were toy replicas of emergency vehicles that were boxier, clunkier to her eye than what zipped around the streets or skies of New York. And a number of bulky trucklike things with scoops or toothy blades or massive tubes attached.

She didn't see how Whittier could be sure what was missing, or what was where. To her eye, there was no rhyme or reason to the collection, but a bunch of little vehicles with wheels or wings or both cobbled together as if waiting for a traffic signal to turn green.

But he was a guy, and her experience with Roarke told her a guy knew his toys very well.

"I haven't moved it. I'd remember." Steve was searching the shelves now, touching various vehicles or machines, scooting some along. "I can't think why my wife would either, or the housekeeper."

"Do you have any of this sort of thing elsewhere on the premises?" Eve asked him.

"Yes, a few pieces here and there, and the main collection upstairs in my office, but . . . "

"Why don't you take a look? Peabody, could you give Mr. Whittier a hand?"

"Sure. My brothers have a few model toys," Peabody began as she led Steve out of the room. "Nothing like what you've got here."

Eve waited until their voices had faded. "How much is this kind of deal worth?" She waved her thumb toward the shelves as she turned to Roarke.

"It's a bit out of my milieu, but antique, nostalgic, novelty collections of any kind have value." He picked up a small, beefy truck, spun the wheels. The quick smile confirmed Eve's theory that such matters were indeed guy things. "And the condition of the pieces add to it. These are all prime, from what I can see. You're thinking the toy's been lifted."

"Strong possibility."

He set the truck down but didn't release it until he'd pushed it gently back and forth. "If Trevor Whittier stole it from his father, if the diamonds were indeed hidden inside it—and that's where you're heading?"

"Past heading. I'm there. I don't think you should be playing with those," she added when he reached for the tractor.

He made a sound that might have been disappointment or mild embarrassment, then stuck his hands in his pockets. "Then why kill? Why break into Samantha's house? Why not be toasting your good fortune in Belize?"

"Who says he knows they're in there?" She watched Roarke lift a brow. "Look at his profile. He's a lazy, self-centered opportunist. I'm betting if Whittier does a check of his collection, he'll find several of the better pieces missing. Stupid bastard might just have sold them, and the diamonds along with them."

She wandered up and down the shelves, scanning the toys. "Samantha Gannon's ex has a collection."

"Does he now?" Roarke nodded. "Does he, really?"

"Yeah. Not as extensive as this, at least not the collection I saw in his office. Put Trevor Whittier together with the ex." She put the tips of her index fingers together. "Point of interest, antique toys and games. Gannon's ex had an advance copy of the book, and might very well have talked about it."

"Intersections," Roarke said with a nod. "It really is a small little world, isn't it? The ex buys pieces from Whittier's son, or at least knows him, socializes perhaps, shares this interest. Because of that, he mentions the book, talks it up. Samantha's grandmother owned an antique store. I believe she still does. Another sort of intersection, another common thread that might've prompted a conversation."

"Worth checking. I want an all-points out on Trevor Whittier. I want to sweep him up and into Interview, and

I want a damn warrant to search his place. All of that's going to take some fast talking." She frowned toward the doorway. "What do you think? Will Whittier keep quiet, or will he try to warn Trevor we're looking for him?"

"I think he'll try to cooperate. That would be his first instinct. Do the right thing. He won't consider, or believe, his son's a murderer. It won't be in his scope. In trouble, yes, in need of help. But not a cold-blooded killer. If he begins to think in that direction, I don't know what he might do."

"Then let's keep him busy as long as we can."

She called Baxter and Trueheart in to handle Whittier. They'd accompany him to his downtown offices, where he kept a few pieces of his collection.

"I need you to wait for the wife," Eve directed Baxter. "Keep her with you. I don't want either of them to have the opportunity to contact the son. Let's keep him out of this mix as long as we can. We get some luck, and we pick him up before he knows we're looking for him."

"How long do you want them wrapped up?"

"Try to get me a couple hours. I need to get a warrant for Whittier junior's place, and I want to get to Chad Dix. I'm going to send a couple uniforms out to Long Island, where Whittier's mother's living. Just to be safe."

"We'll stall. Maybe he'll let us play with the fire truck."

"What is it with guys and little trucks?"

"Come on, you had your dollies and tea parties." A lesser man would have shrunk under her withering stare. "Okay, maybe not."

"Keep them wrapped," Eve ordered as she started out. "If it starts to unravel, I want to hear about it."

"Yeah, yeah. I bet this sucker has a working siren."

Eve heard the high-pitched scream of it as she passed into the foyer. "Excuse my idiot associate, Mr. Whittier. We appreciate your cooperation."

"It's fine. I want this straightened out." He managed a smile. "I'll just go and . . . " He gestured toward his den. "I'll just make sure the detective doesn't . . . "

"Go right ahead. You're waiting for the wife," Eve said in an undertone to Trueheart. "If the son happens by, keep him here, contact me."

"Yes, sir."

"Peabody, with me."

"No place I'd rather be." Peabody glanced at Roarke. "You coming with us?"

"I doubt the lieutenant has use for me at the moment."

"I'll probably get around to you."

"My hope eternally springs."

She paused on the sidewalk. "If you want to stay available, I'll let you know when we have Trevor in custody."

"I appreciate it. Meanwhile, I could do a little search among known collectors and see if a piece fitting the description has been on the market in the last few months."

"That'd cover some bases. Appreciate it. Let's get the commander to wheedle a warrant for us. I want to talk to Chad Dix. Proving a connection there adds a couple of bars to the cage."

Roarke lifted Eve's chin with his hand—a gesture that had her wincing, and Peabody wandering discreetly away. "You're very steely-minded on this one, Lieutenant."

"No touching on the job," she muttered and nudged his hand aside. "And I'm always steely-minded."

"No. There are times you run on guts and wear yourself out emotionally, physically."

"Every case is different. This one's by the stages.

Unless Trevor's figured it all out by now, he's not a particular threat to anyone. We'll have his parents under wraps, and I'm sending a couple of uniforms to keep tabs on the grandmother's place. We've got Gannon protected. Those are his most obvious targets. I'm not dealing with wondering who some psycho's going to kill next. Puts a little more air in my lungs, you know?"

"I do." Despite her earlier warning, he touched her again, rubbing a thumb along the shadows under her eyes. "But you could still use a good night's sleep."

"Then I'll have to close this down so I can get one." She hooked her thumbs in her front pockets, sighed heavily because she knew it would amuse him. "Go ahead, get it over with. Just make it quick and no tongues allowed."

He laughed, as she'd expected, then leaned down to give her a very chaste kiss. "Acceptable?"

"Hardly even worth it." And the quick gleam in his eye had her slapping a hand on his chest. "Save it, pal. Go back to work. Buy a large metropolitan area or something."

"I'll see what I can do."

At Eve's signal, Peabody stepped up to the car. "It must really set you up, having a man like that look at you the way he does every day."

"At least it doesn't keep me off the streets." She slid in, slammed her door. "Let's cook this bastard and maybe we can both get home on time for a change."

Trevor detested visiting his grandmother. The concept of age and illness disgusted him. There were *ways,* after all, to beat back the worst symptoms of the aging process. Face and body sculpting, youth treatments, organ transplants.

Looking old was, to his mind, a product of laziness or poverty. Either was unacceptable.

Illness was something to be avoided at all costs. Most physical ailments were temporary and easily rectified. One simply had to take proper care. Mental illness was nothing but an embarrassment to anyone associated with the patient.

He considered his grandmother a self-indulgent lunatic, overly pampered by his father. If so much time and money wasn't wasted making her comfortable in her mad little world, she'd straighten up quickly enough. He knew very well it cost enormous amounts of money—his inheritance—to keep her in the gilt-edged loony bin, to pay for her housing, her food, her care, her meds, her attendants.

Pissed away, he thought, as he drove his new two-seater Jetstream 3000 into the underground parking facility at the rest home. The crazy old bat could easily live another forty years, drooling his inheritance, what was rightfully his, away.

It was infuriating.

His father's sentimental attachment to her was equally so. She could have been seen to, decently enough, in a lesser facility, or even a state-run project. He paid taxes, didn't he, to subsidize those sort of facilities? What was the *point* of not using them since he was paying out the nose for them in any case?

She wouldn't know the damn difference. And when he was in charge of the purse strings, she damn well would be moved.

He took a white florist box out of the trunk. He'd take her the roses, play the game. It would be worth his time and the investment in the flowers she'd forget ten minutes after he gave them to her, if she knew anything. If by some miracle she remembered knowing anything.

It was worth a shot. Since the old man seemed to know nothing, maybe his crazy old mother had some lead buried in her fogged brain.

He took the elevator to lobby level, gearing himself up for the performance. When he stepped off, he wore a pleasant, slightly concerned expression, presenting the image of a handsome young man paying an affectionate duty call on an aged and ailing relative.

He moved to the security desk, setting the box of flowers on the counter so the name of the upscale city florist could be read by the receptionist. "I'd like to see my grandmother. Janine Whittier? I'm Trevor. I didn't call ahead as it's an impulse visit. I was passing the florist's and I thought of Grandma and how much she loves pink roses. Next thing I knew I was buying a dozen and heading here. It's all right, isn't it?"

"Of course!" The woman beamed at him. "That's so sweet. I'm sure she'll love the flowers nearly as much as she'll love seeing her grandson. Just let me bring up her schedule and make certain she's clear for visits today."

"I know she has good days and bad days. I hope this is a good one."

"Well, I see here she's been checked into the second-floor common room. That's a good sign. If I could just clear you through." She gestured toward the palm plate.

"Oh, sure. Of course." He laid his hand on it, waited while it verified his identification and his clearance. Ridiculous precautions, he thought. Who in hell would want to break into an old people's home? It was the sort of thing that added several thousand a year to the tab.

"There you are, Mr. Whittier. I'll just scan these." She ran a hand-held over the roses to verify the contents, then gestured. "You can take the main staircase to the second floor, or the elevator if you prefer. The common area is to the left, down the hall. You can speak to one of the attendants on duty. I'm sending up your clearance now."

"Thank you. This is a lovely place. It's such a comfort to know Grandma's being so well looked after."

He took the stairs. He saw others, carrying flowers or gifts wrapped in colorful paper. Staff wore what he assumed were color-coded uniforms, all in calming pastels. In this unrestricted area, patients wandered, alone or with attendants. Through the wide, sunny windows he could see the extensive gardens below, with the winding paths where more patients, attendants, visitors strolled.

It amazed him, continuously, that people would work in such a place, whatever the salary. And that those who weren't paid to be here would visit, voluntarily, on any sort of regular basis.

He himself hadn't been inside the place for nearly a year and sincerely hoped this visit would be the last required of him.

As he glanced at the faces he passed he had a moment's jolt that he wouldn't recognize his grandmother. He should have refreshed his memory before the trip out, taken a look at some photographs.

The old all looked the same to him. They all looked doomed. More, they all looked useless.

A woman being wheeled by reached out with a clawlike hand to snatch at the ribbon trailing from the florist's box.

"I love flowers. I love flowers." Her voice was a pipe tooting out of a wizened face that made Trevor think of a dried apple. "Thank you, Johnnie! I love you, Johnnie!"

"Now, Tiffany." The attendant, a perky-looking brunette, leaned over the motorized chair, patted the ancient woman on the shoulder. "This nice man isn't your Johnnie. Your Johnnie was just here yesterday, remember?"

"I can have the flowers." She looked up hopefully, her bony hand like a hook in the ribbon.

Trevor had to battle back a shudder, and he shifted to prevent that hideously spotted hand from making contact with any part of him. "They're for my grandmother." Even as bile rose in his throat, he smiled. "A very special lady. But . . . " Under the pleased and approving eye of the attendant, he opened the box, took out a single pink rosebud. "I'm sure she wouldn't mind if you had one."

"That's so kind of you," the attendant responded. "There you are now, Tiffany, isn't that nice? A pretty rose from a handsome man."

"Lots of handsome men give me flowers. Lots of them." She stroked the petals and lost herself in some blurry memory.

"You said you were here to see your grandmother?" the attendant prompted.

"Yes, that's right. Janine Whittier. They told me downstairs she was in the common room."

"Yes, she is. Miss Janine's a lovely lady. I'm sure she'll be glad to see you. If you need any help, just let me know. I'll be back shortly. I'm Emma."

"Thank you." And since he couldn't be sure Emma wouldn't be useful, he braced himself and leaned down to smile in the old woman's face. "It was nice to meet you, Miss Tiffany. I hope to see you again."

"Pretty flowers. Cold eyes. Dead eyes. Sometimes shiny fruit's rotted at the core. You're not my Johnnie."

"I'm sorry," Emma whispered, and wheeled the old woman away.

Hideous old rag, Trevor thought and allowed himself that shudder before he walked the rest of the way into the common room.

It was bright, cheerful, spacious. Areas were sectioned off for specific activities. There were wall screens set to a variety of programs, tables arranged for game playing, visiting, crafts, seating areas for visiting as well, or for passing the time with books or magazines.

There were a number of people in attendance, and the noise level reminded him of a cocktail party where people broke off into groups and ignored the talk around them.

When he hesitated, another attendant, again female, came over. "Mr. Whittier?"

"Yes, I . . . "

"She's doing really well today." She gestured toward a table by a sunny window where two women and a man appeared to be playing cards.

He had a moment's panic as he wasn't certain which woman was his grandmother, then he saw that one of them wore a skin cast on her right leg. He'd have been told, endlessly, if his grandmother had injured herself.

"She looks wonderful. It's such a comfort to know how well she's being taken care of, and how content she is here. Ah, it's such a nice day—not as hot as it was. Do you think I could take her out into the gardens for a walk?"

"I'm sure she'd enjoy it. She'll need her medication in about an hour. If you're not back, we'll send someone out for her."

"Thank you." Confident now, he strolled over to the

table. He smiled, crouched. "Hi, Grandma. I brought you flowers. Pink roses."

She didn't look at him, not even a glance, but kept her focus on the cards in her bony hands. "I have to finish this game."

"That's all right." Stupid, ungrateful bitch. He straightened, holding the box of flowers as he watched her carefully select and play a card.

"Gin!" the other old woman called out in a surprisingly strong, steady voice. "I beat the pants off you again." She spread out her hand on the table and had their male companion swearing.

"Watch that language, you old goat." The winner turned in her chair to study Trevor as the man carefully counted points. "So you're Janine's grandson. First time I've seen you. Been here a month now, and haven't seen you visit. I'm only in for six weeks." She patted the skin cast. "Skiing accident. My granddaughter comes in every week, like clockwork. What's wrong with you?"

"I'm very busy," he said coldly, "and I don't believe it's any of your concern."

"Ninety-six my last birthday, so I like to make everything my concern. Janine's son and daughter-in-law come in twice a week, sometimes more. Too bad you're so busy."

"Come on, Grandma." Ignoring the busybody, Trevor laid his hands on the back of Janine's chair.

"I can walk! I can walk perfectly well. I don't need to be dragged around."

"Just until we get outside, in the gardens." He wanted her out, and quickly, so he laid the white box across her lap and aimed her chair toward the doorway. "It's not too hot out today, and nice and sunny. I bet you could use the fresh air."

Despite the cleanliness of the place, the floods of money that went into maintaining it, all Trevor could smell was the decay of age and sickness. It turned his stomach.

"I haven't finished counting my points."

"That's all right, Grandma. Why don't you open your present?"

"I'm not scheduled for a walk in the gardens now," she said, very precisely. "It's not on my schedule. I don't understand this change." But her fingers worried the top off the box as he steered her into the elevator.

"Oh, they're lovely! Roses. I never had much luck with roses in the garden. I always planted at least one rosebush wherever we were. Remember, honey? I had to try. My mother had the most beautiful rose garden."

"I bet she did," Trevor said without interest.

"You got to see it that once." She was animated now, and some of the beauty she'd once claimed shone through. Trevor didn't see it, but he did notice the pearl studs at her ears, the expensive shoes of soft cream-colored leather. And thought of the waste.

She continued to gently stroke the pink petals. Those who saw them pass saw a frail old woman's pleasure in the flowers, and the handsome, well-dressed young man who wheeled her.

"How old were you, baby? Four, I think." Beaming, she took one of the long-stemmed beauties out of the box to sniff. "You won't remember, but I do. I can remember so clearly. Why can't I remember yesterday?"

"Because yesterday's not important."

"I had my hair done." She fluffed at it, turning her head from side to side to show off the auburn curls. "Do you like it, baby?"

"It looks fine." He decided, on the spot, that even millions in diamonds wouldn't induce him to touch that ancient hair. How old was the bag of bones anyway? He did the math, just to occupy his mind, and was surprised to realize she was younger than the bitch at the card table.

Seemed older, he decided. Seemed ancient because she was a lunatic.

"We went back, that one time we went back." She nodded her head decisively. "Just for a few hours. I missed my mother so much it nearly broke my heart. But it was winter, and the roses weren't blooming, so you didn't get to see them again."

She laid a rosebud against her cheek. "I always planted a garden, a flower garden wherever we went. I had to try. Oh, it's bright!" Her voice quivered as he pushed the chair outside. "It's awfully bright out here."

"We'll go into the shade in just a minute. Do you know who I am, Grandma?"

"I always knew who you were. It was hard, so hard for you to keep changing, but I always knew who you were, baby. We kept each other safe, didn't we?" She reached back, patted her hand on his.

"Sure." If she wanted to think he was his father, that was fine. Better, in fact. They had a link between them unlike any other. "We kept each other safe."

"Sometimes I can barely remember. It goes in and out, like a dream. But I can always see you, Westley. No, Matthew. No, no, *Steven*." She let out a relieved breath as she latched onto the name. "Steven now, for a long time now. That's who you wanted to be, so that's who you are. I'm so proud of my boy."

"Do you remember the last time he found us? My father? Do you remember the last time you saw him?"

"I don't want to talk about that. It hurts my head." And her head swiveled from side to side as he wheeled her down the path, away from others. "Is it all right here? Are we safe here?"

"Perfectly safe. He's gone. He's dead, long dead."

"They *say*," she whispered, and it was clear she wasn't convinced.

"He can't hurt you now. But you remember that last time he came? He came at night, to the house in Ohio."

"We'd think we were safe, but he'd come. I'd never let him hurt you. Doesn't matter what he does to me, even when he hits me, but he won't touch you. He won't hurt my baby."

"Yes. Yes." Jesus, he thought, get *over* it. "But what about that last time, in Ohio? In Columbus."

"Was that the last time? I can't remember. Sometimes I think he came but it was a dream, just a bad dream. But we had to go anyway. Couldn't take a chance. They said he was dead, but how could they know? He said he'd always find you. So we had to run. Is it time to run again?"

"No. But when we were in Columbus, he came. At night. Didn't he?"

"Oh God, he was just there. There at the door. No time to run. You were scared, you held my hand so tight." She reached back again, squeezed Trevor's hand until the bones rubbed together. "I wouldn't leave you with him, not even for a minute. He'd snatch you away if he could. But he didn't want you, not yet. One day, he'd tell me. One day I'd look around and you'd be gone. I'd never find you. I couldn't let him take you away, baby. I'd never, never let him hurt you."

"He didn't." Trevor ground his teeth with impatience. "What happened the night he came to the house in Columbus?"

"I'd put you to bed. Frodo pajamas. My little Lord of the Rings. But I had to wake you up. I don't know what he'd have done if I'd refused. I brought you downstairs, and he gave you a present. You liked it, you were just a little boy, but still, you were frightened of him. 'Not to play with,' he said, 'but just to keep. One day it might be worth something.' And he laughed and laughed."

"What was it?" Excitement danced up Trevor's spine. "What did he give me?"

"He sent you away. You were too young to interest him yet. 'Go back to bed, and mind what I say. Keep it with you.' I can still see him standing there, smiling that horrible smile. Maybe he had a gun. He might've. He might've."

"Keep what?"

But she was beyond him, she was back fifty years into the fear. "Then it was just the two of us. Alone with him, and he put his hand on my throat."

She reached up with her own as her breath stuttered. "Maybe this would be the time he'd kill me. One day he'd kill me, if I didn't keep running. One day he'd take you away from me, if we didn't hide. I should go to the police."

She balled a fist, thumped it on the box. "But I'm too afraid. He'll kill us, kill us both if I go to the police. What could they do, what? He's too smart. He always said. So it's better to hide."

"Just tell me about that night. That one night."

"That night. That night. I don't forget. I can forget yesterday, but I never forget. I can hear him inside my head."

She put her hands to her ears. "Judith. My name was Judith."

Time was running out, he thought. They'd come looking for her soon, to give her medication. Worried that they'd come sooner if anyone saw her having her little fit, or heard her sniveling, he pushed the chair farther down the path, deeper into the shade.

He forced himself to touch her, to pat her thin shoulder. "Now, now. That doesn't matter. Just that one night matters. You'll feel better if you tell me about that one night. I'll feel better, too," he added, inspired. "You want me to feel better, don't you?"

"I don't want you to worry. Oh baby, I don't want you to be afraid. I'll always take care of you."

"That's right. Tell me about the night, the night in Ohio, when he came and brought me a present."

"He looked at me with those horrible cold eyes. Go ahead and run, run all you want, I'll just find you again. If the boy didn't have the present with him when he found us again, he'd kill both of us. No one would ever find us. No one would ever know. If I wanted to stay alive, if I wanted the boy to stay alive, I'd do exactly what he said. So I did. I ran, but I did what he said in case he found us again. Did he come back? In my dreams he kept finding us."

"What did he bring, damn it?" He gave the chair a vicious shake, then came around to shove his face close to hers. "Tell me what he brought."

Her eyes went wide and glassy. "The bulldozer, the bright yellow bulldozer. Kept it in the box, years and years in the box like a secret. You never played with it. Then you put it on your shelf. Why did you want it on the shelf? To show him you'd done what he told you?"

"Are you sure?" He gripped her shoulders now, the frail frame with its thin and brittle bones. "Are you goddamn sure?"

"They said you were dead." Her color went gray, her breath short and harsh. "They said you were dead, but you're not. I knew, I knew you weren't dead. I see you. Not a dream. You came back. You found us again. It's time to run. I won't let you hurt my baby. Time to run."

She struggled, and her color went from gray to dangerously red. Trevor let her shove him back, and watched dispassionately as she gained her feet. The roses spilled out of the box, strewn over the path. Eyes wild, she set off in a hitching run. Then she stumbled, fell like a limp doll into the colorful flowers and lay still in the streaming sun.

Chapter 14

Eve faced the same receptionist at Dix's offices, but the procedure moved along at a much brisker pace. The woman took one look at Eve crossing the lobby and came to attention in her chair.

"Detective Dallas."

"Lieutenant." Eve held up her badge to refresh the woman's memory. "Clear me for Chad Dix's level."

"Yes, of course. Right away." Her gaze skimmed back and forth from Eve's face to Peabody's as she cleared security. "Mr. Dix's office is on—"

"I know where it is," Eve interrupted, and strode to the elevator.

"Does it feel good to strike fear in the hearts of all people?" Peabody wondered. "Or does it feel just?"

"It feels good and just. You'll get there one day,

Peabody." Eve gave Peabody's shoulder a bolstering pat. "You'll get there."

"It's my life's ambition, sir." They stepped in. "You're not figuring Dix is part of this."

"Guy hides a fistful of diamonds in a toy truck where they've potentially sat for half a century? Nothing would surprise me. But no, Dix lacks imagination. If he has the thing, or has knowledge of its location, it's probably a fluke. If Dix knew about the diamonds and wanted more info, he'd have stuck to Samantha Gannon, played Romeo and pumped her for more data instead of twiddling his thumbs while she broke it off. No need for Tina Cobb as he had access to Gannon's place and could've conducted a dozen searches while they were still an item."

"She wouldn't have told him about Judith and Westley Crew, even if they'd stayed an item."

"No. Samantha's a stand-up. Gives her word, keeps it. Dix, though, he's a whiner. The book took Samantha's focus off him, so he's annoyed with the book. She gets media play and cocktail talk about it, so he's annoyed with her. The diamonds, as far as he's concerned, are nothing but a fluffy fantasy, and they inconvenienced him. But he's the direct link between Trevor Whittier and the Gannons. He's the twist of fate that brought it to a head."

They walked off the elevator where the perky assistant was waiting. "Lieutenant, Detective. I'm sorry, Mr. Dix isn't in the office at this time. He had an outside meeting and isn't expected back for another hour."

"Contact him, call him in."

"But—"

"Meanwhile, I need his office."

"But—"

"You want me to get a warrant? One that has your

name on it along with his, so you can both spend a few hours downtown on this bright, sunny day?"

"No. No, of course I don't. If you could just give me some idea of the nature of business you—"

"What was the nature of my business last time?"

The woman cleared her throat, glanced at Peabody. "She said murder."

"Same goes." Without waiting for assent, Eve headed in the direction of Dix's office. The assistant scrambled at her heels.

"I'll allow you inside, but I insist on being present the entire time. I can't just give you free rein. Mr. Dix deals with a great deal of confidential material."

"I'm just here to play with his toys. Call him in."

The woman unlocked the doors, then marched directly to Dix's desk to use his 'link to make the call. "He isn't answering. It's transferring to his voice mail. Mr. Dix, this is Juna. Lieutenant Dallas is in the office. She insists on speaking to you right away. If you could return my call ASAP and let me know how you want to proceed. I'm calling from your office 'link. Don't touch that!"

Her voice spiked as Eve reached out for one of the mechanical trucks. Even the cool stare Eve shot over her shoulder didn't penetrate.

"I mean it, Lieutenant. Mr. Dix's collection is very valuable. And he's very particular about it. You may be able to have me taken down to the precinct or station house or whatever you call it, but he can fire me. I need this job."

To placate the woman, Eve hooked her thumbs in her back pockets. "Any of these things a bulldozer, Peabody?"

"That little one there." Peabody used a jerk of her chin

to point. "But it's too small, and it's red. Doesn't fit Whittier's description."

"What about this?" Eve reached out, stopping just an inch from touching as the assistant's breath caught on a thin scream.

"That's a—what do you call it—cougar? Mountain lion? Bobcat!" she exclaimed. "It's called a bobcat, and don't ask me why. And there's a pumper thingee—fire truck—and, way iced, an off-planet shuttle and an airtram. See, he's got them set up in categories. Farm machines, air transports, ground transports, construction equipment, all-terrains. Look at all the little pedals and controls. Aw, look at the little hay baler. My sister has one on her farm. And there's little farm people to ride it."

Okay, maybe it wasn't just a guy thing. "That's real sweet. Maybe we should just sit on the floor here and play with all the pretty toys instead of spending our time trying to catch the mean old murdering bastard."

"Just looking," Peabody said under her breath. "To ascertain that the object in question is not in this location."

Eve turned to the assistant. "This the lot?"

"I don't know what you mean."

"Is this the whole of Mr. Dix's collection?"

"Oh no. Mr. Dix has one of the most extensive collections in the country. He's been collecting since he was a child. This is just a sampling; he keeps the most valuable at his home. He's even loaned some of the rarer pieces to museums. Several of his pieces were included in a show at the Met two years ago."

"Where is he?"

"As I said, he has an outside meeting. He should be back—"

"Where?"

Now the assistant sighed. "He's lunching with clients at the Red Room, on Thirty-third."

"He calls in, you tell him to stay where he is."

Dix had already finished his meeting and was enjoying a post-lunch martini. He'd been pleased to see Trevor's name pop on his 'link ident as the meeting had been winding down. And delighted to stretch the tedious business lunch into an entertaining personal meeting.

Enough that he'd ignored the call from his office. He deserved a break after the morning he'd put in.

"Couldn't have timed it better," he told Trevor. "I was stuck with a couple of stuffy old-liners with more money than imagination. I spent ninety minutes listening to them whine about taxes and brokerage fees and the state of the market." He sampled a fat, gin-soaked olive.

Technically, his rehabilitation forbade alcohol. But hell, a martini wasn't Zoner or poppers, for God's sake. And, as Trevor had pointed out, he deserved a small indulgence. "I'm more than ready for a break."

They sat in the dark-paneled, red-cushioned bar of the restaurant. "Didn't have a chance to talk to you much at the dinner party the other night. You left early."

"Family business." Trevor shrugged and sipped at his own martini. "Duty call on the old man."

"Ah. I know how that goes. Did you hear about this mess with Samantha? I wasn't able to talk about anything else all night. Everyone was pestering me for details."

Trevor schooled his face into a puzzled blank. "Samantha?"

"My ex. Samantha Gannon."

"Oh. Sure, sure. Long redhead. You split?"

"Ancient history. But the cops come to my office, female storm trooper bitch. Samantha's out of town, book tour. You remember that, right? The book she wrote about that old diamond heist and her family?"

"It's all coming back to me. Fascinating really."

"It gets more. While she's gone, somebody breaks into her place and kills her friend. Andrea Jacobs. Hot number."

"Christ, what a world."

"You said it. A damn shame about Andrea. You had to like her. The cops are all over me." The faint pride in the tone had Trevor smiling into his drink.

"Over you? Don't tell me the morons thought you had anything to do with it."

"Apparently. They call it routine, but I was this close to calling a lawyer." He lifted his hand, putting his thumb and forefinger together. "Later, I hear Samantha's cleaning girl got herself killed, too. You can bet I'm going to have to come up with an alibi for that one, too. Idiot cops. Jesus, I didn't even know Sam's cleaning girl. Besides, do I look like some psycho? You must've heard about all this. It's all over the news."

"I try not to watch that sort of thing. Depressing, and it has nothing to do with me. Want another?"

Dix glanced at his empty glass. He shouldn't, really. But . . . "Why the hell not? You're behind."

Trevor signaled for another drink for Dix, smiled as he lifted his barely touched martini. "I'll catch up. What does Samantha have to say about all this?"

"I haven't been able to talk to her. Can you beat that? She's gone incommunicado. Nobody knows where the hell she is."

"Somebody must," he countered.

"Not a damn soul. Smart money says the cops got her stashed somewhere." Scowling, he nudged his empty glass aside. "Probably get another damn book out of it."

"Well, she'll surface soon enough. Meanwhile, I wanted to talk to you about a piece I sold you a few months ago. The scale-model bulldozer, circa 2000."

"Beautiful piece, prime condition. I don't know how you parted with it." He grinned as he counted down the time to the second drink with a few cocktail nuts. "Even for the price you scalped me for."

"That's just the thing. I had no idea when I sold it that it was given to my father by his father. When I saw him the other night, the old man brought it up. Sentimental blah, blah, blah. He wants to come over and see it, among some of the others. I didn't have the heart to tell him I'd sold it."

"Well . . . " Dix picked up his fresh drink. "You did."

"I know, I know. I'll buy it back for the full price, and add a kicker. I don't want a big, ugly family crisis over it so it's worth it to me."

"I'd like to help you out, Trev, but I really don't want to sell it."

"Look, I'll double what you paid me for it."

"Double." Dix's eyes gleamed over the rim of his glass. "You must really want to avoid a family crisis."

"It pays to keep the old man happy. You know about his collection."

"And envy it," Dix admitted.

"I can probably talk him out of a couple of pieces."

Considering, Dix bit an olive off his swizzle stick. "I'm looking for a well driller. Circa 1985. The article they did on him in *Scale-Model Mag* said he had one, primo."

"I'll get it for you."

Dix made a sound somewhere between interest and denial. Trevor curled his hand into a fist, imagined ramming it over and over into that smug face until the blood poured.

He'd wasted enough time.

"Okay, then do me a favor. Let me borrow it for a week. I'll pay you a thousand for the use of it, and I'll get the well driller, make you a good deal on it." When Dix said nothing, just continued to sip gin, Trevor felt his control fray. "For fuck's sake, you make a grand for nothing."

"Don't get twisted. I didn't say no. I'm just trying to figure your angle. You don't even like your father."

"I can't stand the stupid son of a bitch, but he's not well. He may only have a few months left."

"No shit?"

Going with the idea, Trevor shifted on his seat, leaned in. "He finds out I sold that piece, he's going to blow. As it stands, I inherit the collection. He finds out about this, he'll probably leave it to some museum. That happens, I won't be able to sell you any of the prime pieces, will I? I lose, you lose, friend."

"When you put it that way . . . One week, Trev, and we're going to write this up. Business is business, especially when it's between friends."

"No problem. Finish your drink and we'll go get it now."

Dix checked his wrist unit. "I'm really late getting back to the office."

"So you'll be later *and* a thousand richer."

Dix lifted his glass in a toast. "Good point."

Eve's communicator signaled as she hunted for a parking spot on Thirty-third. "Dallas."

"Baxter. We got a hitch here."

"Doesn't anybody use public transportation or just stay the hell home!" Annoyed with the traffic, the jammed curb, she whipped over, flipped up her ON DUTY light and ignored the blasts of horns. Double-parked, she jerked a thumb at Peabody to get out. "What hitch?"

"Just got a call from the care facility where Whittier's mother's living. She fell or passed out. Took a header into a flower bed."

"She bad?" Eve asked as she climbed over to get out curbside rather than risk life and limb getting out the driver's-side door.

"Banged up her head, from what I'm getting, maybe fractured her elbow. They got her stabilized and sedated, but Whittier and his wife both want to go see for themselves."

"Let them go, have a couple of uniforms you pick take them and stick with them."

"There's more. Here's the kicker. She wasn't outside strolling down the garden path alone. Her grandson paid her a visit."

"Son of a bitch. Is he with her now?"

"Bastard walked off, left her lying there. Didn't tell anybody. He signed in, Dallas. Signed in, brought her flowers, talked to a couple of the attendants. He knew there was a record of him being there, but he took off. The uniforms you sent out missed him by a good half hour."

"I want the place locked down, searched."

"Already in progress."

"Left himself open." She swung into the restaurant. "He knows what he's looking for now and where to find it. He doesn't care about leaving tracks. You'll need to take the Whittiers, handle the scene there. I've got a line on something here. I'll get back to you."

"He left her lying there," Peabody repeated.

"She's lucky he didn't take the time or trouble to finish her. He's got the prize in his sights. He'll move fast now. Chad Dix," she said to the restaurant hostess. "Where's his table?"

"I beg your pardon?"

"Don't bother, I'm in a hurry." Eve slapped her badge on the podium. "Chad Dix."

"Could you be any more indiscreet?" the hostess demanded, and pushed the badge back at Eve.

"Oh yeah. Want to see?"

The hostess touched a section on her reservation screen. "He was at table fourteen. It's been turned over."

"Get me his server. Damn it." Stepping to the side, Eve yanked out her 'link and called Dix's office. "Did he come back?"

"No, Lieutenant, he's running a little late. He hasn't returned my call as yet."

"When and if, I want to hear immediately." Eve broke the connection and turned to the young, brutally clean-cut waiter. "Did you see Dix, table fourteen, leave?"

"Table for three, two of them left together about a half hour ago. One guy—guy who paid—took a call right as the meal was winding up. Excused himself. He walked over toward the restrooms. I heard him say he'd meet somebody in the bar in ten. Sounded happy about it."

"This bar?"

"Yeah. I saw him go over, get a table."

"Thanks."

Eve worked her way through the tables into the bar section, scanned the area. She snagged a waitress's elbow.

"There was a guy in here. Around thirty. About six feet, one-eighty, dark hair, medium complexion, poster-boy looks."

"Sure. Gin martini, extra dry, three olives. You just missed him."

"Was he with anyone?"

"Long, lean dream machine. Dark blond hair, great suit. Nursed half a martini to the other guy's two. Left together maybe five, ten minutes ago."

Eve turned on her heel and charged for the door. "Get Dix's home address."

"Already on it," Peabody told her. "Do you want to pull Baxter and Trueheart back?"

"No, take too long to get them back, dump the Whittiers." Eve dove into the car, swung her long legs over. "This could turn into a hostage situation in a finger snap."

"We can't be sure they're heading for Dix's home address."

"It's best guess. Tag Feeney and McNab. We'll call for more backup if it turns ugly." Since she was hemmed in by traffic, she jammed the vehicle into a straight vertical, smacked sirens and peeled out into a one-eighty six feet off the ground. "Upper East, isn't it?"

"Yeah, I got it here. Goddamn sucky navi system." Peabody cursed, rapped her fist on the dash and had the map shuddering into place across the windshield.

"You're making progress, Detective."

"Learned from the best. Sixth is your best bet. Jeez, watch the glide cart."

She missed it by a good two inches, and used the in-dash 'link to contact Roarke. "Suspect is believed to be heading to Chad Dix's residence, with Dix," she began without preamble. "We believe he's learned the location of the diamonds. Baxter and Trueheart are halfway to Long Island with the Whittiers. Feeney and McNab are being tagged. Depending on how this shakes, I might be able to use a security expert, even a civilian. You're closer than Feeney."

"What's the address?"

Peabody called it out and grabbed onto the chicken stick on her door. "ETA's five minutes, unless we end up a smear on the pavement prior to that."

"I'll be there."

Eve punched it up Sixth, weaving around vehicles with drivers too stubborn or too stupid to make way for the sirens. She was forced to slam the brakes to avoid mowing down a mob of pedestrians who surged into an intersection at the WALK sign.

They streamed by, ignoring the scream of sirens and the vicious blast of cursing she poured out her open window. Except for one grizzled old man who took the time to give her the finger.

"God love New Yorkers," Peabody commented when her heart kicked back to beating again. "They just don't give a shit."

"If I had time, I'd get Traffic to haul in every last one of those *jerks*. Goddamn it!" She rammed for vertical again, but this time the car only shuddered, shook an inch off the ground and dropped again with a thump.

"We'll be clear in a minute."

"He's going to get him inside. He's going to get him inside the apartment. Once he does . . . "

Uptown, Trevor paid off the cab in cash. It occurred to him on the way up with Dix babbling a bit drunkenly beside him that he might not be able to get out of the city, out of the country immediately and he'd already left too much of a trail.

The cops had already interviewed and dismissed good old Chad, so they were unlikely to bother with him again anytime soon. But there wasn't any point in leaving a credit trail in a cab to Dix's front door.

This was smarter. Fifteen minutes, twenty, he'd walk out with millions. He'd stroll right by the doorman and down the block, catch a cab and pick up his car from the lot on Thirty-fifth.

He needed time to get back to his own place, pick up his passport and a few essentials. And he wanted a few minutes, at least a few, to admire the diamonds in the privacy of his own home. After that, he'd vanish. Simple enough.

He'd planned all of it already. He'd vanish, not unlike Samantha Gannon had done the last few days, but with a great deal more style.

A private shuttle to Europe, where he'd rent a car with a forged ID in Paris and drive himself to Belgium and a gem dealer he'd found through the underground. He had more than enough money for that leg of the trip, and once he'd sold some of the diamonds, he'd have plenty more for the rest.

Another transaction in Amsterdam, a trip to Moscow for a third.

Crisscrossing his way from point to point, using various identifications, selling off the gems here and there—never too many at a time—until, in six months perhaps, they were liquified and he could live the life he'd always deserved to live.

He'd require some face sculpting, which was a shame as he liked his face quite a bit. But sacrifices had to be made.

He had his eye on an island in the South Seas where he could live like a king. Like a fucking god, for that matter. And there was an exciting and palatial penthouse on the sumptuous off-planet Olympus Resort that would suit him very well as a pied-à-terre.

He would never, never have to pay lip service to the rules again. Never have to kowtow to his sniveling parents, pretend an interest in his mother's obnoxious relatives or spend all those tedious hours every week in some box of an office.

He'd be free, as he was meant to be free. Claiming his rightful legacy at long, long last.

"Damn office again."

Trevor tuned in to see Dix frowning at his beeping pocket 'link.

"Screw them." Trevor laid a restraining hand on Dix's. "Let them wait."

"Yeah, screw them." With the gin sliding through his bloodstream, Dix chuckled, dropped the 'link back in his pocket. "I'm so damn indispensable, I'll have to up my fees."

He strolled into the building beside Trevor. "In fact, I think I'll take the rest of the day off. Let somebody else run on the wheel for a while. You know, I haven't had a vacation in three months. Fricking nose to the fricking grindstone."

He used his passcode to access the elevator. "You know how it is."

"That's right." As Trevor stepped into the elevator with him, his heart began to trip lightly in his chest.

"Dinner party tonight. Jan and Lucia. You going to make that?"

It all seemed so petty to him now, so bland, so *small.* "Bored."

"I hear that. Gets so it's the same thing, day after day. Same people, same talk. But you've got to do something. Could use a little excitement though, something different. Something unexpected."

Trevor smiled as they stepped off the elevator. "Careful what you wish for," he said, and laughed and laughed as Dix unlocked his door.

Eve screeched to a stop outside Dix's building. She was out of the car with her badge held up before the doorman could sputter an objection.

"Chad Dix."

"He just came in. About ten minutes ago, with a companion. I'm afraid you can't park—"

"I'm going to need a blueprint of the building and of the apartment."

"I can't help you with—"

She cut him off simply by holding up a hand, and looked over as Roarke pulled up. "I need the blueprints, and I need your security to shut down the elevators, block the stairwells on every floor. Roarke." She jerked her head, knowing he'd get results quicker. "Talk the talk. Peabody, let's get that backup."

She yanked out her communicator to contact her commander and apprise him of the situation.

By the time she was finished, she was ready to confer with McNab and Feeney in the security office. The diagram of the building was up on screen.

"We send a uniform up to the other units on this floor. We determine what other tenants are in residence and move them out quick and quiet. Then we lock down the floor again. Make that happen," she said to Peabody.

"Yes, sir."

"Emergency evac in Dix's unit, here." She tapped a finger on the screen. "Can that be sealed from this location?"

"Sure." Feeney jerked a thumb toward McNab to put him on that detail.

"He won't be going anywhere," Eve stated. "Got him locked, got him boxed. But that doesn't help Dix. We wait and Whittier remains unaware of our presence, maybe he just walks out, but odds are he kills Dix, takes his prize, then tries to walk. That's his style, that's his pattern. We move in, we've got a civilian in the crosshairs. We let Whittier know we're here and he's sealed in, he's got a hostage."

"Has to be alive to be a hostage."

She met Feeney's gaze. "Yeah, but he doesn't have to stay that way. Big place," she continued, studying the diagram of the apartment. "Chad's got himself a big-ass place. No telling where they are in it."

"They came in chummy," Feeney reminded her. "Maybe he takes the toy, leaves Dix alive."

She shook her head. "Self-preservation comes first. Dix is too big a risk, so he has to eliminate him. Easier to do it now. He's killed twice before and gotten away clean."

To better absorb the whole of it, she stepped back from the screen. "We seal it up, we seal it up tight. Isolate him. Let's go with decoy first. Delivery. See if we can get Dix to open the door. He opens it, we get him out, move in. He doesn't, we assume he's dead or incapacitated and we take the door."

She pushed at her hair. "We work on getting eyes and ears in there, but we try the decoy now. This turns into a hostage situation, you take the negotiations?" she asked Feeney.

"I'll get it set up."

"Okay, somebody get me a package. McNab, you're playing messenger. I want three of the tactical team up, positioned here, here, here." She tapped the screen again. "Feeney, security and the coms are on you. McNab, let's move."

She looked at Roarke. "Can you ditch the locks on the door without letting anyone inside know?"

"Shouldn't be a problem."

"Okay." She rolled her shoulders. "Let's rock."

Chapter 15

Inside the apartment, Dix suggested another drink. "Since I'm blowing off the day, I might as well make it worthwhile."

Calculating, Trevor watched him get out a martini shaker. The doorman had seen him come inside. Security disks would show him entering. If he needed a little extra time, it might be wise to set the stage for an accident. Alcohol in the bloodstream, a slip in the bathroom? He could and would be gone before they found the body. Gain a little more of a buffer while they investigated what would appear, on the surface, to be a drunken fall.

My God, he was clever. Wouldn't his grandfather be proud?

"Wouldn't say no to a drink. I'd really like to see the piece."

"Sure, sure." Dix waved him off while he mixed drinks.

He could send a text message from Dix's 'link to his office, Trevor decided. Set it to transmit ten minutes after he left the building. Security and the doorman would both verify his exit if need be, and the message would appear—until they dug deeper—to have been sent by Dix himself, alive and well, and alone in his apartment.

God was in the details.

He could knock him out, anywhere, then cart him into the bath, angle him, let him fall so that his head hit the corner of the tub, say.

Bathrooms were death traps, after all.

"What's the joke?" Dix asked as Trevor began to laugh.

"Nothing, nothing. Little private moment." He took the glass. His prints wouldn't matter. In fact, all the better that they show up on a glass. Nice, companionable drink with a friend. Not trying to hide a thing.

"So, what's wrong with your father?"

"He's an anal-retentive, stiff-necked, disapproving asshole."

"A little harsh, seeing as he's dying."

"What?" Trevor cursed himself as he remembered. "Being dead doesn't change what he is. I'm not playing the hypocrite over it. Sorry he's sick and all that, but I've got to live my own life. Old man's already had his, such as it is."

"Jesus." With a half laugh, Dix drank. "That's cold. I've got issues with my father. Hell, who doesn't? But I can't imagine just shrugging it off if I knew he was going to kick. Pretty young for taking the slide, isn't he?" He squinted as he tried to remember. "Can't have hit even seventy yet. Guy's just cruising into his prime."

"He hasn't ever been prime." Because it amused him, Trevor spun out the tale. Lying was nearly as fun as cheating, and cheating came very close to stealing. Killing didn't give quite the same rush. It was so damn messy. It was more of a needs-to-be-done kind of chore. But he was beginning to believe he'd enjoy ending Dix.

"Some genetic deal," he decided. "His mother passed it to him. Son of a bitch probably passed it to me. Some brain virus or happy shit. He'll go loony before he kicks. We'll have to put him away in some plush cage for mental defectives."

"God, Trevor, that's really rough." A glimmer of the man Samantha Gannon had enjoyed eked through the haze of gin. "I'm sorry. Really sorry. Look, forget the money. I didn't know it was something like this. I wouldn't feel right taking money for the loan when you've got all this on your head. Just to keep it clean, I'll draw up a paper, a receipt, but I can't take any money for it."

"That's big of you, Chad." It got better and better. "I don't want to trade on sympathy."

"Look, forget it. Your father's got a sentimental attachment to the piece, I get that. I'm the same way myself. I couldn't enjoy owning it if I thought about him being upset, under the circumstances, that it was sold off. When, ah, the rest of the collection comes to you, and you want to unload any of it, just keep me in mind."

"That's a promise. Hate to cut this short, but I really should get moving."

"Oh, sure." Dix drained the last of his drink, set the glass aside. "Come on back to the display room. You know, the reason I took this apartment was for this room. The space, the light. Samantha used to say I was obsessed."

"She's your ex, what do you care what she used to say?"

"Miss her sometimes. Haven't found anyone else who interests me half as much as she did. Talk about obsessions." He stopped, blocking the doorway. "She got so wrapped up in that book she couldn't think about anything else. Didn't want to go out, barely noticed if I was around. And what's the big deal? Just a rehash of family stories, and that bullshit about diamonds. Who cares? Could it be more yesterday?"

Yes, Trevor thought, it would be a pleasure to kill this tedious moron. "You never know what'll juice the unwashed masses."

"You're telling me. The thing's selling like it was the new Word of the Lord. You were pretty interested," he remembered. "Did you ever read that copy I passed you?"

"Scanned through it." Another reason to snip this thread, he reminded himself. And quickly. "It wasn't as compelling as I'd thought it would be. Like you said, it's yesterday. I'm a little pressed for time now, Chad."

"Sorry, sidetracked." He turned toward the wide etched-glass door. Through it Trevor could see the floating shelves, the glossy black cabinets all lined or filled with antique toys and games. "Keep it locked and passcoded. Don't trust the cleaning service."

The lock light continued to blink red, and the computer's voice informed him he'd entered an incorrect passcode.

"That's what I get on three martinis. Hold on a sec."

He reentered while Trevor stood vibrating behind him. He'd spotted the shining yellow bulldozer, parked blade-up on a wide, floating shelf.

"You're going to need a box for it," Dix commented as he rekeyed. "I keep some stored in the utility closet off the kitchen. Some padding there, too."

He paused, leaned on the glass door until Trevor imagined bashing his head against it. "You're going to have to promise to return it in the same condition, Trev. I know your father's careful, and you've got a decent collection yourself, so you know how important it is."

"I won't be playing in the dirt with it."

"I actually did that when I was a kid. Can't believe it now. Still have a couple of trucks and one of the first model airbuses. Bunged up pretty bad, but sentimental value there."

The light went to green, and the doors slid open. "Might as well get the full effect. Lights on full."

They flashed on, illuminated the nearly invisible shelves from above and below. The brightly painted toys shone bright as jewels with their ruby reds, sapphire blues, ambers and emeralds.

Trevor's gaze tracked across, and he noted the wide curved window, without privacy screen. Casually, he crossed over, as if studying the collection, and checked the windows on the building next door.

Screened. He couldn't be sure, not a hundred percent sure there wasn't someone on the other side looking over. He'd have to make certain Dix was out of view when he put him down.

"Been collecting since I was ten. Seriously since I was about twenty, but in the last five years I've really been able to indulge myself. Do you see this? Farm section. It's an elevator, John Deere replica in pressed steel at one-sixteenth scale. Circa 1960. Mint condition, and I paid a mint for it, but it was worth it. And this over here . . . " He took a few steps, swayed. "Whew. Gin's gone to my head. I'm going to grab some Sober-Up. Look around."

"Hold on." That wouldn't do, not at all. Trevor wanted the alcohol, and plenty of it, in his system. Added to that, the impairment of it would make it simpler to kill him. "What's this piece?"

It was enough to draw Dix's interest, to have him shift direction and move just out of the line of sight of the side window. "Ah, game department," Dix said cheerfully. "It's a pinball machine, toy-sized version, baseball theme. Circa 1970. Be worth more in the original box, but there's something to be said for the fact it saw a little action."

"Hmm." Trevor turned around, grinned broadly. "Now, that's a hell of a piece."

"Which?" Dix turned as well. "In the military section?"

Trevor slipped his accordion baton from his pocket. "The tank?"

"Oh yeah, that's a jewel."

As Dix took a step, Trevor snapped his wrist to extend the baton. He swung it up in an arc, then brought it down across the back of Dix's skull.

Dix fell as Trevor had positioned him, away from the shelves and out of the line of sight of the unprotected window.

"Spending this much time in your company," Trevor said as he took out a handkerchief and meticulously cleaned off the lethal wand, "I've discovered something I only suspected previously. You're an unbearably tedious geek. The world's better off without you. But first things first."

He stepped over the body, toward the toy that had

once been his father's. As he reached out, the doorbell buzzed.

His heart didn't leap, but stayed as steady as it had when he'd fractured Dix's skull. But he spun around, and calculated. To ignore it—and how he wanted to ignore it, to take what was his and see it at last—would be a mistake.

They'd been seen coming into the building, riding up in the elevator. In a building like this there would be security cameras in the halls outside. He'd have to acknowledge whoever was at the door and dismiss them.

More irritated than uneasy, he hurried to answer the summons. He engaged the security screen first and studied the thin young man in an eye-searing pink shirt covered with purple palm trees. The man looked bored and was chewing what appeared to be a fist-sized wad of gum. He carried a thick zip-bag. Even as Trevor watched, the man blew a bubble the size of a small planet and hit the buzzer again.

Trevor flicked on the intercom. "Yes?"

"Delivery for Dix. Chad Dix."

"Leave it there."

"No can do. Need a sig. Come on, buddy, I gotta get back on my horse and ride."

Cautious, Trevor widened his view. He saw the purple skinpants, the pink air boots. Where *did* these people get their wardrobes? He reached for the locks, then drew his hand back.

Wasn't worth the risk. There'd be too many questions if he accepted a package, if he signed Dix's name, or his own, for that matter.

"Leave it with the downstairs desk. They'll sign. I'm busy."

"Hey, buddy—"

"I'm busy!" Trevor snapped, and disengaged the intercom. He watched, just to be sure, and sneered as the messenger flipped up his middle finger and walked out of view.

Satisfied, he switched off the screen. It was time he accepted his own special delivery, long overdue.

"Shut down the coms and screens," Eve ordered Feeney through her communicator. "We'll have to take the door."

"Shutting them down."

She turned to McNab. "Nice job. I'd've bought it."

"If that was Dix and he wasn't under duress, he'd have opened the door." McNab drew his weapon from the base of his spine and holstered it at his side.

"Yeah. Take care of the locks," she told Roarke. "Weapons on stun," she ordered the team. "I don't want a hostage taken down. Hold fire until my command. Peabody and I go in first. You take the right. McNab, you're left. You, you, you, fan out, second wave. I want this door secured behind us. Roarke?"

"Nearly there, Lieutenant." He was crouched, delicately disarming locks and alarms with tools as thin as threads.

She squatted beside him, lowered her voice. "You're not going in."

"Yes, I don't believe I heard my name in today's lineup."

She suspected he was armed—illegally—and that he would—probably—be discreet about it. But she couldn't justify the risk. "I can't take a civilian through the door until the suspect is contained. Not with this many cops around."

He shifted his gaze and those laser blue eyes met hers.

"You don't need to explain or attempt to quell even my infamous ego."

"Good."

"And you're in."

She nodded. "You're a handy guy to have around. Now step back so we can take this asshole."

She knew it was hard for him to do just that, to stand aside while she went through the door. Whittier was almost certainly armed, and he would kill without hesitation. But Roarke straightened, moved away from the team.

She'd remember that, she thought—or she'd try to remember that—when things got heated between them as they tended to do. She'd remind herself that, when it mattered to her, he'd stepped aside so she could do her job.

"Feeney? Emergency evac?"

"It's down. He's boxed."

"We're on the door. Peabody?"

"Ready, sir."

With her weapon in her right hand, Eve eased the unsecured door open with her left. With one sharp nod, she booted it, went in low and fast.

"Police!" She swept, eyes and weapon, as Peabody peeled to the right and McNab came in from behind and shot left. "Trevor Whittier, this is the police. This building is surrounded. All exits are blocked. Come out, hands up and in full view."

She used hand signals to direct her team to other areas, other rooms as she moved forward.

"You've got nowhere to go, Trevor."

"Stay back! I'll kill him. I have a hostage. I have Dix, and I'll kill him."

She held up a closed fist, signaling her team to stop, to hold positions, then eased around the corner.

"I said I'll kill him."

"I heard you." Eve stayed where she was, looking through the open glass doors. Light glittered on the toy-decked shelves and on the blood smeared on the white floor.

Trevor sat in the center of it, the prize he'd killed for beside him. He had an arm hooked around Dix's neck, and a knife to his throat.

Dix's eyes were closed, and there was blood on the otherwise spotless floor. But she could see the subtle rise and fall of Dix's chest. Alive then. Still alive.

They looked like two overgrown boys who'd played just a little too hard and rough.

She kept her weapon trained and steady. "Looks like you already did. Kill him."

"He's breathing." Trevor dug the point of the knife into flesh, carving a shallow slice. Blood dribbled over the blade. "I can change that, and I will. Put down that weapon."

"That's my line, Trevor. There are two ways you can leave this room. You can leave it walking, or we can carry you out."

"I'll kill him first. Even if you stun me, I'll have time to slit his throat. You know it, or you'd have hit me already. You want to keep him alive, you back out. You back out now!"

"Kill him and the only thing I put down is you. Do you want to die today, Trevor?"

"You want him to die?" He jerked Dix's head back, and stirring slightly, Dix moaned. "If you don't clear this place, that's what's going to happen. We start negotiating, and we start now. Back out."

"You've been watching too many vids. You think I'm

going to deal with you over a single civilian who's probably going to die anyway from the looks of things? Grab some reality, Trev." She smiled when she said it, wide and white. "I got pictures in my head of the two women you killed. It'd just fucking make my day to end you. So go ahead, finish him off."

"You're bluffing. Do you think I'm *stupid*?"

"Yeah, actually. You're sitting there on the floor trying to talk me into negotiating when you're holding a knife, and I have this handy little thing. You know what they do when they're on full? It's not pretty. And I'm getting a little tired of this conversation. You want to die over a toy truck, your choice."

"You have no idea what I have. Clear the others out. I know there are others out there. Clear them out, and we'll talk. I'll make you the deal of a lifetime."

"You mean the diamonds." She gave a quick, rude snort. "Jesus, you *are* stupid. I gave you too much credit. I've already got them, Trevor. That's a plant. Set you up. I set you up and used that clown for bait. Worked like a charm. It's just an old toy, Trevor, and you fell for it."

"You're lying!" There was shock now, and there was anger, clear on his face.

As his head whipped around toward the bright yellow truck, and his knife hand lowered a fraction, Eve shot a stream into his right shoulder. His arm spasmed, and the knife fell from his shaking fingers.

Even as his body jerked back in reaction, she was across the room, with her weapon pressed to his throat. "Gee, you caught me. I was lying."

She was glad he was conscious, glad she could see it sink in. Tears of rage gathered in the corners of his eyes as she dragged him clear of Dix.

"Suspect's contained. Get medical in here!" It gave her a dark satisfaction to flip him onto his belly, to drag his hands back for the restraints.

She'd lied about the diamonds, but not about the pictures in her head. "Andrea Jacobs," she said in a whisper, close to his ear. "Tina Cobb. Think about them, you worthless fuck. Think about them for the rest of your miserable life."

"I want what's mine! I want what belongs to me!"

"So did they. You have the right to remain silent," she began, and flipped him back over so she could watch his face while she read him his rights.

"You got all that?"

"I want a lawyer."

"There you go, being predictable." But she wanted a few moments with him first. She looked over her shoulder where the medical techs were readying Dix for transport. "How's he doing?"

"Got a good chance."

"Isn't that happy news, Trev? You may only get an attempted murder hit on this one. That's no big after the two first degrees. What's a few years tacked onto two life terms anyway?"

"You can't prove anything."

She leaned close. "Yes, I can. Got you with both murder weapons. Really appreciate your bringing them both along today."

She watched his eye track over to where Peabody was bagging the baton.

Leaning back again, she laid her hand on the bulldozer, rolled it gently back and forth. "You really figure they're in here? All those shiny stones? Be a joke on you, wouldn't it, if your grandfather pulled a fast one. Maybe this is just a kid's toy. Everything you did, all the years you'll pay for it would be for nothing. You ever consider that?"

"They're in there. And they're mine."

"That's a matter of debate, isn't it?" Idly, she worked the lever that brought the blade up and down. "Pretty freaking arrogant of him to pass this to a kid. Guess you take after him."

"It was brilliant." There were lawyers, he thought. His father would pay for the best. "Better than a vault. Didn't they do exactly what he told them? Even after he was dead, they kept it."

"Got me there. You want me to tell you where you weren't brilliant? Right from the start. You didn't do your homework, Trevor, didn't dot all your *i*'s. Your grandfather wouldn't have been so sloppy. He'd have known Samantha Gannon had a house sitter. Those diamonds slipped through your fingers the instant you put that knife to Andrea Jacobs's throat. Sooner really. Then killing Tina Cobb on your father's job site."

She enjoyed watching his face go gray in shock. It was small of her, she admitted, but she enjoyed it. "That was sloppy, too. You just needed a little more forethought. Take her over to New Jersey, say. Romantic picnic in the woods, get what you needed from her, take her out, bury her." Eve shrugged. "But you didn't think it through."

"You can't trace her back to me. No one ever saw—" He cut himself off.

"No one ever saw you together? Wrong. I got an eyewitness. And when Dix comes out of it, he'll tell us how he talked to you about Gannon's book. Your father will fill in the blanks, testifying how he told you about your grandfather, about the diamonds."

"He'll never testify against me."

"Your grandmother's alive." She saw his eyes flicker. "He's with her now, and he knows you left his mother, the woman who spent her life trying to protect him, lying in the dirt like garbage. What would it have cost you? Fifteen minutes, a half hour? You call for help, play the concerned, devoted grandson. Then you slip away. But she wasn't worth even that much effort from you. When you think about it, she was still protecting her son. Only this time, she protected him from you."

She lifted the bulldozer, held it between them. "History repeats. You're going to pay, just the way your grandfather paid. You're going to know, just the way he knew, that those big, bright diamonds are forever out of his reach. Which is worse? I wonder. The cage or the knowing?"

She got to her feet, stared down at him. "We'll talk again soon."

"I want to see them."

Eve picked up the truck, tucked it under her arm. "I know. Book him," she ordered, and strolled away while Trevor cursed her.

Epilogue

It wasn't what she'd call standard procedure, but it seemed right. She could even make a case for logical. Precautions and security measures had to be taken, and paperwork filed. As all parties were cooperative, the red tape was minimal.

She had a room full of civilians in conference room A, Cop Central. Plenty of cops, too. Her investigative team were all present, as was the commander.

It had been his idea to alert the media—that was the political side that irked her, even though she understood the reasoning. Understanding or not, she'd have a damn press conference to deal with afterward.

For now, the media hounds were cooling their heels, and despite the number of people in the room, it was very quiet.

She'd put names to faces. Samantha Gannon, of

course, and her grandparents, Laine and Max, who stood holding hands.

They looked fit, she thought, and rock steady. And unified. What was that like? she wondered. To have more than half a century together and still have, still need that connection?

Steven Whittier and his wife were there. She hadn't known exactly what to expect by mixing those two elements, but sometimes people surprised you. Not by being morons or assholes, that never surprised her. But by being decent.

Max Gannon had shaken Steven Whittier's hand. Not stiffly, but with warmth. And Laine Gannon had kissed his cheek, and had leaned in to murmur something in his ear that had caused Steven's eyes to swim.

The moment—the decency of that moment—burned Eve's throat. Her eyes met Roarke's, and she saw her reaction mirrored in them.

With or without jewels, a circle had closed.

"Lieutenant." Whitney nodded to her.

"Yes, sir. The New York Police and Security Department appreciates your cooperation and your attendance here today. That cooperation has, in a very large part, assisted this department in closing this case. The deaths of . . ."

She'd had very specific, very straight-lined statements prepared. She let them go, and said what came into her mind.

"Jerome Myers, William Young, Andrea Jacobs, Tina Cobb. Their deaths can never be resolved, only the investigation into those deaths can be resolved. It's the best we can do. Whatever they did, whoever they were, their lives were taken, and there's never a resolution to murder.

The officers in this room—Commander Whitney; Captain Feeney; Detectives Baxter, McNab, Peabody; Officer Trueheart—have done what can be done to resolve the case and find justice for the dead. That's our job and our duty. The civilians here—the Gannons, the Whittiers, Roarke—have given time, cooperation and expertise. Because of that, it's done, and we move on."

She took the bulldozer from the box she'd unsealed. It had been scanned, of course. She'd already seen what was in it on screen. But this, she knew, was personal.

"Or in this case, we move back. Mr. Whittier, for the record. This object has been determined to be your property. You've given written permission for it to be dismantled. Is that correct?"

"Yes."

"And you've agreed to do this dismantling yourself at this time."

"Yes. Before I . . . I'd like to say, to apologize for—"

"It isn't necessary, Steven." Laine spoke quietly, her hand still caught in Max's. "Lieutenant Dallas is right. Some things can never be resolved, so we can only do our best."

Saying nothing, he nodded and picked up the tools on the conference table. While he worked, Laine spoke again. Her voice was lighter now, as if she'd determined to lift the mood.

"Do you remember, Max, sitting at the kitchen table with that silly ceramic dog?"

"I do." He brought their joined hands to his lips. "And that damn piggy bank. All it took was a couple whacks with a hammer. Lot more work involved here." He patted Steve's shoulder.

"You were a cop before," Eve put in.

"Before the turn of the century, then I went private. Don't imagine it's all that different. You got slicker toys and tools, but the job's always been the job. If I was born a few decades later, I'd've been an e-man." He grinned at Feeney. "Love to see your setup here."

"I'd be glad to give you a personal tour. You're still working private, aren't you?"

"When a case interests me."

"They almost always do," Laine put in. "Once a cop," she said with a laugh.

"Tell me about it," Roarke agreed.

Metal pieces clattered to the table and cut off conversation.

"There's padding inside." Steve cleared his throat. "It's clear enough to get it out." But he pushed away from the table. "I don't want to do it. Mrs. Gannon?"

"No. We've done our part. All of us. It's police business now, isn't it? It's for Lieutenant Dallas now. But I hope you'll do it fast, so I can breathe again."

To solve the matter, Eve lifted the detached body of the truck, reached in to tug out the padding. She laid it on the table, pulled it apart and picked up the pouch nested inside.

She opened the pouch and poured the stones into her hand.

"I didn't really believe it." Samantha let out a trapped breath. "Even after all this, I didn't really believe it. And there they are."

"After all this time." Laine watched as Eve dripped the glittering diamonds onto the pouch. "My father would have laughed and laughed. Then tried to figure how he could palm a couple of them on his way out the door."

Peabody edged in, and Eve gave her a moment to

goggle before she elbowed her back. "They'll need to be verified, authenticated and appraised, but—"

"Mind?" Without waiting, Roarke plucked one up, drew a loupe out of his pocket. "Mmm, spectacular. First water, full-cut, about seven carats. Probably worth twice what it was when it was tucked away. There'll be all sorts of interesting and complicated maneuvers, I imagine, between the insurance company and the heirs of the original owners."

"That's not our problem. Put it back."

"Of course, Lieutenant." He laid it with the others.

It took Eve more than an hour to get through the feeding frenzy of the media. But it didn't surprise her to find Roarke in her office when it was done. He was kicked back in her chair, his elegantly shod feet on her desk while he fiddled with his PPC.

"You have an office of your own," she reminded him.

"I do, yes, and it has a great deal more ambiance than yours. Then again, a condemned subway car has more ambiance than yours. I watched your media bout," he added. "Nice job, Lieutenant."

"My ears are ringing. And the only feet that are supposed to be on my desk are mine." But she left his there, sat on the corner.

"This is tough on the Whittiers," he commented.

"Yeah. It's a hard line they've drawn. I guess it's not easy, whatever the circumstances, to turn your back on your son. Junior's not going to sponge off Mom and Dad for his legal fees. He's going down, all the way down, and they have to watch it."

"They loved him, gave him a good home, and he wasted it. His choice."

"Yeah." The images of Andrea Jacobs and Tina Cobb held in her head a moment, then she put them away. "Just answer one question, no bullshit. You didn't switch that diamond, did you?"

"You wired?" he said with a grin.

"Damn it, Roarke."

"No, I didn't switch the diamond. Could have—just for fun, of course, but you get so cross about that sort of thing. I think I'll buy you a couple of them though."

"I don't need—"

"Yammer, yammer, yammer," he said with a wave of his hand, and had her eyes going huge. "Come sit on my lap."

"If you think that's even a remote possibility, you need immediate professional help."

"Ah well. I'm going to buy some of those diamonds," he continued. "They need the blood washed from them, Eve. They may only be things, as Laine Gannon said, but they're symbols, and they should be clean ones. You can't resolve death, as you said. You do what you can. And when you wear the stones that cost all those lives, they'll be clean again. They'll be a kind of badge that says someone stood for the victims. Someone always will. And whenever you wear them, you'll remember that."

She stared at him. "God, you get me. You get right to the core of me."

"When I see you wear them, I'll remember it, too. And know that someone is you." He laid a hand over hers. "Do you know what I want from you, darling Eve?"

"Sweet-talk all you want, I'm still not sitting in your lap in Central. Ever."

He laughed. "Another fantasy shattered. What I want from you is the fifty years and more I saw between the

Gannons today. The love and understanding, the memories of a lifetime. I want that from you."

"We've got one year in. Second one's going pretty well so far."

"No complaints."

"I'm going to clock out. Why don't we both ditch work for the rest of the day—"

"It's already half-six, Lieutenant. Your shift's over anyway."

She frowned at her wrist unit and saw he was right. "It's the thought that counts. Let's go home, put a little more time into year two."

He took her hand as they walked out together. "What's done with the diamonds until they're turned over to whoever might be the legal owner?"

"Sealed, logged, scanned and locked in an evidence box that is locked in one of the evidence vaults in the bowels of this place." She slanted him a look. "Good thing you don't steal anymore."

"Isn't it?" He slung a friendly arm around her shoulders as they took the glide. "Isn't it just?"

And deep, deep under the streets of the city, in the cool, quiet dark, the diamonds waited to shine again.

A heroic belch of thunder followed the strange little man into the shop. He glanced around apologetically, as if the rude noise were his responsibility rather than nature's, and fumbled a package under his arm so he could close a black-and-white-striped umbrella.

Both umbrella and man dripped, somewhat mournfully, onto the neat square of mat just inside the door while the cold spring rain battered the streets and sidewalks on the other side. He stood where he was, as if not entirely sure of his welcome.

Laine turned her head and sent him a smile that held only warmth and easy invitation. It was a look her friends would have called her polite shopkeeper's smile.

Well, damn it, she *was* a polite shopkeeper—and at the moment that label was being sorely tested.

If she'd known the rain would bring customers into the

store instead of keeping them away, she wouldn't have given Jenny the day off. Not that she minded business. A woman didn't open a store if she didn't want customers, whatever the weather. And a woman didn't open one in Small Town, U.S.A., unless she understood she'd spend as much time chatting, listening and refereeing debates as she would ringing up sales.

And that was fine, Laine thought, that was good. But if Jenny had been at work instead of spending the day painting her toenails and watching soaps, Jenny would've been the one stuck with the Twins.

Darla Price Davis and Carla Price Gohen had their hair tinted the same ashy shade of blond. They wore identical slick blue raincoats and carried matching hobo bags. They finished each other's sentences and communicated in a kind of code that included a lot of twitching eyebrows, pursed lips, lifted shoulders and head bobs.

What might've been cute in eight-year-olds was just plain weird in forty-eight-year-old women.

Still, Laine reminded herself, they never came into Remember When without dropping a bundle. It might take them hours to drop it, but eventually the sales would ring. There was little that lifted Laine's heart as high as the ring of the cash register.

Today they were on the hunt for an engagement present for their niece, and the driving rain and booming thunder hadn't stopped them. Nor had it deterred the drenched young couple who—they'd said—had detoured into Angel's Gap on a whim on their way to D.C.

Or the wet little man with the striped umbrella who looked, to Laine's eye, a bit frantic and lost.

So she added a little more warmth to her smile. "I'll be

with you in just a few minutes," she called out, and turned her attention back to the Twins.

"Why don't you look around a little more," Laine suggested. "Think it over. As soon as I—"

Darla's hand clamped on her wrist, and Laine knew she wasn't going to escape.

"We need to decide. Carrie's just about your age, sweetie. What would *you* want for your engagement gift?"

Laine didn't need to transcribe the code to understand it was a not-so-subtle dig. She was, after all, twenty-eight, and not married. Not engaged. Not, at the moment, even dating particularly. This, according to the Price twins, was a crime against nature.

"You know," Carla piped up, "Carrie met her Paul at Kawanian's spaghetti supper last fall. You really should socialize more, Laine."

"I really should," she agreed with a winning smile. *If I want to hook up with a balding, divorced CPA with a sinus condition.* "I know Carrie's going to love whatever you choose. But maybe an engagement gift from her aunts should be something more personal than the candlesticks. They're lovely, but the dresser set's so feminine." She picked up the silver-backed brush from the set they were considering. "I imagine another bride used this on her wedding night."

"More personal," Darla began. "More—"

"Girlie. Yes! We could get the candlesticks for—"

"A wedding gift. But maybe we should look at the jewelry before we buy the dresser set. Something with pearls? Something—"

"Old she could wear on her wedding day. Put the candlesticks *and* the dresser set aside, honey. We'll take a look at the jewelry before we decide anything."

The conversation bounced like a tennis ball served and volleyed out of two identical coral-slicked mouths. Laine congratulated herself on her skill and focus as she was able to keep up with who said what.

"Good idea." Laine lifted the gorgeous old Dresden candlesticks. No one could say the Twins didn't have taste, or were shy of heating up their plastic.

She started to carry them to the counter when the little man crossed her path.

She was eye to eye with him, and his were a pale, washed-out blue reddened by lack of sleep or alcohol or allergies. Laine decided on lost sleep as they were also dogged by heavy bags of fatigue. His hair was a grizzled mop gone mad with the rain. He wore a pricey Burberry topcoat and carried a three-dollar umbrella. She assumed he'd shaved hurriedly that morning as he'd missed a patch of stubbly gray along his jaw.

"Laine."

He said her name with a kind of urgency and intimacy that had her smile turning to polite confusion.

"Yes? I'm sorry, do I know you?"

"You don't remember me." His body seemed to droop. "It's been a long time, but I thought . . . "

"Miss!" the woman on her way to D.C. called out. "Do you ship?"

"Yes, we do." She could hear the Twins going through one of their shorthand debates over earrings and brooches, and sensed an impulse buy from the D.C. couple. And the little man stared at her with a hopeful intimacy that had her skin chilling.

"I'm sorry, I'm a little swamped this morning." She

sidestepped to the counter to set down the candlesticks. Intimacy, she reminded herself, was part of the rhythm of small towns. The man had probably been in before, and she just couldn't place him. "Is there something specific I can help you with, or would you like to browse awhile?"

"I need your help. There isn't much time." He drew out a card, pressed it into her hand. "Call me at that number, as soon as you can."

"Mr. . . . " She glanced down at the card, read his name. "Peterson, I don't understand. Are you looking to sell something?"

"No. No." His laugh bounced toward hysterical and had Laine grateful for the customers crowded into the store. "Not anymore. I'll explain everything, but not now." He looked around the shop. "Not here. I shouldn't have come here. Call the number."

He clamped a hand over hers in a way that had Laine fighting an instinct to jerk free. "Promise."

He smelled of rain and soap and . . . Brut, she realized. And the aftershave had some flicker of memory trying to light in her brain. Then his fingers tightened on hers. "Promise," he repeated in a harsh whisper, and she saw only an odd man in a wet coat.

"Of course."

She watched him go to the door, open the cheap umbrella. And let out a sigh of relief when he scurried out into the rain. *Weird* was her only thought, but she studied the card for a moment.

His name was printed, Jasper R. Peterson, but the phone number was handwritten beneath and underscored twice, she noted.

Pushing the card into her pocket, she started over to give the traveling couple a friendly nudge, when the sound of screeching brakes on wet pavement and shocked screams had her spinning around. There was a hideous noise, a hollow thud she'd never forget. Just as she'd never forget the sight of the strange little man in his fashionable coat slamming against her display window.

She bolted out the door, into the streaming rain. Footsteps pounded on the pavement, and somewhere close was the crunching sound of metal striking metal, glass shattering.

"Mr. Peterson." Laine gripped his hand, bowed her body over his in a pathetic attempt to shield his bloodied face from the rain. "Don't move. Call an ambulance!" she shouted and yanked off her jacket to cover him as best she could.

"Saw him. Saw him. Shouldn't have come. Laine."

"Help's coming."

"Left it for you. He wanted me to get it to you."

"It's all right." She scooped her dripping hair out of her eyes and took the umbrella someone offered. She angled it over him, leaned down closer as he tugged weakly on her hand.

"Be careful. I'm sorry. Be careful."

"I will. Of course I will. Just try to be quiet now, try to hold on, Mr. Peterson. Help's coming."

"You don't remember." Blood trickled out of his mouth as he smiled. "Little Lainie." He took a shuddering breath, coughed up blood. She heard the sirens as he began to sing in a thin, gasping voice.

"Pack up all my care and woe," he crooned, then wheezed. "Bye, bye, blackbird."

She stared at his battered face as her already chilled skin began to prickle. Memories, so long locked away, opened. "Uncle Willy? Oh my God."

"Used to like that one. Screwed up," he said breathlessly. "Sorry. Thought it'd be safe. Shouldn't've come."

"I don't understand." Tears burned her throat, streamed down her cheeks. He was dying. He was dying because she hadn't known him, and she'd sent him out into the rain. "I'm sorry. I'm so sorry."

"He knows where you are now." His eyes rolled back. "Hide the pooch."

"What?" She leaned closer yet until her lips almost brushed his. "What?" But the hand she had clutched in hers went limp.

Paramedics brushed her aside. She heard their short, pithy dialogue—medical codes she'd grown accustomed to hearing on television, could almost recite herself. But this was real. The blood washing away in the rain was real.

She heard a woman sobbing and saying over and over in a strident voice, "He ran right in front of me. I couldn't stop in time. He just ran in front of the car. Is he all right? Is he all right? Is he all right?"

No, Laine wanted to say. He's not.

"Come inside, honey." Darla put an arm around Laine's shoulders, drew her back. "You're soaked. You can't do anything more out here."

"I should do something." She stared down at the broken umbrella, its cheerful stripes marked with grime now, and drops of blood.

She should have settled him down in front of the fire. Given him a hot drink and let him warm and dry himself in front of the little hearth. Then he'd be alive. Telling her stories and silly jokes.

But she hadn't recognized him, and so he was dying.

She couldn't go in, out of the rain, and leave him alone

with strangers. But there was nothing to be done but watch, helplessly, while the paramedics fought and failed to save the man who'd once laughed at her knock-knock jokes and sung silly songs. He died in front of the shop she'd worked so hard to build, and laid at her door all the memories she thought she'd escaped.

She was a businesswoman, a solid member of the community, and a fraud. In the back room of her store, she poured two cups of coffee and knew she was about to lie to a man she considered a friend. And deny all knowledge of one she'd loved.

She did her best to steady herself, ran her hands through the damp mass of bright red hair normally worn in a shoulder-sweeping bob. She was pale, and the rain had washed away the makeup, always carefully applied, so freckles stood out on her narrow nose and across her cheekbones. Her eyes, a bright Viking blue, were glassy with shock and grief. Her mouth, just a hair too wide for her angular face, wanted to tremble.

In the little giltwood mirror on the wall of her office, she studied her reflection. And saw herself for what she was. Well, she would do what she needed to do to survive. Willy would certainly understand that. Do what came first, she told herself, then think about the rest.

She sucked in a breath, let out a shudder, then lifted the coffee. Her hands were nearly steady as she went into the main shop and prepared to give false testimony to Angel's Gap's chief of police.

"Sorry it took so long," she apologized as she carried the mugs to where Vince Burger stood by the little clinker fireplace.

He was built like a bear with a great shock of white-blond hair that stood nearly straight up, as if surprised to find itself on top of the wide, comfortable face. His eyes, a faded blue and fanned with squint lines, were full of compassion.

He was Jenny's husband, and had become a kind of brother to Laine. But for now she reminded herself he was a cop, and everything she'd worked for was on the line.

"Why don't you sit down, Laine? You've had a bad shock."

"I feel sort of numb." That was true enough, she didn't have to lie about everything. But she walked over to sip her coffee and stare out at the rain so she wouldn't have to meet those sympathetic eyes. "I appreciate your coming in to take my statement yourself, Vince. I know you're busy."

"Figured you'd be more comfortable."

Better to lie to a friend than a stranger, she thought bitterly. "I don't know what I can tell you. I didn't see the actual accident. I heard . . . I heard brakes, screams, an awful thud, then I saw . . . " She didn't shut her eyes. If she shut them, she'd see it again. "I saw him hit the window, like he'd been thrown against it. I ran out, stayed with him until the paramedics came. They were quick. It seemed like hours, but it was only minutes."

"He was in here before the accident."

Now she did close her eyes, and prepared to do what she had to do to protect herself. "Yes. I had several customers this morning, which proves I should never give Jenny a day off. The Twins were in, and a couple driving through on their way to D.C. I was busy when he came in. He browsed around for a while."

"The woman from out of town said she thought you knew each other."

"Really?" Turning now, Laine painted a puzzled expression on her face, as a clever artist might on a portrait. She crossed back, sat on one of the two elbow chairs she'd arranged in front of the fire. "I don't know why."

"An impression," Vince said with a shrug. Always mindful of his size, he sat, slow and careful, in the matching chair. "Said he took your hand."

"Well, we *shook* hands, and he gave me his card." Laine pulled it out of her pocket, forced herself to keep her attention on Vince's face. The fire was crackling with warmth, and though she felt its heat on her skin, she was cold. Very cold. "He said he'd like to speak with me when I wasn't so busy. That he might have something to sell. People often do," she added, offering Vince the card. "Which is how I stay in business."

"Right." He tucked the card into his breast pocket. "Anything strike you about him?"

"Just that he had a beautiful topcoat, and a silly umbrella—and that he didn't seem like the sort to wander around small towns. Had city on him."

"So did you a few years ago. In fact . . ." He narrowed his gaze, reached out and rubbed a thumb over her cheek. "Still got some stuck to you."

She laughed, because it's what he wanted. "I wish I could be more help, Vince. It's such an awful thing to happen."

"I can tell you, we got four different witness statements. All of them have the guy running straight out into the street, dead in front of that car. Like he was spooked or something. He seem spooked to you, Laine?"

"I wasn't paying enough attention. The fact is, Vince, I basically brushed him off when I realized he wasn't here to shop. I had customers." She shook her head when her voice broke. "It seems so callous now."

The hand Vince laid over hers in comfort made her feel foul. "You didn't know what was coming. You were the first to get to him."

"He was right outside." She had to take a deep gulp of coffee to wash the grief out of her throat. "Almost on the doorstep."

"He spoke to you."

"Yes." She reached for her coffee again. "Nothing that made much sense. He said he was sorry, a couple of times. I don't think he knew who I was or what happened. I think he was delirious. The paramedics came and . . . and he died. What will you do now? I mean, he's not from around here. The phone number's New York. I wonder, I guess I wonder if he was just driving through, where he was going, where he was from."

"We'll be looking into all that so we can notify his next of kin." Rising, Vince laid a hand on her shoulder. "I'm not going to tell you to put it out of your mind, Laine. You won't be able to, not for a while. I'm going to tell you that you did all you could. Can't do more than all you could."

"Thanks. I'm going to close up for the day. I want to go home."

"Good idea. Want a ride?"

"No. Thanks." It was guilt as much as affection that had her rising on her toes to press a kiss to his cheek. "Tell Jenny I'll see her tomorrow."

His name, at least the name she'd known, was Willy Young. Probably William, Laine thought as she drove up the pitted gravel lane. He hadn't been her real uncle—as far as she knew—but an honorary one. One who'd always had red licorice in his pocket for a little girl.

She hadn't seen him in nearly twenty years, and his hair had been brown then, his face a bit rounder. There'd always been a spring in his step.

Small wonder she hadn't recognized him in the bowed and nervy little man who'd come into her shop.

How had he found her? *Why* had he?

Since he'd been, to her knowledge, her father's closest friend, she assumed he was—as was her father—a thief, a scam artist, a small-time grifter. Not the sort of connections a respectable businesswoman wanted to acknowledge.

And why the hell should that make her feel small and guilty?

She slapped on the brakes and sat, brooding through the steady *whoosh* of her wipers at the pretty house on the pretty rise.

She loved this place. Hers. Home. The two-story frame house was, strictly speaking, too large for a woman on her own. But she loved being able to ramble around in it. She'd loved every minute she'd spent meticulously decorating each room to suit herself. And only herself.

Knowing, as she did, she'd never, ever have to pack up all her belongings at a moment's notice to the tune of "Bye Bye Blackbird" and run.

She loved being able to putter around the yard, planting gardens, pruning bushes, mowing the grass, yanking the weeds. Ordinary things. Simple, *normal* things for a woman who'd spent the first half of her life doing little that was normal.

She was entitled to this, wasn't she? To being Laine Tavish and all that meant? The business, the town, the house, the friends, the *life*. She was entitled to the woman she'd made herself into.

It wouldn't have helped Willy for her to have told Vince the truth. Nothing would have changed for him, and everything might have changed for her. Vince would find out, soon enough, that the man in the county morgue wasn't Jasper R. Peterson but William Young, and however many aka's that went with it.

There'd be a criminal record. She knew Willy had done at least one stint alongside her father. "Brothers in arms," her father had called them, and she could still hear his big, booming laugh.

Because it infuriated her, she slammed out of the car. She made the house in a dash, fumbled out her keys.

She calmed, almost immediately, when the door was closed at her back and the house surrounded her. Just the quiet of it, the scents of lemon oil rubbed into wood by her own hand, the subtle sweetness of spring flowers brought in from her own yard stroked her frayed nerves.

She set her keys in the raku dish on the entry table, pulled her cell phone out of her purse and plugged it into the recharger. Slipped out of her shoes, out of her jacket, which she draped over the newel post, and set her purse on the bottom step.

Following routine, she walked back to the kitchen. Normally, she'd have put on the kettle for tea and looked through the mail she'd picked up from the box at the foot of the lane while the water heated.

But today, she poured a big glass of wine.

And drank it standing at the sink, looking through the window at her backyard.

She'd had a yard—a couple of times—as a kid. She remembered one in . . . Nebraska? Iowa? What did it matter, she thought and took a healthy gulp of wine. She'd liked the yard because it had a big old tree right in the middle, and he'd hung an old tire from it on a big thick rope.

He'd pushed her so high she'd thought she was flying.

She wasn't sure how long they'd stayed and didn't remember the house at all. Most of her childhood was a blur of places and faces, of car rides, a flurry of packing up. And him, her father, with his big laugh and wide hands, with his irresistible grin and careless promises.

She'd spent the first decade of her life desperately in love with the man, and the rest of it doing everything she could to forget he existed.

If he was in trouble, again, it was none of her concern.

She wasn't Jack O'Hara's little Lainie anymore. She was Laine Tavish, solid citizen.

She eyed the bottle of wine and with a shrug poured a second glass. A grown woman could get toasted in her own kitchen, by God, especially when she'd watched a ghost from the past die at her feet.

Carrying the glass, she walked to the mudroom door, to answer the hopeful whimpering on the other side.

He came in like a cannon shot—a hairy, floppy-eared cannon shot. His paws planted themselves at her belly, and the long snout bumped her face before the tongue slurped out to cover her cheeks with wet and desperate affection.

"Okay, okay! Happy to see you, too." No matter how low her mood, a welcome home by Henry, the amazing hound, never failed to lift it.

She'd sprung him from the joint, or so she liked to think. When she'd gone to the pound two years before, it had been with a puppy in mind. She'd always wanted a cute, gamboling little bundle she'd train from the ground up.

But then she'd seen him—big, ungainly, stunningly homely with his mud-colored fur. A cross, she'd thought, between a bear and an anteater. And she'd been lost the minute he'd looked through the cage doors and into her eyes.

Everybody deserves a chance, she'd thought, and so she sprang Henry from the joint. He'd never given her a reason to regret it. His love was absolute, so much so that he continued to look adoringly at her even when she filled his bowl with kibble.

"Chow time, pal."

At the signal, Henry dipped his head into his bowl and got serious.

She should eat, too. Something to sop up some of the wine, but she didn't feel like it. Enough wine swimming around in her bloodstream and she wouldn't be able to think, to wonder, to worry.

She left the inner door open, but stepped into the mudroom to check the outside locks. A man could shimmy through the dog door, if he was determined to get in, but Henry would set up the alarm.

He howled every time a car came up the lane, and though he would punish the intruder with slobber and delight—after he finished trembling in terror—she was never surprised by a visitor. And never, in her four years in Angel's Gap, had she had any trouble at home, or at the shop.

Until today, she reminded herself.

She decided to lock the mudroom door after all, and let Henry out the front for his evening run.

She thought about calling her mother, but what was

the point? Her mother had a good, solid life now, with a good, solid man. She'd earned it. What point was there in breaking into that nice life and saying, "Hey, I ran into Uncle Willy today, and so did a Jeep Cherokee."

She took her wine with her upstairs. She'd fix herself a little dinner, take a hot bath, have an early night.

She'd close the book on what had happened that day.

Left it for you, he'd said, she remembered. Probably delirious. But if he'd left her anything, she didn't want it.

She already had everything she wanted.

Max Gannon slipped the attendant a twenty for a look at the body. In Max's experience a picture of Andrew Jackson cut through red tape quicker than explanations and paperwork and more levels of bureaucracy.

He'd gotten the bad news on Willy from the motel clerk at the Red Roof Inn where he'd tracked the slippery little bastard. The cops had already been there, but Max had invested the first twenty of the day for the room number and key.

The cops hadn't taken his clothes yet, nor from the looks of it done much of a search. Why would they on a traffic accident? But once they ID'd Willy, they'd be back and look a lot closer.

Willy hadn't unpacked, Max noted as he took stock of the room. Socks and underwear and two dress shirts were still neatly folded in the single Louis Vuitton bag. Willy had been a tidy one, and he'd loved his name brands.

He'd hung a suit in the closet. Banker gray, single-breasted, Hugo Boss. A pair of black Ferragamo loafers, complete with shoe trees, sat neatly on the floor.

Max went through the pockets, felt carefully along the

lining. He took the wooden trees out of the shoes, poked his long fingers into the toes.

In the adjoining bath, he searched Willy's Dior toiletry kit. He lifted the tank lid on the toilet, crouched down to search behind it, under the sink.

He went through the drawers, through the suitcase and its contents, flipped over the mattress on the standard double.

It took him less than an hour to search the room and verify Willy had left nothing important behind. When he left, the space looked as tidy and untouched as it had when he'd entered.

He considered giving the clerk another twenty not to mention the visit to the cops, then decided it might put ideas in his head.

He climbed into his Porsche, switched on Springsteen and headed to the county morgue to verify that his strongest lead was on ice.

"Stupid. Goddamn, Willy, I figured you for smarter than this."

Max blew out a breath as he looked at Willy's ruined face. *Why the hell did you run?* And what's in some podunk town in Maryland that was so important?

What, Max thought, or who?

Since Willy was no longer in the position to tell him, Max walked back out to drive into Angel's Gap to pick up a multimillion-dollar trail.

If you wanted to pluck grapes from the small-town vine, you went to a place where locals gathered. During the day, that meant coffee and food, at night, alcohol.

Once he'd decided he'd be staying in Angel's Gap for

at least a day or two, Max checked into what was billed as The Historic Wayfarer's Inn and showered off the first twelve hours of the day. It was late enough to pick door number two.

He ate a very decent room-service burger at his laptop, surfing the home page provided by the Angel's Gap chamber of commerce. The Nightlife section gave him several choices of bars, clubs and cafes. He wanted a neighborhood pub, the kind of place where the towners knocked back a beer at the end of the day and talked about each other.

He culled out three that might fit the bill, plugged in the addresses for directions, then finished off his burger while studying the printout map of Angel's Gap.

Nice enough place, he mused, tucked in the mountains the way it was. Killer views, plenty of recreational choices for the sports enthusiast or camping freak. Slow enough pace for those who wanted to shake the urban off their docksiders, but with classy little pockets of culture—and a reasonable drive from several major metro areas should one be inclined to spend the weekend in the Maryland mountains.

The chamber of commerce boasted of the opportunities for hunting, fishing, hiking and other manner of outdoor recreation—none of which appealed to the urbanite in Max.

If he wanted to see bear and deer in their natural habitat, he'd turn on The Discovery Channel.

Still, the place had charm with its steep streets and old buildings solid in their dark red brick. There was a nice, wide stretch of the Potomac River bisecting the town, and the interest of the arching bridges that spanned it. Lots of church steeples, some with copper touches gone soft green with age and weather. And as he sat, he heard the long, echoing whistle of a train signaling its passing.

He had no doubt it was an eyeful in fall when the trees erupted with color, and pretty as a postcard when the snow socked in. But that didn't explain why an old hand like Willy Young had gotten himself mowed down by an SUV on Market Street.

To find that piece of the puzzle, Max shut down his computer, grabbed his beloved bomber jacket and headed out to go barhopping.

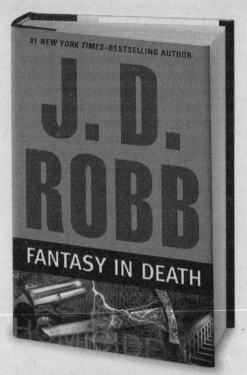